SHATTERED HEARTS

HUDSON YARDS SERIES: BOOK TWO

TINA SPENCER

Editing and Proofreading: Rachel's Top Edits, Heather Doig

Cover Art: Cass at Opulent Designs

Dev Edits: Jasmine M.

To those silently battling against everything that has tried to shatter you. One day, you'll touch your wounds and feel nothing but scars.

"He's more myself than I am. Whatever our souls are made of, his and mine are the same."

— **Emily Bronte**

SPOTIFY PLAYLIST

Stay- Hurts
Paid For Love- Ilan Bluestone, Gid Sedgwick
Tattoo- Topic Remix- Loreen, Topic
Let Me Touch Your Fire - ARIZONA
you should see me in a crown - Billie Eilish
Don't Blame Me - Taylor Swift
AMERICAN HORROR SHOW - SNOW WIFE
Fetish (feat. Gucci Mane) - Selena Gomez, Gucci Mane
Ruin My Life - Zara Larsson
Before You Leave Me - Alex Warren
Happiness Amplified - Above & Beyond, Richard Bedford
Iris - Goo Goo Dolls
Blue and Yellow - The Used
Dive Deep (Hushed) - Andrew Belle
I Feel Like I'm Drowning - Two Feet

CONTENT WARNINGS

Shattered Hearts is a **DARK** hockey romance. The contents are heavy at times and may be triggering for some readers. To avoid spoilers, I have put all the triggers warnings on my website (www.tinaspencerbooks.com) and at the end of this page. I'm also active on socials if you have any questions or would like to discuss the triggers before you read the book. Your mental health matters, please take care of it.

This is book two and the final installment of The Hudson Yards DUET (Dominik and Zoe's story). Book one, Shattered Obsession, ends on a cliffhanger. Please read Shattered Obsession prior to reading this book or you will be utterly lost.

If you're like me and want the shock factor then please skip the following trigger warnings. Otherwise, I hope you enjoy the ride.

*

*

*

*

*

Graphic sexual content, which include BDSM and kinks such as, voyeurism, exhibitionism, rough sex, choking, bondage, rope play, snowballing, switch, degradation, praise, adult toys, pain/ pleasure, CNC, forced submission, dub-con, dual masturbation, orgasm control, orgasm denial, cum play, and more.

- Stalking
- Primal play
- Mask kink
- Mention of parental abuse and childhood neglect
- Suicidal thoughts and ideations
- Mention of past thoughts of abortion (not FMC)
- Mental illness (depression, anxiety and intrusive thoughts)

PROLOGUE
DOMINIK LEWIS

High School - Boston

A NEW BEGINNING. *This will be a fresh start.*

That's what mom kept repeating on the car ride over, with our entire belongings thrown in the trunk as we made our way to Boston. She said it so many times I lost count. If I was legal drinking age, I would have recorded it so I could turn it into a drinking game later. I think she was trying to convince herself more than me. You hear something enough; you believe it.

This is a new beginning and the start of my hopefully very long hockey career. I should feel excited about the opportunity to progress and play with bigger teams. I'm definitely way ahead of the game for my age. But right now, I just feel numb to it all and I don't know why.

Because coming here also meant a new start without dad. A life where he didn't choose us. I have to grow up remembering how he didn't fight for me. For my mom.

A reminder that I wasn't good enough.

He was always a shitty dad. Never present, always said I'd never make it into the NHL and he barely showed up at my games. But it still fucking hurts to know we're not good enough.

That I'm not enough. Maybe I'll never be.

My mom is pretending to be okay with this. She wants to stay strong for me and keeps telling me he's going to come see us, see Boston and fall in love with the city. As if that's enough. She can pretend all she wants, but I also hear her crying herself to sleep at night and it kills me to know she's in so much pain. It makes me want to throat punch the guy.

I'm going to build a better life for us, for her, and prove that piece of shit excuse for a father wrong. Everything we left behind in Minnesota, everything I scarified to get here will be all worth it one day soon. I'm going to make sure of it, using all the negativity thrown at me as fuel.

"Alright sweetheart, you're all set."

Looking up at the school administrator, I force out a smile. She's an older lady, clearly a lifer, and the permanent smile on her face shows how much she enjoys her job. Her glasses sit on the edge of her nose, giving her this serious yet quirky look. She smells like those fake flowers you forget about and leave to collect dust for ages. The same ones grandma always had at her house. As she leans closer, sliding a bunch of colorful papers my way, I notice her name tag reads 'Mary'.

"Your first class is Mathematics with Mr. Castor," Mary explains.

"Cool. Thanks."

I repeat her name in my head four times, knowing I'll probably forget it as soon as I walk out of here. I'm good with faces, but names disappear as soon as they enter my brain.

"You're welcome, honey. Do you have everything you need?"

I shrug. "I think so."

She pushes up her wide glasses, observing me politely. "You

know, Dominik, this is a close knit community and a lot of us are hockey fans. We're all very excited you're here."

Shuffling the stack of papers in front of me, I hide my smile, feeling my face turn red. You'd think I'd be used to the compliments by now, but it still doesn't feel real to me. I don't know why I thought I could slip under the radar for a bit.

"Thank you, ma'am."

She nods, her smile growing wider. "My husband and I have seen some of your clips on YouTube. Very impressive. I think you're going to go far, son."

The attention makes my skin itch. I'm not accustomed to it, especially the compliments tied to my hockey skills. Hockey isn't just something I do; it's ingrained in me, part of my identity. It's not that I haven't put in the effort for those stats, but playing hockey isn't a choice for me—it's a necessity. In these situations, I'm at a loss for words. Mom's advice echoes in my mind: smile and say thank you. So, that's what I do.

"Do you know how to get to your class?" Mary finally says.

"I'll figure it out. Thanks again."

I don't know where any of my classes are since I literally just stepped inside this building, but if she's willing to let me go, then I plan on slipping out and finding my way around. I'm not one to ask for help. Maybe I'll get lost and skip algebra altogether. That wouldn't be a bad thing.

Showing up in the middle of the school year is not ideal, but we had no other option. Mom and I packed up as soon as we got the news that I got picked to play for one of the top junior teams in Boston. It feels absolutely unreal to have this opportunity at such a young age. It's going to propel my hockey career forward by several years, and I'm looking forward to getting started later this week.

"It's a big school, dear. I think I should get someone to show you to all your classes."

Oh no. I was so close. "It's okay. I'll find it and if I get lost or have any issues, I'll come right back here. Promise."

She narrows her gaze at me. "Give me five minutes and I can walk you down to class myself."

Goddamn it.

Mary turns, talking to her colleague, who's tucked away at the desk in the back, her nails clicking furiously against her keyboard. I realize this might be my one and only opportunity to slip out of here.

Turning to open the door, it swings open abruptly, nearly smacking me in the face. My heart slams on the brakes as soon as I see her face. It feels as if time has slowed down, everything around me moving in slow motion. Like that crazy scene from 'The Matrix', where Neo is dodging bullets in slow motion.

She has to be the most beautiful girl I've ever seen.

"Oh good, Zoe! Can you do me a favor, sweetie?"

I'm trying to figure out why my heart is beating a thousand miles a minute. I was fine a minute ago. This has never happened to me before, what even is this feeling? I've seen plenty of girls before.

But it's never been like this.

I watch Zoe smile and nod at Mary. They're talking, but I can't hear anything. All I'm focused on is her eyes, her lips and the way she smiles. Zoe reaches up, tucking her hair behind her ear, and I feel the movement all over my body as tingles rush down my legs.

Zoe.

Her name is just as beautiful as her.

I can't believe I'm blatantly gaping at this random girl who just walked into the office. What is wrong with me? Am I even blinking? She's looking at me, likely thinking I've had a stroke or that I'm insane. And all I can seem to think about is what it would feel like to wrap my arms around her. To taste her lips.

I bet she smells nice.

Green eyes so round and vivid, they are instantly unforgettable. Her hair is an amazing golden color, as if the sun touched it itself. And she's got the softest looking lips, so pink and luscious... they're perfect. They remind me of comfortable hotel pillows you can sink into.

Everything about her is perfect.

Is this what love feels like because god fucking damn it, I'm a goner.

As her eyes sparkle, she brightens up with a smile, revealing the cutest dimple on her right cheek that holds me captive. Just like the rest of her.

She says hi, I'm pretty sure I mumble a response. Maybe it was a grunt.

She laughs, the sound setting my heart on fire. "I'll take that as a yes."

"Dominik, are you okay, son?" Mary is talking to me.

"Yes, ma'am!" I exclaim, my voice coming out a little choppy.

Mary glares at me, probably wondering if I'm having a brain aneurysm or some shit. I don't know, Mary, maybe I am because I don't even know what's happening to me right now.

"Zoe is going to show you to Mr. Castor's class."

"Okay." I breathe out, turning back towards the beautiful girl I can't seem to stop obsessing over.

"Have a great first day at Winchester High!"

Zoe steps out into the hall, and I follow her. My hands are so clammy, I wipe them against my jeans a thousand times before deciding to give up. I have never been this nervous around a girl before.

"So, Dominik...where are you from?" Zoe asks.

The sound of our footsteps padding softly against the linoleum floor follows behind us.

"Saint Paul. Minnesota."

You need serious help.

Zoe doesn't scoff or judge. She just laughs. Genuinely laughs as if I've told a joke and it makes me so happy. Just hearing her laugh like that. I don't even know this person and hearing her laugh makes me light up, easing the tension off my shoulders.

"First day nerves, huh? You're going to fit in just fine here. I can already tell. Everyone will love you." I watch her eyes travel down my body as she takes me in, before they land back on my face. She bites the corner of her lip, shaking her head ever so slightly.

"Does that include you?" I question, watching her cheeks flush a beautiful shade of pink.

That one move just made my fucking month.

"Why Boston?" She ignores my question.

"Fresh start." I shrug.

She grins. "Not hockey?"

I laugh, rubbing the back of my neck. Looks like the entire school already knows. Did they send a newsletter before I arrived?

The hallway is utterly empty, except for the two of us. School is in session, and I'd like to know why Zoe was out of class to begin with. I also have to find my locker at some point, but I don't dare interrupt whatever brief minutes I get with her. Hoping she makes a wrong turn or goes the long way so I can get to know her a little better.

I made up my mind about how this was going to go the minute she walked through those doors.

She's going to be mine.

"Does the entire school know?"

She sighs, cringing. "Sort of."

My shoulders droop. "Ah shit. I didn't want to make a big deal out of it."

"I totally get it, but everyone loves hockey around here. You'll be a superstar."

Yeah, that's what I'm worried about.

Sweet notes of orange and vanilla brush against me as Zoe leans in close, glancing over my shoulder at my schedule as I try to remain calm, telling myself it's just a girl. A strand of golden hair brushes the back of my hand and I nearly lose my will.

I can't take my eyes off her. Noticing ever freckle, every line, everything.

She is...god, she feels like everything.

"Oh! My brother Aaron is in Mr. Castor's class. You'll meet him. He's super nice." Zoe exclaims, beaming with excitement.

A brother. My age. That could be nice.

"Are you in the same class?" I ask.

"No. I'm two years younger."

I try but cannot hide my disappointment. Thankfully Zoe doesn't notice. She's too busy pulling her phone out of her back pocket. Her cheeks turn red and a smirk appears on her face. A pang of jealously stabs me right in the chest because I know that look. I know when a girl smiles like that.

It doesn't even matter if she has a crush on someone else or even a boyfriend. I'm going to change all of that soon.

She's going to be mine. And we'll become high school sweethearts. Going through life together and one day, I'll marry her. Mark my fucking words.

Zoe stops at an old oak door. Turning to face me, she tucks her phone in her pocket and glances up. Taking in a strained breath, I try to focus on anything but those jade eyes of hers.

I could just get lost in those eyes for hours.

"Well, this is it." She whispers, her eyes sweeping across my chest and biceps. A subtle hint of red splashes her cheeks and hope blooms in my chest. Maybe she doesn't have a boyfriend. Maybe she was just texting a friend.

"Thank you, Zoe. It was nice to meet you. I'll see you around?"

"See you around. Say hi to Aaron for me."

She turns, pulling her phone out from her back pocket again. I stand there, unmoving as I gaze after her, and just before she rounds the corner she looks back...her eyes locking onto mine. I capture the sight of her in that very second like a picture, tucking it safely away in my mind.

Something shifts. My bones feel it the second it occurs, as if it flips my entire world upside down and I am instantly taken by it.

There is no denying it.

I'm obsessed, and I won't stop until Zoe is mine.

1

DOMINIK

What does a heart sound like as it shatters? Everything else makes itself known upon impact; every other collision or breakage echoes with resounding noise. The crashing of metal, the splintering of glass, or the thud of a puck against a stick, all announce their presence with a cacophony. But when a heart breaks, it's eerily silent. It's as if the universe itself holds its breath, acknowledging the painful moment.

A moment of agonizing silence.

Maybe it's the haunting stillness that makes it more unbearable.

And I'm standing in the aftermath of it, staring at Zoe sitting in my closet, her beautiful face contorted with pure disgust as the truth finally dawns on her.

"You're sick. A sick fucking freak."

I'm losing her with each passing second.

You've already lost her.

The thought of a world without her completely breaks my heart.

I can't lose her. I won't.

"I need to leave," Zoe whispers to herself.

I stand frozen in place, not knowing what the hell to do right now.

"Please don't."

I'm trapped in a nightmare.

I can't let her walk away from me again.

"How could you do this to me?" Her voice cuts straight through my heart.

Rushing over to where Zoe is sitting in the closet, I get down on my knees and crowd her. Cradling her face in my hands as her eyes remain shut, tears cascading down her cheeks, dropping one after the other.

Tears caused by pain I've inflicted on her.

"I didn't mean to hurt you. You have to believe that. It's never been a choice when it comes to you."

As I watch her fall apart in my hands, fresh tears well up in my eyes. I can't remember the last time I cried. It might have been after I finally came to terms with the fact that my father was never coming back, that I wasn't enough for him to want to stay. Or maybe it was the time I left Boston, knowing I couldn't see Zoe again. I left my heart that day with her in Boston.

In both instances, I'd cried to release the suffocating emotions, and when it was over, I felt numb, as if nothing had happened.

My father abandoning me altered my brain chemistry.

Pain like that always changes you. Sometimes, it's overnight, instantaneous as the cracks settle in. Other times, it can take minutes, hours, days, maybe even weeks to realize how different things are. Until one day I looked in the mirror and didn't even recognize myself.

It's been a long time since I've cried, but sitting here, watching the woman I love sobbing over pain I've caused brings me to tears. I don't bother concealing them as my thumb wipes away her wet cheeks only for new tears to replace the ones I dried.

I've cared about her for such a long time. Why did it take me this long to realize that this feeling is actually love? My unwavering need for Zoe has fueled everything I've done.

I should have protected her.

"No," Zoe mutters under her breath.

Her hands press into my chest, and her eyes finally open before she pushes me away.

"You don't get to fucking touch me. *No!*" Her scream fills the closet as she gets to her feet, racing out with the masks still in her hands.

"Zoe, please. Let me explain."

I'm following her out of the closet and into my bedroom when she turns around. Her cheeks are red, her eyes puffy, and her chest heaving.

"Explain what exactly, Dom? The countless times you lied to my face? How you kept lying this entire time? Or do you want to explain the fact that you fucked me in Boston, in disguise, while knowing exactly who I was? Or better yet, let's talk about the fact that you've been stalking me for years! Is that why you got close to Aaron? So you could be near me?"

"Yes," I blurt out. "It started out that way, but he's like a brother to me. That has never been a lie."

"How could you do that to me? How could you do that to Aaron?" Zoe struggles to contain her anger.

Her questions replay in my mind, but I'm drawing a blank. I don't know what to say to make this better. I'm not sure anything I say right now could.

Shaking my head, I take a step toward her. "I know. I'm the world's biggest piece of shit. You think I don't know that? I...I'm a different person around you."

"So, this is my fault somehow?"

"No, that's not what I'm saying. What I did was wrong, but I knew if I removed my mask, it would change everything. I needed that night to be ours, as Runi and Parvaneh. I needed to be with you without reality getting in the way. Hiding in plain sight, lying to you like that, tracking your conversations online, keeping tabs on you...these were all wrong, and I'm sorry for them. But I'm not sorry for that night with you in Boston because it was the best night of my life. I never thought I'd get the chance to be with you. To taste your lips, to hold you, to feel you... That night was just ours."

She can't even look at me. "That night was a lie. It was all a lie."

"That's not true. It's never been a lie. Not for me."

Zoe winces. Her glare turns dark as she holds up the masks from that night. The one with the red light from *The Purge* and the other I wore during the masquerade ball, matte black covering half my face.

"It was never real. You ruined it for me when you hid the truth from me. Using me. Was that what last night was too? Taking whatever it is you want from me whenever you feel like it?"

This is wrong. It's all coming out wrong.

"It's not like that, Zoe. I wish you could see inside my head. I've been hiding for so long, trying to run from this and from what I want the most. I know you can feel that. Maybe if you could see, you'd know what it means to want you like this."

"Don't!" she screams. "I don't want to fucking hear it."

I approach her, taking the masks from her hands and throwing them onto the floor.

"I can't stop. I've never been able to. Don't you see that? You're everything I've ever wanted, the closest to happiness I'll ever get, Zo. I can't let you go. Ever since the moment I laid eyes on you."

"No."

"This is it for me. I won't lose you again."

"Get away from me." She pulls away, taking everything I said and throwing it onto the floor next to the masks that are staring up at us.

"I won't," I state calmly, leaning against the door and blocking her in.

Zoe abruptly stops crying, using the back of her hands to wipe her tear-stained face. Taking two steps toward me, she gradually regains control of her breathing. The trembling in her body subsides, as though every ounce of emotion has drained from her. It's as if she reached a point of emptiness where she's drained every ounce of her feelings.

"I never want to see your face again. Get out of my way."

That's too fucking bad.

They say everything that happens to us is the result of our feelings. How we allow something to affect us through emotion. And this is about to break me into a thousand little pieces. But I can't show her that, because Zoe isn't in the right state of mind to listen to reason.

I'll have to force her to see. I just need a bit of time.

"We have a deal. And I'm sure you wouldn't want your brother to know what's been going on."

"Are you fucking threatening me?"

"I don't want to, but if that's what it takes, so be it. You show up in New York, and everything goes to shit. Do you really want your brother to deal with that?"

Zoe looks shell-shocked, speechless even, but it only lasts a second before she schools her features and smooths down her hair, nodding. "You're right. Aaron can't find out about any of this. Not right now. He'd blame me."

Merely saying those words was enough to make her believe me. They sank into her mind like butter, revealing just how fragile she is right now. Maybe she has always been this way, unable to risk losing the one and only person she believes cares for her. But she couldn't be more wrong. I will always be there for her, even if she hates me forever. And I have a feeling Tristan would drop everything to be by her side too. But when you've been abandoned for so long, your perception of reality becomes distorted. And what happened in that closet only worsened things. I wish I could take back my words, reassure her that she's wrong. Aaron wouldn't blame her, and if he did, I would set him straight. For now though, I have to use her insecurities and fears to my advantage.

"He would."

Zoe's chin quivers, but she doesn't drop her gaze. Even if she forgives me one day for this, I never will.

"We don't have to tell him. If you play along," I continue.

"I hate you," she spits out, her anger hot enough to power up an entire hockey arena.

"Let's—" I start, but Zoe raises her hand, stopping me.

"I'm done listening to you, Dominik. This is how it's going to go down. We keep this between us. In two months, you will come to my work event's grand opening. I'll stage a public breakup at the event. And after that, no one will remember me, and we will go our separate ways."

"You're an idiot if you think that's going to happen." I'm going to be sick.

"Leave me the fuck alone in between games and events. Or I'll make your life a living hell."

"Zoe," I whisper.

"After our agreement is over, I never want to see your face again."

I am in a state of shock, unable to speak as she pushes me aside and abruptly leaves my room. The front door slams as I remain rooted in place, replaying everything over and over again.

Different scenarios, different versions of us in different timelines. I wish I could go back and do this all differently.

I never want to see your face again.

I sink to my knees and cradle my face in my hands, letting the weight of her absence and everything that occurred in the last twenty-four hours finally engulf me.

2

ZOE JACKSON

I don't think hate would even describe how I feel about Dominik right now. And I want to feel it all, but truthfully, I feel nothing.

Absolutely nothing.

I'm completely numb. Unable to grasp what just happened.

Everything I thought I knew just feels like one giant lie.

I punch the elevator button with my finger, knowing it will not make the damn thing show up any faster, but the anger within me is blinding.

Where am I even going? Up to my brother's empty penthouse? I have no one to talk to about this. I'm all alone. Always alone.

You'd think I would be used to this feeling by now. That I could turn it off. But the feeling of betrayal and hurt never gets easier. Time never heals those parts of me, never dulls the pain, and I hate that more than anything else.

I hate myself for letting my situation affect me in this way.

I hate Dominik for throwing my brother into the mix because he knows Aaron is all I have left. He knows I would do anything to make sure this doesn't reach him. If Aaron found out what

Dominik did, he would commit murder. And guess whose fault it would be? Mine.

I am the common denominator in every disaster.

My mother was amazing for reminding me how much of a mistake I am. How my existence made her life so complicated. How my dad couldn't even look at me.

I just want to run away.

The one thing that was mine is no longer mine. It's a secret I share with my brother's best friend. A secret he's known for the last six years, but I never did, not until now. And not because he wanted me to know, either. Dominik would have likely hidden this forever if I hadn't rooted through his closet.

The elevator doors chime, and I enter, finding it difficult to meet my own gaze in the numerous mirrors staring at me.

You're a worthless piece of shit, and you will always be a worthless piece of shit.

My breathing becomes rapid, each breath shallow and unsteady. The tears well up, threatening to spill over. The elevator walls close in around me, suffocating and confining. I want to crumble right here, in this small space, and drown in the overwhelming emotions running through me. The weight of it all threatens to consume me. But I'm the same powerless, waste of space I've always been. Trying to make myself smaller and smaller but failing to let go of the one weakness that haunts me. Hope, my forever burden and a constant reminder of something I'll never have.

I'm tired of feeling everything. I want to turn it all off, and I know exactly what will help me drown out the noise right now.

The elevator comes to a halt at the top floor, and just as the doors open, the familiar *ding* rings out. Aaron's penthouse comes into full view as I quickly wipe the tears off my face, vowing to leave the pathetic version of myself behind in the elevator as the doors shut. I'm done entertaining that bitch.

I don't even bother calling out to Aaron. I know he's not here. What would he think if I called him right now and told him what happened? What his best friend did to me in Boston? What he did to me last night on his couch?

As if wanting me all this time makes any of this okay. I should hate that the most, but what's even more fucked up is that I don't. Hearing his confession, seeing the box, and the reasons behind is not as terrible as it should be. What the fuck is wrong with me?

Are we really going to open that can of worms, today of all days?

Dominik is disgusting and sick and fucking twisted. End of discussion.

He's a psychopath, and he shattered every fond memory that was linked to my one mystery man, Runi.

Runi is no longer this amazing experience that opened me up to the world of BDSM. Dominik knew who I was and used it to his advantage that night.

He gave you exactly what you wanted, and you agreed for him to stay in the mask. You are just as much to blame for this as he is.

Kindly shut the fuck up, brain. Please and thank you.

Pacing Aaron's living room, my eyes fall to his liquor cart and the vast collection of alcohol sitting neatly on the glass.

I need a break, just for today. Just enough to give myself some quiet before I have to face Dominik again. The alcohol will numb my emotions and help me forget about this, maybe even fall asleep peacefully. I grab the bottle of gin and crack it open, almost vomiting on the spot as I begin chugging. The fucking thing tastes like cleaning solution, burning my throat on its way down, but I welcome the pain.

Sliding down the wall, I sit in the living room, my eyes focusing on one of Aaron's giant abstract paintings as I force the gin down. And soon enough, with each passing minute, I start to feel less. The numbness finally taking over my senses.

But there is one thing I can't seem to force away. And that's the fact that no one has ever wanted me so much they'd do all the things Dominik did. I have never mattered, was always a second thought, yet I'm supposed to believe that someone like Dominik has always desired me? So much so that he couldn't stay away? That his actions were driven by his intense need?

Why? No one has ever wanted me that way.

It must be something else. Some other reason.

Does it even matter? It was wrong.

Yes, wrong in every way, and it shouldn't matter. Because he lied and took advantage of me. He invaded my privacy and with-held information from me. He masked his true identity and took something from me that wasn't his. Consent or not, it was wrong.

Right?

Then why does it feel like this? Why don't thoughts of last night disgust me as I sit here in the aftermath?

It doesn't matter. I want to get through the next two months and then erase Dominik from my memory. A part of me wants to run away from this place and never look back. If only it were that easy.

3

ZOE

I'm in excruciating pain.

I want to die. Actually, I'm pretty certain I am dying...a slow, painful death.

All because of a certain blonde.

"Come on! One more round. You can do it. Choose your hard," the instructor yells over the loud EDM music as all the workout junkies pedal faster on their spin bikes.

Everyone but me... How am I this out of shape? I go for runs regularly, but this type of workout is next-level. It feels like a training camp for *The Hunger Games*.

Via convinced me to come to this new spin club during our lunch hour instead of waiting in line at our favorite food truck like we normally do. I wanted to stuff my face with a burger but somehow got roped into sweating my ass off.

She promised me I'd feel better during *and* after the workout. But Via is a big, fat liar.

I don't feel better. It feels like Death is about to take me home and have his way with me.

Although, I will admit, focusing on how not to die in the last forty-five minutes has been a welcome distraction. It's the first time I haven't actively thought about what happened last week in Dominik's apartment.

It's been a week of avoidance on my part and him doing everything he can to get me to talk to him. Texts. Calls. Emails. Showing up at Aaron's. Work visits. Flower deliveries. And messages on all my fucking devices.

The man has serious issues. He's relentless. I'm secretly happy he's suffering, though.

One would expect that after days of being completely ignored by someone, you would get the hint and back off. But not Dominik Lewis. If anything, my silence only seems to fuel his persistence. Unfortunately for him, I couldn't care less.

He could buy me all of Manhattan, and it wouldn't matter to me. I'm still not interested in talking to him about what happened. I'm over it. Over him and any words he may throw my way.

Words mean nothing. Everything I need to know about Dominik is in his track record. He's a selfish asshole who only cares about his happiness. He tapped into the most vulnerable parts of me, made me believe he was someone else and...

Except that's where I get stuck, because the more I think about that night in Boston, the more I realize he never had his way with me in the way he wanted to. I never asked him about his desires. He was honest about his mask and how he wanted to keep it on. That night was about me and my needs. He gave me the experience I desired. And I let him. I agreed to his conditions.

But you didn't know it was him.

I've gone over every detail, every conversation I had with Runi. Every touch. Glance. Kiss. Every single moment.

I've exhausted myself with how much I've thought about it. Which means I also remember him telling me his mask had to stay on and that he couldn't expose his face to me. I brushed past it, knowing everyone in that place wanted to stay anonymous. That was the entire theme of the night. Why didn't I take a pause then? Look further into his words? Because I didn't care at the time. Which means I'm to blame here, too. I was too curious and hungry to pass up a night with him.

I would have stopped. Knowing it was Dominik behind the mask—I would have left.

But would you really?

Yes, I'd like to think that I would have. Because it was never like that with him.

None of it makes sense.

"Great job, everyone! You were all so wonderful today. I'm so proud of you for showing up and choosing to be a better version of yourself. Grab a drink and turn down the dial. We're rolling into our cool down," the instructor shouts, reminding me where I am at this moment.

"Thank fuck," I grunt, taking a swig from my water bottle.

"That was amazing, wasn't it? How do you feel?" Via is glistening under the blue studio lights, covered in a dusting of sweat. Her blonde bob is half pulled back. She's wearing spandex shorts and a black sports bra, her abs and perky tits on full display. She's in amazing shape. Probably because she can't sit still and spends her free time at places like this. I wish I were like that or had that kind of drive.

Even I wouldn't kick her out of bed. How she's single in New York is beyond me, but I haven't been brave enough to dig that deep into her personal life yet.

"I feel like I'm going to kill you as soon as we leave this studio," I huff out, taking twice as long to finish my sentence in between breaths.

She laughs. "It's normal. Your first few times are tough, but if you stick with it, you'll be a spin addict in no time."

Doubtful.

I take another drink of water, occupying my mouth before I say something rude. Reaching down to tuck my bottle back into the cup holder, I catch the eyes of a lean biker on the other side of the room. He smiles, and I catch myself smiling back.

The tempo slows down, and all the bikes hum slowly to the music as we work to get our heart rates down.

"How's Dom, your famous hockey player boyfriend?" Via is leaning in, her eyes bouncing back between me and the mystery biker across the room.

"Fine, I guess. We're taking it slow. I'm not holding my breath."

"Commitment issues much?" Via laughs. "You know, you're kind of famous, so maybe don't wave at strange men."

"Hey, don't judge. I'm just trying to be nice."

Via arches a sweaty brow at me. "He wants to take you home and have a second workout with you. There is nothing nice about how that man is staring at you."

"And why is that my problem?"

"It's not, and I'm not judging . . . trust me. But I'm just wondering if you want to share Dom with the rest of us normal, dick-deprived folks way down here."

I throw my towel at her, and she snatches it from the air. "You can try, but I doubt he'd want to."

"Can I at least come to a game and meet a few of his single, hopefully older, teammates? Or younger. I'm not picky." She pouts as the class ends, and we all get off the bikes.

Bringing her to a game rather than going alone is actually a great idea. Much better than asking Aaron, who will most likely suspect something is up between Dom and me.

I've been avoiding my brother like the plague. My parents finally left a few days ago, and I silently moved back in while he wasn't around. We've been mostly communicating via text or notes around the house. It's awkward, and I hate it.

He's been putting in extra hours since he had to spend some time with our parents. Am I pissed off that he seemed to prioritize spending time with them over me? Yes, absolutely. Who wouldn't be? Am I going to bring it up with him? Fuck no. I'd rather only eat slimy grass for a month.

"Yes, great idea. You're coming to the next game."

"Wait, really?" Via asks surprisingly.

I try not to focus on the sheer amount of sweat all over my body as we head for the changing room. "Yes. I've been wanting to ask you anyway, but figured I should give you some time to figure out if you're going to run away from me or not."

"Fuck off. You're stuck with me," Via remarks genuinely.

I pause and have to remind myself that I've heard those words before. I give her a tight smile, grabbing the complimentary toiletries bag and a towel from my locker.

"When is the next game?" Via says from behind me.

"They are away this week, but I think there is a game next week. I'll text Dom and get him to add your name."

Except it's Noa I'll be texting because I'd rather chop off my arm than talk to *him*.

"Thanks, Zoe! You're the best. Also, you're my new spin partner... We come here three days a week."

Groaning, I rest my head against the shower wall, regretting my decision to be nice to Via from day one.

"I heard that!" she says cheerfully, right before her shower turns on.

How she peeled off her sweaty sports bra that quickly is beyond me. I'm going to be wrestling with mine for the next ten minutes.

Double groan.

"OKAY, this chunky monkey protein smoothie tastes so much better after that workout."

I'm having a moment with my chocolate and peanut butter smoothie from the spin club's smoothie bar. This might be the best thing I've ever fucking had.

"I told you. A million bucks."

I feel amazing actually, but I'm not admitting that to Via. Over my dead body.

She was right about the after workout high, and I knew that all along. It's like a runner's high. That sweat session followed by a lavender shower and a healthy smoothie has me feeling like a whole new person as we stride into Blooms.

"What's going on?" Via says, puzzled.

Looking around, I notice most people aren't at their desks, and there seems to be some sort of commotion coming from the back of the office.

I see the sea of purple and black as soon as we round the corner. My jaw hits the floor as I take in black and purple roses scattered everywhere.

"What the actual fuck."

Yeah, what she said.

When I say everywhere, I mean absolutely everywhere. Glass vases overflowing with roses sit on every surface. Black and purple petals cover the floor, office chairs, keyboards, desk phones.

It seems like a troll's vomit has completely covered the inside of Tracy's pristine office.

"Tell me I'm imagining this," I whisper.

"Nope. Thousands and thousands of roses. This is so sweet, but so overwhelming."

"Zoe! I'm going to need you to speak now!" Tracy's stern voice comes from right behind me, forcing me to jump out of my skin. I nearly drop my smoothie on the floor as I turn, seeing the furious, blue vein popping out of her forehead.

She shoves a small card against my chest. When I look down at the words, all the good energy I was feeling from that workout drains out of me.

A rose for everyday we've been apart. I counted from the very beginning.
Yours,
Dom

He's trying to get me fired. I'm filled with such anger that I don't even know where to begin untangling this mess. There are roses on every surface and every inch of this floor. When did he even do this? Did someone help him?

Jesus fuck.

Looks like I won't be the one dying from a slow, painful death today, after all.

"Holy shit, Zoe. He's so in love. And I hate you so much, but love this for you. You must be a total vixen in bed," Via whispers, grabbing my elbow and dragging me to our desks while we walk over crisp rose petals.

The significance of the purple roses does not evade me, and I think that makes me more angry. That he knows so much about me and the inner workings of my brain.

The entire place smells like a flower garden. The floor and the white desks are barely visible amidst the sea of vibrant colors.

Everyone is staring at me, and I desperately wish to disappear. Whispers circulate and fuel the perpetual rumor mill.

I hate attention, and Dominik has given me all of it right now.

"Who is all this for?"

"Zoe. The new girl Greg got rid of in Boston."

"I heard she's dating Dominik Lewis."

"The Slashers captain?"

"Yes."

"No way. I don't believe that for a second."

Assholes. The entire lot of them are complete assholes.

"Hey, don't listen to them. They're just words. What they think of you has nothing to do with you and everything to do with the type of people they are."

Glancing at Via, I find her worried gaze on me. Her hand wraps around my fist as she stops me from picking the skin around my nails, a nervous habit I picked up years ago to stop me from having mental breakdowns.

"This sucks," I say, kicking roses away from my office chair and reaching under my desk for a black garbage bag. I was supposed to come in quietly, keep my head down, and get my work done. Prove to everyone here that everything they heard from Greg's office whores isn't true. Now I don't even know where I stand.

Tracy is probably going to fire me by the end of the week.

"What are you doing?" Via asks, standing behind her desk and holding a giant wicker basket. Where did she even get that? I haven't seen that basket before.

"I'm going to start cleaning up. What are *you* doing?" I say, staring at the basket.

"Oh, fuck no, you're not throwing all these flowers out. No girl gets treated like this! Dominik should teach classes to shitty men on dating apps."

Little does she know this is all fake. An act Dom is putting on to prove how amazing he is and that he's not a lying piece of shit.

My phone buzzes in my pocket. Pulling it out, I notice he's already messaged me six times.

The last message makes me see red.

I can't ignore it, not with the stench of roses all around me.

DOM

One way or another, you're going to come around, Zoe. You belong to me. I hope you enjoy the roses.

ME

Fuck. You. When are you doing to get the message that I hate your guts?

DOM

I'm not going anywhere.

ME

You should. Go play in traffic and lose my number while you're at it.

DOM

Don't even think about blocking me again. You tried that several times, and I just end up getting a new phone. Unlimited funds means unlimited resources to annoy you.

ME

You're an asshole.

DOM

But I'm your asshole.

EXHAUSTED, I give up and notice Via's stupid smile as she bends down, picking up roses and placing them gently into her basket like she's lazily walking through a flower garden. Is everyone completely oblivious to this? Am I the only one who wants to strangle Dominik for all this shit?

Enough is enough. I'm putting an end to this tonight.

ME

> I have to clean up this mess now. My boss is pissed with me, and I'm probably going to get fired. So thank you for that. Thank you for continually ruining my life. What do you want from me, Dom?

Bubbles appear and disappear. My heart picks up speed, and I can't tell if it's from anger or anticipation to see his next words. He's been hounding me every day. Telling me everything that he's been feeling from day one, that first day we met at the admin office in high school. So many details I never even thought twice about that he has apparently been replaying in his head for years. But I don't believe any of it. Because if you truly love someone, you set them free. That's what they say, don't they? Although I never really believed in that shit. I may not have ever experienced love before, but I imagine if someone consumes your entire mind and body, then there is no way in hell you'd hurt or lie to them. You wouldn't give up on them.

DOM

> I just want you.

ME

> Never going to happen.

DOM

> We'll see.

Isn't that what he's doing right now? Not giving up on you?
It's not the same because for pure love to exist, it has to be

reciprocated, not born from hate and deceit. We're standing in the middle of a graveyard surrounded by nothing but our disastrous endings.

4
ZOE

The elevator doors open up to my brother's dark and quiet penthouse suite. It's eerily silent, which is a warm welcome after the stressful day I had. I'm craving the quiet a lot lately, realizing that I'm more comfortable in the dark. More comfortable within the borders of my thoughts where it's safe, predictable, painless.

It might seem lonely, but I recognize this type of loneliness. I've lived with it for so long that it's familiar and comforting. It might be dark, but I welcome the pain. I know how to handle it. Some days, I just want to drown in the void until it consumes me in full.

I want to turn it all off until there is nothing left of me.

This space is better than hope or false promises. What I hate is the illusion that hope lingers somewhere nearby. Trusting someone and then getting treated like trash, like a punch in the gut when I'm already down. It's a relentless cycle that reinforces the belief in my worthlessness. I stay away from emotions and attachments because they always lead to disappointment. But even when I shut down, failure still finds a way in. Because at the end of the day, we're all left with ourselves, headed for the same inevitable fate.

So, what's the point?

Some days I'm not even sure why I bother. Some days I invite those dark thoughts in, wondering what it would be like to just not wake up tomorrow. To not feel anything at all, fade into darkness and never return.

I want to never remember these days—the pain, the memories. To slip away and cease to exist.

My palm stings as I reach for the liquor cabinet in my brother's empty apartment. I spent a solid hour today picking up rose heads and petals with Via at the office, long after the hushed chatter had died down. There weren't even any thorns on the roses. All the stems had been removed. Not even one full flower to cut myself on accidentally. What bullshit is that? I wonder if Dominik did that on purpose. Does he know about my old habits too?

Others might not understand, but the pain feels good, especially when nothing else does. It's a reminder that I can feel something.

I wish I could be someone else for a day. That's exactly why I'm grabbing my brother's half-empty bottle of vodka and planning to cuddle with it tonight. I have picked up drinking again. Whenever something happens that destroys a part of me, I can't sleep very well, and the only proven method that helps me pass out is alcohol.

I only take what I need, and I always make sure to replace exactly what I take. It's important to me not to exploit my brother's kindness by stealing his alcohol, especially after he let me stay at his place. I also don't want anyone to know I'm turning into a bit of a boozer. It's managed because I'm aware of it. Besides, it's only until I can make my brain forget all the nonsense that's messing with my sleep.

Just like that night in Boston and again in Dominik's apartment, he took something from me that I'm not sure I'll ever be able to recover. He stole Runi from me, all the while showing me a glimpse of who he truly is. It's difficult to ignore the possibility that he and I might be more alike than I had initially thought. Maybe he sees me in ways that I can't see myself.

And I don't want to think about that. I don't want to think about Dominik at all, so vodka it is until he no longer occupies my brain.

Glancing around the pristine, white kitchen, I notice the lingering scent of freshly baked bread, but my hunger subsides as I flick off the vodka cap and take a large swig. I nearly spit it all back up, but I push through the sting and swallow the burn. The first sip is always the most challenging, but by the fifth one, the taste barely registers.

It's the first week of February, but as I take in the New York skyline adorned with twinkling remnants of holiday lights, a subtle warmth washes over me. An unfamiliar feeling, yet a comforting one. The lingering decorations, like specks of magic suspended in the cold winter air, offer a respite from the haunting memories that usually accompany the Christmas season for me.

Boston during Christmas felt suffused with obligation and pressure. It was a lot. But here, in this vibrant city of dreams, the energy is entirely different. The dazzling display of lights, which used to overwhelm me, now softly murmurs stories of happiness and awe.

Walking over to the plush couch, I sink into it, allowing its softness to envelop me as I cradle the Gray Goose bottle. Raising it to my lips, I take another sip, becoming more captivated by the New York skyline.

I hate the holidays or any reminders of the season, but sitting here, half drunk, I realize maybe I hate it a little less this year. It's funny how my past doesn't seem so haunting now that I'm not walking by dark reminders every day. Reminders of my terrible childhood and everything I didn't get to experience. It's not as heavy here. Maybe I can create better memories. Write a better ending for myself.

I feel so small, sitting here with my stupid problems while witnessing an entire world taking place.

I wonder what it's like to be in one of the other lit up apartments right now. Thousands of tiny squares illuminating life right from where I'm sitting. I wonder what's beyond each window. An older, happy couple, or maybe a new couple who just moved in together. Their stories are worlds apart, yet they are neighbors, sharing the same space and air. The same walkways and elevators. We do that a lot as humans. Pass one another by, but none of us really know what lurks beneath the masks we wear. We only allow certain people to peek beyond the door.

What if we all stripped away our masks and openly exposed all our hidden truths? Imagine a world where everyone embraced their true selves, free from societal expectations and constraints. I can't even imagine a place filled with that type of authenticity and acceptance. I have only ever felt that way once in my life... and it wasn't even real.

Taking another swig, I rest my head back on the couch and close my eyes, hoping the room will stop spinning soon.

Skipping dinner was a bad idea. I might hug the toilet later, but right now, I feel good. Actually, I feel little of anything, which is exactly why I've been drowning myself in liquor more often than not these days. I'd much rather feel nothing than everything all at once.

I'm not sure how long I remain like that, head kicked back, eyes closed, and just listening to the fake crackling of the electric fireplace. When I open my eyes, there is a hazy image of Dominik staring down at me. His hair is longer, dark as night as it drapes loosely around his face, highlighting his beautifully sharp features. His chest tattoo is on display with the few buttons on his shirt undone. I just want to run my fingers down his chest and bite the skin. He pins his dual colored eyes on me, a beautiful blend of blue and gold, almost shimmering in the night. His expression is unreadable with the blanket of fog around him.

Is it me, or does he keep getting more beautiful with time?

I really hate that about him.

It must be the dream effect. This has to be a dream. That's why I reach up and spin my finger through his loose waves.

"Can't even leave me alone here, huh? I was hoping I wouldn't think about you tonight. Now you're imposing on my dreams, too."

"You're drunk." His voice sounds pained.

"Can't be drunk if I'm passed out and dreaming. Or maybe that was the point all along." I shrug.

A grunt. "Why are you drinking alone in the dark?"

"Dream Dominik rarely talks. He's normally busy with his mouth occupied in other places."

Is he arching a brow at me? And is that a smile? Why is he so attractive, even upside down and blurry? It's not fair.

"Where would you like my mouth occupied?"

Tingles erupt all over my skin. It's okay if it's just a dream, right? I can indulge. No one will know.

"My mouth. Neck. Chest. Stomach... In between my legs. Everywhere," I whisper, running my fingers down his hard arm. "I hate you, but you're a great fuck."

"Am I?" He smirks.

I take a deep breath. "Mm-hmm... Our sex dreams are out of this world. And I hate when I wake up wanting you, but it's my dirty little secret. I can hate you all I want during the day, but at night, it's a different story. And it doesn't matter."

"What doesn't matter?" he asks.

The course of my hand changes direction, heading for his pants. "What you're about to do to me."

Fingers tighten around my wrist, and my hand is pulled away. A second later, the cold liquor bottle disappears from its resting spot beside me on the couch.

"Are you taking me to bed, handsome?"

"Yes. You need sleep." A quiet observation.

"No. I need cock. I need your cock. Your massive cock." I giggle.

"This is my fault."

"Yes, it is your fault."

"I will make it right. I'll fix everything. I'm sorry," Dominik whispers.

"You're not sorry, though. You couldn't help yourself. Isn't that what you said? That you wanted me so badly you had to have me. Why didn't you just try talking to me like a real person? Telling me you wanted me? Asking me out on a date? Telling me you had a crush on me? You think I would have rejected you?"

"Come on, Zoe. Let's go to bed." Dream Dom ignores my questions.

"Answer me." I yank my arm away and try to sit up, but the weight of the entire room falls on my body. Maybe my bed is right here on this couch tonight.

"Christ, Zo."

"Answer me."

The couch dips, and I hear him take in a strained breath. This version of Dominik feels very real tonight. That, or I've overdone it with the alcohol again.

"You were the one thing I wanted desperately but was told I could never have. And when you showed up that night, it felt like we could begin again without our past getting in the way. I couldn't stop myself then, and I can't stop myself now. There is no stopping this. But I can't force you into it. You have to come to me on your own."

Dream Dominik is saying words I'm not prepared to hear. Words that are meaningless in reality, because if he truly felt that way, he wouldn't have waited so long to tell me. Real Dom is just sorry he got caught in all the lies.

There is no stopping this.

"There is no 'this,'" I say, pointing blindly in the air. "I'm not yours."

"That's where you're wrong, little butterfly. You've always been mine. You belong to me."

I want to yell at him, but my eyelids feel so heavy right now. A second later, I feel my body being hoisted up, tucked against Dominik as he carries me away. He smells so good, like cedar and Irish Spring soap. Forget the toilet and the vodka bottle. I want to cuddle with him tonight, right after I get a little taste.

What happened to hating him?

It feels nice this way, taking a break in my dream to not hate a ridiculously gorgeous man. Who I now know is the only man responsible for the best sex of my life. Sometimes, I tire of being angry. Sometimes, I just want to think about Dominik's cock stretching me. For just tonight, I want to feel like I belong to him.

You've always been mine.

Just another drunken dream night.

"Then show me how I'm yours."

"Fuck," he whispers, his grip tightening around me.

"You're so prettyyyyy. It's just ridiculously unfair." The words feel heavy on my tongue as I hear them float into the air. "Do you know how unfair that is? I've never told you that before because I don't want to feed your massive ego, but you're in my dream, so it doesn't count. You're pretty. So fucking pretty, it hurts."

Dream Dominik says nothing, but I hear a slight chuckle as I rest my head against his chest while we float through the house.

"Have you had any food?" He sounds distant.

I shake my head as my body rests on a piece of cloud. Opening my eyes, I watch Dominik sit on the edge of the fluffy, white cloud as he takes off my shoes.

"Are you going to touch me now?"

He looks up at me, shocked. "No."

I huff, turning my face and closing my eyes again. "That's rude. Why are you being so rude to me tonight? Don't you want me?"

"I always want you," he breathes. "But not like this. Not when you won't even remember me tomorrow."

"You're hard to forget. I wish that wasn't the case, but sadly... it is." I sigh. "Besides, it's not like my remembering stopped you before."

I feel his body shift. "You didn't want it last time?"

I could lie, tell him he forced himself on me, but that would be entirely untrue. Because that night in his apartment, I wanted it more than he did. If he opened up to me, I would have fucked him until sunrise.

"I wanted it. I think about it all the time. Think about you."

"I thought you hated me."

Vodka has a funny way of wiping out all the filters in my brain. Words don't even require a processing time. They just shoot right out of my mouth.

"Yes, I do, but that doesn't stop me from wanting you. I'll never tell you that. Dream you is fine because in the morning, I'll wake up, and none of this will be real. We'll go back to hiding from and hating one another."

"This is real, Zoe. And I've never hated you. I could never hate you," he says, helping me out of my sweater.

"You're not really here. You never have been. There is always a ticking timer in every person I meet."

Dominik's hand is around my hair as he fans it behind me, setting it free from my sweater, which is still stuck to me. "I'm never leaving. No matter what you say or do, I will always be here. Watching, waiting. No one else matters. It's just you and me. You're stuck with me."

No one ever stays.

No one ever has and no one ever will. The thought burrows deep inside my chest, twisting and turning as the weight of it settles over me like a blanket.

I wish I didn't yearn for everything I convince myself I hate. It's a paradox—I crave the very things I feign disinterest in, creating a self-imposed restraint to protect myself from the ache of knowing I'll never feel them. Touch them. Live the life I truly want. It's a game of denial, isn't it? We all construct these fronts to cover our vulnerabilities and to avoid pain. How am I any different from the rest?

"I'm here, Zoe. I've always been here, and I always will. You can't get rid of me. No matter how much you say you hate me or how hard you try to push me away, it's not going to work. I'll wait forever if that's what it takes. I will force it out of you if I have to. Burn the entire world down to prove to you that it's real. That this has always been real."

"Wow... You're really poetic tonight," I scoff.

"I mean every single word," Dominik says.

"Nothing has changed," I whisper, knowing my sense of reality and what exists are vastly different.

"Everything has changed."

I feel Dominik's warm palm press against my beating heart, and when I turn to look at him, he's inches away, staring at me like he could lift us right out of this dream state. Like he could turn this into a reality and give me everything I've always wanted.

"What happened?" He pulls open my fingers to reveal the fresh cuts from earlier today.

I may have gotten a little carried away earlier after everyone left the office.

I try to make a fist, but he doesn't let me. "Nothing."

"Did you do this on purpose?" he pushes.

"No. I'm fine. It was from all the roses earlier," I lie.

"There were no thorns on the stems of the flowers." His voice is darker somehow.

I don't have a response. My head is all fuzzy, so I simply shrug.

"Why?"

"I don't know," I whisper.

"Yes, you do."

I blink several times, trying to clear the fog from my brain and come up with some sort of clever lie. He's staring down at my hand, the pads of his fingers gently tracing over the angry wounds.

"Why did you do it?" Dominik asks again.

"I don't know. Sometimes I like the pain. It feels good, a reminder that I can feel something else."

As our eyes meet, he lifts my hand to his lips, pressing a gentle kiss against my skin.

"I'm sorry, Zoe. For everything. I'm sorry."

"Stop. I don't want your apology." I sigh. "You're being such a bore. Stop bumming me out in my dream. This isn't real, remember? Sex me up, mister."

Dominik moves instantly, pressing into me as the back of his hand grips my hair, tilting my face up and forcing me to stare into his hazel and blue eyes.

Here we go. Finally, this dream is about to get good. I can't help but smile, biting the edge of my lip and trying to hold back the excitement coursing through me.

"I wish I could wipe that smirk off your face, show you just how real this is. Make you feel so many things that don't involve as much pain. I'm going to take it all away, show you just how much you matter to me, but not right now. Not like this. I'm not about to fuck you while you're so drunk you think you're stuck in a dream with me."

It's impossible for me not to giggle at how ridiculous all of this is. The sheer absurdity of the universe deciding to place him in my drunken dream is just so laughable.

"I'm keeping track of all the ways I'm going to punish you when you finally give in to me. When you finally beg me to fuck you." His grip tightens in my hair, and I involuntarily arch my back, pressing our chests together as a slow shiver crawls up my legs, settling in between my thighs.

"I love it when you do that. But I'm never going to beg you," I whisper against his lips, running the tip of my tongue along his jaw.

"Fuck, Zoe. You're going to regret that."

And then he's gone. Vanishing into the thin air, or that's what it feels like, because by the time I blink, he's nowhere to be found.

When I blink again, he's back, holding a glass of water and a plate with two croissants. My stomach gurgles instantly.

"Drink this and eat these slowly."

The room is spinning faster and faster, so I don't bother fighting with dreamy Dom and do as I'm told. Like a good girl.

I watch as he floats around my room, gathering a few things. He scribbles something on a piece of paper, folds it, and shoves it behind his back. I forget to ask him what he's doing before I even take another bite.

Time becomes a fluid concept as I lie down, beginning to drift off into sleep as someone plays with my hair.

"Are you going to regret saying all this to me tomorrow?"

It's Dominik, but his voice sounds far away, as if he's calling out to me from the bottom of a well. I'm too far gone to respond to him, but I hope I remember this dream and the way he showed up for me tonight. I don't feel so alone. It's nice to be cared for, even if none of it is real. But then again, why would I want the memories of what this feels like to follow me for days? Maybe a sliver of what him touching me feels like will linger, but then again, maybe not.

"I won't remember any of this, so there will be nothing to regret," I say right as darkness grabs hold of me.

"Wow, you're really taking this boyfriend gig seriously. How much did this cost you?"

Tristan flashes his phone screen at me, showing me a video trending online of Zoe's office covered in black and purple roses. I love that video, because ten seconds in, a stunned Zoe comes into view. Just standing there in the middle of the room, trying to process what's in front of her. It hasn't even been a full week, but the fight we had in my bedroom closet after she found the masks has made it feel like an eternity. The memories of that incredible night are some of my favorites.

It used to be the best night of her life too until she discovered the truth. But I made a mistake out of desire. I didn't want to hurt her, not intentionally. And I'm going to prove to her how real this is, even if it takes an eternity. Especially after everything she said to me last night.

I'm going to show her how much I fucking love her. The ideal depiction of genuine love. It's about not giving up. No matter how dark or difficult it may seem, even when it feels impossible, the outcome will always be worth the struggle.

I'm done fighting this connection. I'm not interested in wasting any more time. I just haven't figured out a way to tell Aaron yet. Not that it's any of his business, but I know how much this means to Zoe, and I don't want to make things worse.

Speak of the devil, Aaron strides through his foyer, a disheveled mess. His hair's in disarray, his tie dangling haphazardly around his neck. The telltale signs of a sleepless night show beneath his eyes. I'd joke about him getting lost in the company of a few women last night, but I'd wager good money he burned the midnight oil, hammering out contracts and doing god knows what else. He's been pulling overtime, compensating for lost hours while his parents were in town, or so he claims. He hadn't prioritized Zoe when she first arrived, but his parents, he made time for. And now he's leaving his sister alone to drink herself to death in his big ass penthouse.

Why have I been so worried about pissing Aaron off? Maybe I'm in the mood to piss him off for the way he's been treating Zoe lately. Has he forgotten the way his parents treated Zoe her entire life? I know that's not entirely fair to Aaron, but time and distance have made him forget the past. He's become softer and more forgiving around his parents, and I'm over it.

I repeatedly peek to see if Zoe is finally ready to leave her room. It's already six a.m., and I'm sure she'll be late for work today considering how much alcohol she had last night.

Taking out my phone, I open the tracker to make sure she's still in her room. Seeing the green dot on the map brings me some level of comfort. I couldn't simply abandon her after what happened last night. She's all by herself, resorting to alcohol to numb her feelings. Aaron is never around, and Zoe isn't one to ask for help. I want to respect her privacy and give her the time and space she needs, but this is just a precautionary measure. I don't plan on continuously checking on her whereabouts, unless it becomes necessary.

And one day, I'll tell her about it. I don't plan on keeping secrets from her anymore.

"Do you two not have your own homes? Oh, wait. Yes, you do. Right in this fucking building," Aaron remarks aggressively.

"Good morning to you too, sweetheart. Do you need a hug?" Tristan coos.

"Maybe a kick in the balls," I mutter under my breath, but Tristan catches it, narrowing his eyes at me inquisitively.

Aaron runs a hand down his tired face, dropping his briefcase onto one of the kitchen stools. "I haven't slept in thirty hours, but I finally sold that billion dollar property. The paperwork for that was a fucking nightmare, so excuse me if I'm a little tired."

"You should hit the shower and get two days of sleep."

I bark out a laugh. "Right. You mean five hours, max?"

Aaron nods as he pours himself a cup of coffee.

"It's nice you're spending all this time at the office right after kicking your sister out. That's what she needs right now...to spend all her time in a new city alone with your endless collection of alcohol."

Aaron whips around, splashing coffee on the floor and not even noticing it. Tristan's eyes follow the mess, and he takes two steps back, unsure if the rest is going to end up on his expensive suit.

Bring it on, Aaron. It's been ages since we've had it out.

"She...what?"

"Yeah. I found her completely drunk last night, hallucinating and hugging your bottle of Gray Goose."

"Fuck," Tristan mutters under his breath.

"Why didn't you text me?" Aaron barks accusingly.

"No need. I had it under control." From the edge of my coffee mug, I raise my eyes to meet his gaze, noticing how his frustration intensifies while I remain composed.

"What is your problem, Dom?"

"You're my problem, Aaron. Why the fuck have you been ignoring Zoe? Hasn't she been through enough? First, you throw her to the side as if she doesn't matter because you're too scared to stand up to your parents and tell them she's living with you. Why didn't you force them to stay at a hotel if it bothered them so much? You don't think that hurt Zoe?"

"Dominik," Tristan tries to interject, but I don't even look at him as I bolt up out of my stool.

"I'm not ignoring her." With a noticeable force, Aaron grinds his teeth and slams his coffee mug onto the stone countertop.

"Sure seems that way. Did you know she's been drinking nightly?"

"And since when do you give a shit about my sister, Dominik?"

We're standing mere inches apart, our anger so intense that I am just seconds away from being honest and ending this friendship.

"That's enough. Both of you."

Aaron and I both glance at Zoe, who is clutching her head and squinting in the morning light that floods the entire apartment.

"Is he telling the truth?" Aaron asks.

"No," she groans, shuffling toward the couch and covering her eyes with her arm. "And please, for the love of God, stop yelling. Both of you."

"I'm not yelling. Am I yelling?" Aaron asks Tristan, who shrugs and looks away, refusing to get involved. He's always been the smart one.

"I'm way too tired for all of this commotion today," Zoes grumbles.

"You're not tired. You're hungover."

"Someone tell Dominik I'm not speaking to him," she says as

she lies down on the other side of the couch, her body hidden from view.

"Why?" Tristan asks.

"Yeah, Zoe... Why?" I chime in, not bothering to hide my smirk.

Has she forgotten we're on good terms? She's made a lot of effort to ensure no one finds out just how much she hates me when we're not alone. But a part of me thinks it's all for show. That she doesn't hate me as much as she wishes she did, especially after what she said to "dream Dom" last night.

I'm not saying what happened at the masquerade ball was right, nor was the fact that I hid everything from her for so long. But Zoe agreed to me staying anonymous, and I know she remembers that. I just don't think she hates what happened as much as she's letting on.

But keeping up this front is easier than admitting to herself that there is something real between us.

Her head pokes up for a second, and she gives me the brattiest dagger eyes before she lies back down, groaning in pain by the sudden movement.

Grabbing an empty glass, filling it with ice and Gatorade, I walk over to sit on the wooden coffee table. Waiting for Zoe to lift the throw cushion off her face and look at me. She's going to need to face the room at some point because there is no way in hell Aaron is letting her off the hook that easily, especially not after I opened my mouth.

"Drink this," I order.

"Go away," she whisper yells.

"Are you mad at him for the rose explosion at your office?" Tristan asks, sounding far too amused.

"Yes... Wait, how do you know about that?"

Tristan laughs. "It's all over the internet. You're sort of famous now."

Zoe springs up, forgetting about her splitting headache. I hand her the glass of cold Gatorade, and she takes it without a fight.

"Did you take the Advil on the side of your bed?" I arch a brow at her.

Her brows pull together. "That was you?"

"Did you take it?" I ask again, my tone a bit more firm this time.

She nods, and I stand up, needing to put some distance between us. It hurts to be this close to her and not touch her, hold her, kiss her. After that night on the couch, a dam broke inside me, and everything I've been protecting, everything I've been pushing away, came rushing back but with such a potent force. I can't contain any of it anymore.

I have no desire to distance myself from Zoe, nor can I deceive myself into thinking that I can easily move on from this. That was before. This is now.

I wanted so badly to take her last night, to be with her. Everything she was saying was what I've been dying to hear, and in her drunken state, she finally let me take a peek inside her head. And as much as I wanted to pull more out of her, I knew she wouldn't remember it and she'd likely hate herself more if she learned her tongue was incredibly loose. Given everything that's happened, I want to do things right from here on out. The next time we're together, it's going to be because she wants to be, because she knows who she belongs to.

The next time we're together, it's going to feel real, and she's going to know just how much she means to me.

No more hiding. No more secrets.

I've been completely truthful with her for days, demonstrating my sincerity in every way I can, and there's still so much more to come. Just because she wants to reject all my efforts doesn't mean I'll quit trying. I'm done pretending, done fighting against our current.

"How bad, Tris?" Zoe asks, watching us while we stand in the kitchen.

"What did I miss?" Aaron interrupts, turning toward me, but I ignore him as I reach for my coffee.

"It's good, actually. It's really driving the message home. People think you two are actually a couple and are buying into it."

"Good for who? Him? Is that all the three of you care about? I had to work extra late last night because I was cleaning up roses from every fucking surface of the office. My boss was pissed, and now people are spreading new rumors about me, as if the old ones from Boston weren't enough. There isn't another office for me to get transferred to. Next time, I'm getting fired."

Shit. I should have thought more about this. Now I feel like a total fucking asshole.

"I'm sorry," I utter, nearly choking on my guilt.

"It's too late for that, Dominik. Stick to the original plan. Nothing more, nothing less. I don't need your shitty grand gestures."

She can't even look at me when she speaks.

"Why did you do all this?" Aaron looks up from his phone, glancing away from the video Tristan was talking about.

He's observing me, knowing that something is off. I can sense his suspicion, and truth be told, he's not wrong. Lately, I've been veering off my usual track, wrestling with my thoughts, obsessing over ways to convince Zoe that the person she met at the ball in Boston was the genuine me. It was us, unmasked. Even though I concealed my identity, every moment shared with her and every emotion I harbor for her is unequivocally real. It's always been real, even when I tried to deny it to myself. But she refuses to see any of that, attributing it all to this fake dating arrangement we agreed to right here in this room. The harder I attempt, the more it seems to fail on me. Maybe I should dial it back for a little bit.

"Dominik?" Aaron asks again, and I can feel Zoe and Tristan's eyes on me now too, waiting for my answer.

But all I want to say is how desperate I am for her forgiveness. That I would give anything to start over with Zoe, and I'm terrified that I ruined my chances forever. I can't say any of that though.

"I don't know how to be romantic. I've never done this shit before either. I thought maybe a grand gesture would go over well with Zoe and get some of the Greg rumors off her back."

That sounds believable enough, and it's not entirely untrue.

Tristan makes a noise, running his hand through his auburn hair. "It's okay. We can still turn this around. You're going to have to go to Zoe's office and do some damage control in Dominik fashion. Take a few tickets and warm up to her boss. Turn on your charm. Maybe put on a small display of affection in front of everyone with Zoe. That should kill the Boston office bullshit too. Everyone will chalk up the roses as a total romantic gesture. You'll win extra brownie points with some free tickets and an apology from the team captain himself."

I'm afraid to look at Zoe. "Only if that's okay with you."

She's staring down, playing with her hands. A long silence from her leaves me breathless, realizing that her agreement could finally give us some alone time together. We need to talk, desperately.

"Sure. But get an extra ticket for my friend Via."

"Who's Via? Is she hot?" Tristan jumps in, and I smack his chest.

The jackass can't help himself. Always needing to insert humor into every situation. Fortunately, this time, Zoe responds positively by smiling and playfully throwing the couch cushion at Tristan. It misses him by a long shot.

"I need to pack for the airport. I won't be around until later this week." Chugging back my coffee, I place my empty mug in the sink and turn to see Aaron standing right behind me.

"You're acting weird," he states.

"Am I? Maybe it's you who's off."

"What the fuck crawled up your ass?"

I glance behind Aaron, gritting my teeth and itching to leave. "We're not talking about this right now, or here."

He narrows his eyes, clearly annoyed by my childish behavior, but I don't give a shit. I'm allowed to be pissed at him for the way he's been treating his sister.

"We're going to continue this conversation later."

"Sure thing, boss. And before we do, maybe reassess your actions. You're always telling us to improve and reassess. It's your turn to take your own advice." I subtly gesture toward Zoe with my head as she watches us intently, attempting to listen to our quiet conversation.

Schooling my features, I steal a last look at her before leaving the apartment, longing to turn back and catch her gaze. I'm too scared to turn and look for any signs of hope on her face, fearing that it would crush me to see the opposite. My patience is wearing thin with her silent treatment, especially considering what happened last night.

The fear of losing her is getting to me, but I find a glimmer of hope as I replay her drunken words in my mind. Over and over again like a broken record player.

It's all I've got right now.

6

ZOE

Taylor Swift is blasting in my headphones, and my second coffee has finally kicked in. I'm working on a marketing and communication plan for one of Tracy's new clients, and the ideas are pouring out of me. My shoulders are swaying, and I'm finally in a good mood. Probably because I haven't had the urge to drink alcohol for a few days. I've felt different, not better or in a more forgiving mood, just different.

Or maybe it has everything to do with getting a much-needed break from Dominik. He was gone all last week for hockey, which means no surprise run-ins. Seeing him is inevitable though, since I'm going to his home game and an after party at the end of this week. I took a couple of snaps for Insta during his last game, showing my support from the comfort of my couch with wings and pizza. Things have been getting quieter by the day on the Dom rumor front, and I'm just happy that at least one thing is going according to plan.

Being at work has also been a welcome distraction. Thanks to Via and Tracy, I have plenty to keep me busy.

Suddenly, my headphones are violently tugged off my head.

"Hey!" I exclaim, turning around to find a frantic, wide-eyed Via standing behind me. There is a tiny dollop of cream on her chin from her coffee. "What was that for?"

"I'm going to fucking murder you."

I try to scan my brain quickly, attempting to remember if I forgot something important. Via's heavy panting could easily turn her into a dragon capable of spewing fire.

"What—"

"Shut up." She smacks the side of my head. "When were you going to tell me your boyfriend was going to stop in today?"

Excuse me?

"Why are you staring at me like that? You understand English, right?" Via mocks.

"I don't understand what is happening right now."

Inhaling deeply through her nose and exhaling slowly through her mouth, she uses her arms to aid in a more efficient breathing pattern.

"I know you're working hard to find your Zen right now, so it's probably not the right time to tell you that there is a blob of cream on your chin." Cringing, I chew the corner of my nail, trying not to laugh when Via goes from forced calm to sheer panic.

"That's it. Whatever we had is over in about two hours."

I laugh at her theatrics. "Why two hours? Why not now?"

"Because of that, you dimwad!" she whisper-yells, crouching and pointing her thumb at whatever is beyond our cubicle wall.

Confused, I finally stand from my chair and choke when I see why Via has been losing her mind. "Oh. My. God."

"I know! He's here, and you didn't tell me."

"Does it look like I knew?" I collapse onto my chair, retreating into myself as if that's going to magically make me disappear.

"Why are you behaving like this?"

Wait. I suddenly remember when Tristan suggested Dom should drop in to the office and apologize to Tracy for the flower fiasco, but I figured he'd at least have the decency to give me a heads up.

There is no time for the blame game right now. I need to put on my girlfriend mask and behave. With so many witnesses around, I'm certain Greg will hear about whatever happens before the day ends. This is my chance to shine and give a big, giant middle finger to every asshole who has been talking shit behind my back.

"I just hate surprises, and I didn't know he was coming today. My man loves grand gestures."

Via beams, her eyes shimmering. "Aw, that's so sweet! Who knew such a hot athlete was also incredibly romantic? Everything they said about him online is completely untrue. People are such jealous assholes."

If only she knew. "Mm-hmm, they sure are."

Via constantly surprises me, even when I believe I have her all figured out. She is often the epitome of a posh New Yorker, complete with her high-end pant suits and luxurious handbags. Other times, she is a chaotic mess. She's all over the map but unapologetically genuine. I think that's why I like her so much. She is unbothered by others' judgment and embraces her true self daily. While I wish I could be more like that, I've found it easier to hide from everyone and everything as the years have gone by.

I'm a coward and lie to everyone, including myself.

Sound like someone else you know?

No, not even remotely close. I'm not harming anyone by doing this. Dominik hurt me for his pleasure. There is a difference.

No matter how much you try to lie to yourself with alternative versions of the events, you know he didn't do anything without

*your consent. You crave to be tamed, and now that you know he
can do that, you're scared. Eventually, you'll lose him too.*

Pressing my eyes shut, I shove down the terrible voice in my
head. My fucking anxiety shows up at the worst times.

"Are you okay?" Via whispers, and I feel her icy hand press
against my cheek, her touch helping to pull me back.

One more second. One more breath before I have to slip into
a role, to be someone else for a little while. This isn't for me, it's
for someone else. It's for my brother, because I know how much
Dominik means to him. One more second to let the hateful words
I say to myself wash over me.

Opening my eyes, I smile at Via. "Yes, of course. We might as
well go say hi."

Via's eyes turn into dinner saucers. "Oh my God, absolutely
not. Holy shit. It just dawned on me that you're banging the
captain of the New York Slashers. Holy fuck. Why have I treated
you normally until now?"

Laughing, I roll my eyes and grab her shoulders, pulling her
into a tight hug. I'm not one for random physical contact, but I
think a controlled squeeze might be the only thing that will get
Via to calm down right now.

"It's okay. Take a deep breath. He's just a person like
everyone else."

"Sure. A normal person...on Planet Delulu," she mocks.

"Get a grip, Via." I fix her hair and wipe away the cream on
her chin. Via pokes her head around the corner and takes in a
sharp breath.

"There is a really hot guy with him. Good lord, I should have
put on my hot girl clothes today."

"You're always wearing hot girl clothes." I snicker.

"This isn't funny!"

Stepping away and into the open space, I notice everyone is
staring at the main attraction: Dominik and...my brother? What is

he doing here? He hasn't even bothered to call me in the last couple of weeks since he's been so busy with work. I'm more surprised to see him here than I am to see Dominik.

Shit, now I'm nervous. I turn to face Via, and she bumps into my chest.

"Who is the other guy?" she says way too loudly.

"My brother, and lower your voice."

"That's your brother? Jesus Christ, dude," Via shrieks, fanning herself. I smack my forehead, realizing no matter what I do, she's going to act like a thirsty fan girl.

"You're a lost cause, and also, good luck. He's like a robot."

Before she can respond, the hushed voices around the office grow much louder.

"Oh my God!!! Dominik Lewis is in the lobby talking to Tracy!"

"Shut up!!!"

"I need his autograph for my nephew."

"Holy shit!! He's probably here to see Zoe."

"Who?"

"The new girl."

"So it's true then!"

Why do I have such great hearing? Fuck this. Maybe I'm not ready for this after all. I return to my cubicle and collapse onto my chair, attempting to regulate my breathing and feign productivity by tackling my emails.

"Umm...what do you think you're doing?"

My fingers are practically dripping with sweat as I type. "He can come to me. Besides, he's probably here to apologize to Tracy for getting me in trouble for the mess last week."

"Are you kidding me? She wasn't mad! You're ridiculous," Via hisses behind my ear, but I ignore her. "So that's how you do it, huh? Play hard to get and let the boys come to you," Via keeps talking.

I read the same email for the fifth time, trying not to smile but not really paying attention. My heart is beating a thousand miles a minute. I can almost hear the drumming in my ears.

"Oh, fuck, here they come." Via rushes over to her chair, pulling out a small mirror she keeps in her drawer as she frantically brushes her hair and re-applies lip gloss.

"Are you trying to look good for my boyfriend or my brother?" The word boyfriend catches on my tongue, sounding entirely too foreign coming out of my mouth.

"Dom is friends with other hockey players, and your brother is hot! I haven't had a proper dick in months." She barely whispers the last part before I burst out laughing.

"I—"

Tracy dashes around the corner, gradually slowing down and wearing a huge grin. She takes a quick glance at me, widening her eyes and adjusting her burgundy jacket.

"Ladies, did I miss the memo about celebrity day at the office? What a pleasant treat." Tracy sounds so fake. Her voice is too high and her excitement is undeniable. I wish the barricade was see-through so I could watch the expression on the guys' faces.

"Oh, god...someone needs to help her," Via mutters under her breath, and I squeeze my lips together, swallowing my laugh.

Standing, I pretend to be surprised.

"Celebrity?! No way. Is Henry Cavill here?" I say loudly, ensuring both Dom and Aaron can hear me as I walk out to greet them.

Dominik pulls his hand out from behind him, holding an enormous bouquet of red roses.

Fucking hilarious.

Tracy's eyes dart back and forth between my brother and Dominik. It's unlikely that she has even taken notice of the flowers.

Good, so not a trigger. Phew.

"Oh, it's you two." My face drops before I readjust the smile back on my lips. "What a nice surprise, indeed. What are you guys doing here?"

Aaron moves closer and plants a gentle kiss on my cheek. He looks impressive in a navy suit that seems freshly pressed. His dirty blonde hair is slicked back, and he smells like bergamot and something else I can't place.

"The surprise was Dom's idea. Sorry," he whispers in my ear before pulling away.

"Tracy, this is my brother Aaron, and this is—" I begin to introduce Dom, but she cuts me off.

"Dominik Lewis. What a pleasure to meet you both. I know you probably can't tell, but I'm a big fan."

Oh, we can tell, Tracy. I need to remember to give Tristan a big hug when I see him next. He's a genius.

"I had no idea you were a hockey fan, Tracy. I would have asked Dom to come by sooner if I had known."

Her eyes fly to me. "Are you kidding me?! We're huge hockey fans at my house. We don't miss a game. Especially me since you became the captain... We know you're going to bring the cup home."

Wow, what a compliment.

Beaming with charm, Dominik smiles brightly. Just like before every game, he's putting on the same performance.

"That's the plan. And these are for you, Tracy." Dominik hands the bouquet of roses to my boss, making her light up instantly. I watch her face changing colors, from pink to a burning hot red.

"Oh my gosh, this is so thoughtful. For me? I figured after last week, they would be for Zoe."

And then he finally looks at me, taking my breath away with those eyes.

A week wasn't enough time to build an immunity against him, it would seem.

"Nah, my girl has apparently had her fill of flowers. I'll have to sweep her off her feet in other ways." He winks, and my stupid knees nearly give out.

What is the matter with you? Get a hold of yourself. It's all an act.

It's hard to remember that when he's looking at me like this.

"That's so sweet!" Via pipes up from behind me, clearly needing to get in on the action.

"Sorry... This is Via. Dom, Aaron." I point to the guys, getting flustered by all this attention.

Via and Aaron shake hands, but he quickly pulls away and discreetly wipes his hand on his pants, which doesn't go unnoticed by Via. He clenches and unclenches his hand, forming a fist.

That's strange.

"Nice to meet you both. Zoe has told me so much about you." Even if that hurt Via's feelings, she doesn't let on. I would be crumbling on the inside.

Also, why did she just say that? I squeeze her back, and she smacks my hand away.

"Is that so?" Dominik cuts her a glance before his eyes land on me again. He's a truly remarkable actor. He could give Brad Pitt a run for his money. I must remember to inform him about his incredible lying skills if we ever speak again, or I could tell Tristan and have him relay the message.

I seriously need to stop complimenting him in my head and start becoming physically repulsed by him.

"She's being a goof. Anyway, what are you both doing here?"

Dom's good looks are enhanced by his tight jeans and a perfectly fitting sweater that showcases his tight chest. His peacoat is unbuttoned, and his hair is slightly damp from a recent shower. Now I'm picturing him naked in the shower.

Stop it.

"I needed to see my butterfly. I hope it's okay we dropped in unannounced."

Did he just say the words, "my butterfly?" I watch Aaron glance over at him, his brows furrowed in confusion.

Yes, I'm just as puzzled. This is completely out of my element. We did not rehearse or discuss any of this. This visit was meant for Tracy, not him being all romantic to me in front of everyone else. I hate the attention.

I think my lip is twitching, trying to form a thoughtful smile, but my brain won't allow it.

"Oh, you!" I smack his shoulder, forcing out a laugh. Aaron doesn't miss my awkwardness.

Dominik's smile widens as he delicately guides my hand to his lips. His soft kisses against my skin spark a whirlwind of sensations within me. Though I should resist, I can't help but savor the impact he has on me. That is the thing I despise the most: the way I seem to gravitate toward him.

The way my body reacts to him without me wanting it to.

I've been trying not to think about the way he stood up for me to Aaron or the fact that he checked in on me when I woke up hungover, left me a glass of water and painkillers. I woke up with a splitting headache and fuzzy feelings floating around my head. Memories of something distant I couldn't place.

There was too much Gray Goose involved for me to even attempt to remember the dreams I had that night. All I know is I somehow stripped and put myself to bed. That was a first for me and somewhat of a red flag that I was getting a little too good at being a drunk.

I've always been in favor of using whatever means necessary to numb my emotions, but I don't want to take this too far.

Which is why I haven't reached for any alcohol since that night.

"Of course it's okay! You're welcome anytime. I'm sure a few people in the office will want to take a couple of photos. Maybe an autograph. I know I'd love that! My son will be very jealous," Tracy bursts out.

"We can definitely make that happen. Actually, there is another reason why I wanted to personally stop by. I know I made a huge mess last week, and I wanted to apologize. Maybe hand you these." Dominik reaches inside his coat pocket and pulls out a small stack of tickets, fanning them out in front of Tracy.

"Oh my... Are you serious?"

Someone needs to remind Tracy to take a breath. She looks like she's about to pass out.

"Absolutely. Take your son, the whole family. There are even a couple of extra tickets in case you need to bribe some people around here." Dominik winks, smiling big.

"Holy shit. Those are season tickets," Via exclaims from behind Tracy.

Dominik winks at her next. I catch a glimpse of Via transforming shades, similar to fall's changing days. What is it about this guy that makes everyone lose themselves? He's not that special, sheesh.

"Your name was added to the VIP list. You can come to any game with Zoe."

"*What?!*" Via shrieks.

"Wow," I mutter under my breath. I wonder what else I can pull out of him, since he seems to be dead set on apologizing for God-knows-how-long.

Next thing I know, I'm being strangled from behind. "Thank you. I love you so much."

"I thought you were disowning me after today," I mutter.

"Shut up," Via hisses in my ear.

"This is all so generous, Dominik," Tracy coos, looking at the stack of tickets in her hands.

"Don't mention it. I'm sorry again for the mess."

Tracy glances up, blushing again. "What mess?"

I watch as they all burst into laughter. This is so fake and ridiculous. And not even necessary.

It's crazy how quickly Tracy pivoted from last week to now. How easy it was to buy her forgiveness. It makes me want to escape.

"We're out of printer paper. I'm going to run downstairs real quick."

"Now?" Aaron asks.

"Yep. I have some contracts I need to print out for your meetings this afternoon." I glance at Tracy, who is shamelessly ogling the boys.

"I'll come with you. You can give me a tour." Dominik takes a step toward me, his hand gently sliding behind my back. My body stiffens, instantly on high alert.

"Tracy?" I look at her with pleading eyes.

Please say no. I'm begging you.

"Of course. Take him around!" She doesn't even look at me.

Time for my plan B.

I turn to Aaron. "Do you want to come?"

"No," Dominik instantly blurts out.

Aaron's jaw tightens as he and Dominik stare at one another. Ever since my parents showed up unexpectedly a few weeks ago, they've been extremely tense around each other. Maybe something else is going on, or maybe it's my parents. They are a topic Aaron and I don't dare broach, because the mere thought of them causes me anxiety, and I know Aaron is still close with them. I made the conscious effort years ago to stop bringing our parents up in conversation with Aaron. It's just easier that way. I want to avoid putting my brother in a difficult position or causing him to resent me.

He's the only thing I have left, and if he turns against me too, I'm not sure how I would manage.

Lately, I've felt like there isn't a point to any of this, and that thought alone terrifies me.

Shouldn't I be afraid of the end?

Not when it could be better than this.

Maybe, or maybe there is nothing on the other side. Nothing but darkness. Which is comforting all on its own.

I wonder if other people have such dark intrusive thoughts as well, or am I like this because I'm far too broken?

"It's okay. I have to get to a work meeting. I caught Dom on his way out and wanted to come by to say hi. Can we have dinner this week?" Aaron's voice is stern as he turns his attention back to me.

I nod, and my brother leans forward, planting a kiss on the top of my hair. I feel every single pair of eyeballs on me.

I have to escape from this place before I create another unforgettable scene. In that case, I'll have no choice but to resign and move to Alaska, where no one knows my name. Start over.

"Sure. Dinner sounds good," I force out, giving my brother a quick smile before heading for the stairwell.

My skin is hot, my lungs are compressed, and it feels like my shirt is trying to melt into my skin. My smart watch beeps, signifying an increase in my blood pressure right as I push through the door. I nearly stumble down the stairs, forcing myself to count my breaths as the corners of my vision go black.

When I sense my balance wavering, I lean on the wall and close my eyes, striving to steady my breaths.

What is the matter with me? There is no reason for me to behave like this.

It's all the fake attention. I hate it. I hate being here,

pretending to be someone I'm not. While people see that display of affection, thinking my brother loves me and I have a boyfriend who is head over heels for me, it's all a big facade and none of them can see beyond the deception.

It's suffocating. All of it.

I don't belong in this world. I never have, and I never will.

"Zoe."

Dominik. Shit.

"I'm fine. It's just anxiety." I breathe out.

Struggling against his frigid touch, I try to break free, only to encounter an immovable obstruction.

"You're not fine. Look at me."

"You can leave now."

"Look. At. Me," he growls.

My eyes open slowly, revealing his face just inches from mine. He appears genuinely worried, a bit stunned and uncertain about what to do.

"Let me go," I whisper.

Dominik slowly shakes his head. "Not until you calm your breathing. Just focus on me."

Except I can't focus. I'm drowning, feeling the distance growing wider between my brother and me. Feeling like even Via can't see me. Like everyone hates me. Nothing even happened. This reaction is completely unjustified.

Fuck this anxiety and my stupid asshole brain.

My breathing becomes more erratic, and I can't control the panic attack heading directly my way.

"Zoe."

"I...can't...breathe." I force out each word in between sharp breaths.

"Tell me what to do," he begs.

"Make...it...stop..."

"How?"

I can only shake my head.

I'm not even sure what I'm asking for because I don't even know how to make it stop. Once the thoughts flood me, I lose myself to the anxiety and the vicious cycle until it passes and I realize it's not the end of the world. I hate that I'm exposed right now, dealing with this at work. In front of Dominik.

I don't like anyone seeing this uncontrolled side of me.

Just that realization alone intensifies the discomfort of breathing.

I'm not sure if I'm imagining it or if Dominik's fingers are tightening around my neck. I think I'm imagining his lips on mine as he kisses me with an intensity that has my mind doing a complete 180. One second, I'm falling into the pits of anxious thought, the next, I'm being brought back up. An equal blend of desire and anger has taken the place of sadness.

I pound my fist against his chest, but it only seems to invigorate him. Dominik lifts my leg and securely wraps it around his waist. My treacherous body succumbs to him, melting against his touch. I trace my fingers up his neck, scratching him with my nails as our lips meet in a passionate kiss. Our tongues clash fervently, as if we both crave each other's touch. It's as if we're underwater, relying solely on each other to survive.

Fuck, he feels good, and I hate that more than the panic attack. I'm starved for him, and I hate myself for wanting him like this.

"I hate you," I breathe against his mouth before biting his upper lip.

His grip around my throat tightens, eliciting a moan from me.

"It doesn't feel like you hate me right now, little butterfly." He fists my hair, exposing my neck right as he bends down and licks up to my jaw. Shivers cascade down my body as fresh desire pools in between my legs.

"Don't call me that."

"I'll call you whatever I want, brat."

As I stare up at the bleak stairwell ceiling, listening to the sounds of our breaths, I realize my panic attack is gone and I'm back in my body. Feeling everything right now, aside from dread.

As Dominik and I make eye contact, he releases his hold on my hair and takes a step back.

He's breathless, gaze filled with lust, and the evidence of his arousal is clearly pressing against his pants. There is no way in hell he's going to hide that.

Runi's cock ruined me in Boston. For an entire week, I could hardly walk in a straight line. It felt so good to be reminded of him, and I frequently fantasized about it while pleasuring myself months later. I had never seen or felt a cock like his before, and fuck... That beautiful dick has always belonged to Dominik.

The sting of his lies hits me from nowhere, reeling me back to the present.

"You said to make it stop," he states.

I did, didn't I? I asked for him to make the panic stop, and he somehow knew exactly what would do the trick.

"I didn't mean like that—" The words die on my tongue.

"I know you better than you think, Zoe. Stop fighting it."

"There is nothing here to fight for," I spit out, but Dominik just smiles.

"That's where you're wrong."

He attempts to adjust himself and fails miserably. Running his hand through his onyx hair, he gives me one last, lingering stare before he turns and walks down the stairs.

Leaving me standing there completely dumbfounded.

7

ZOE

I'm still processing everything that took place earlier in the stairwell.

When I finally came to, I followed Dominik down to the basement, but he was nowhere to be found. Either he vanished within the walls or used the elevator to leave the building.

I'm boiling with rage. I almost considered involving the police and getting a restraining order against the man, but there was a disturbing part of me that actually enjoyed being with him like that. Here I am, at my desk, with my panties rendered completely useless, reminding me of how my body reacts to him without my consent.

I gaze at my phone, anticipating an apology text, but it seems unlikely after two hours.

He is infuriating.

Maybe I need to send a text and remind him of what I said before about how no amount of apologies or grand gestures can erase everything he did. Everything he took from me. The beautiful memories he robbed.

What about him saving you from yourself? Or giving you the one thing you've been dreaming about for years?

Not even that.

"Earth to Zoe."

I turn to see Via waving her arms at me.

"Sorry."

She narrows her eyes and flashes me a wicked smile. "Did you two fuck in the stairwell?"

"God, no."

"Well, you seem awfully distracted since you got back up here. You forgot the printing paper, and your hair is all messed up. Oh, and your lipstick is bleeding," Via retorts, glancing at my lips.

In a rush, I snatch my compact mirror from the desk drawer to quickly check.

Crap, she's right. Despite my smudged lipstick from that make-out session, my winged liner remains perfect as I stare back at my own unrecognizable green eyes.

I quickly touch up my lips with my favorite pink-nude lipstick and brush my hair, still feeling the sensation of Dom's fingers. His touch is everything I've been craving for so long. He instinctively knew the perfect amount of pressure, not too gentle or rough, and I didn't have to direct him at all. He's always been good at reading my body, or maybe he's like that with every woman.

Something about our sexual chemistry just works. It always has.

"Thank you for saying something before I went into my back-to-back client meetings."

Via nods, not saying anything else as she rummages around her desk, making far too much noise.

"What are you looking for?" I ask.

"Nothing. Just tidying up a little." She seems cold suddenly.

"How come?"

Via shrugs. "Just feel like it."

Strange, she's never cared much about her space before. "Did something happen?"

She ignores my question, dumping a stack of pens into her drawer and forcing the thing shut.

"So you're really dating Dominik. What's he like?"

"What happened when I left?" I ignore her question this time, changing the subject back.

Via keeps herself occupied with other tasks, not bothering to look up. It seems like she won't respond until she eventually sighs and turns toward me.

"Tracy was flirting with your brother. He brought up your big file from the Boston office. She told him you were leading the launch party, and all the comms for the event. Aaron seemed happy about that and said he was going to attend and bring a few of his upscale clients."

"What? Aaron said that?" I'm genuinely surprised.

"Yep. And then he kept glaring over at my desk and made some sort of comment about cleanliness. When he left, I got a mouthful from Tracy."

Jesus Christ, Aaron. Way to be an asshole.

"Fuck. I'm sorry. He's kind of a jerk." I cringe.

"Tell me about it. How far up is that stick in his butt?"

I burst out laughing. "Honestly, I'm not even sure. He seriously needs to loosen up. He's gotten so much worse since he became a workaholic."

Via gives me a sympathetic stare. "I'm sorry."

"It's okay. We'll figure it out," I say reassuringly.

"You will. He might be an ass, but it's obvious he cares a lot about you."

I blow out a breath. "I'm not sure. I think he more so feels responsible for me, or maybe wants to make sure I don't mess up under his watch."

"Well, do you blame the guy? You sort of turned green and ran out of the room earlier. No explanation or anything."

I've been so distracted today since they showed up. This entire fake dating ordeal needs to end as soon as possible so I can get back to my normal life.

Maybe that's the answer.

I think the rumors have died down enough that we can probably just call the entire thing off. No more grand gestures, surprise visits, or neck squeezes in stairwells. We need a proper cut off so I can block him from everything.

It's impossible to ask him to stay away from me when we're supposed to be a happy couple. The best thing to do is to end things publicly. That way I won't have to see Dom again.

Pulling out my phone, I fire him a text message.

ME

We need to talk.

His response is instant.

DOM

If it's about earlier, I'm sorry. I got carried away.

ME

It's not. Are you free later?

DOM

Yes. My place?

Images of me buck naked on his couch flash in front of my eyes.

No, I can't go back there.

ME
No, come to Aaron's. I'll be home around eight.

"Zoe?" I look away to see a concerned Via staring at me.

"I'm good. Everything is going to be fine."

Her lips tighten into a smile. "If you ever need to talk, I'm here."

"Thank you."

A wave of dread settles in my stomach, and I face my computer. When others notice my messy emotions, I know it's time to tighten my mask and cut off all loose ends. And right now, Dominik is at the top of that list.

I can't have him interfering with my life like this anymore, making things muddier and leaving me with the mess to deal with all on my own. I was fine before him. Okay, maybe not fine, but I was surviving, and now it feels like I'm drowning. I don't need his help with work, and I think our little agreement has done its job. His team is doing fantastic, and he hasn't been benched once. It's time to end this, bring closure, and erase the memories that bind us. The weight on my shoulders lifts as I make peace with this decision and what I need to do.

Real or not, I'm going to call it and put an end to Dominik.

The sound of my phone buzzing on the desk grabs my attention instantly, and my heart races in anticipation of a message from Dominik. It's just the earlier excitement, nothing worth over-analyzing.

But it's not Dominik who texted me. It's my brother.

AARON
Are you okay? What happened?

ME
I'm sorry I ran off. It was nothing. I just needed a minute alone.

Bubbles pop up, disappear and pop up again.

AARON

With Dom?

The last thing I need right now is for my brother to be suspicious.

ME

No. I didn't see him. Did he come looking for me?

AARON

We should talk. I feel like we've had no time to catch up since Mom and Dad arrived.

Yeah, and whose fault is that?

I wait for a long time, trying to figure out what to say to him.

ME

Sure. Whenever you're free.

IT'S LATE. I'm hungry and exhausted as I walk through Aaron's poorly illuminated hallway. As usual, the place is empty. I can't comprehend why my brother would waste millions on a property he never actually uses. If I even make a comment about this, he'll probably start lecturing me about long-term investment and the value of real estate. Those who are wealthy think differently, and Aaron probably views each dollar as an opportunity to triple its value.

But what's the point in being rich and having all this money if you can't even enjoy the things you buy?

I throw my keys onto the kitchen island and grab a cold bottle of water from the fridge. It's twenty past eight, and a faint aroma of coffee lingers in the kitchen. I just remembered—didn't we agree to meet here at eight? It seems Dominik is running late too.

I'm decide to take a quick shower to wash away the dirt and exhaustion from the daily hustle of New York. As I walk toward my bedroom, I noticed a beam of light at the end of the hallway. It's coming from my room. The closer I get, the gentle glow exuding from it intensifies, causing my heart to pound in my chest. The door is slightly ajar, and I strain my ears, hearing faint shuffling noises coming from inside.

My instincts kick into overdrive, and my senses sharpen as I try to make sense of the situation. Who could be in there? My mind races with possibilities, each one more unsettling than the last.

"Hello? Aaron?" I call out, hoping for a response, but I am only met with silence.

A strong sense of fear tightens its grip on me as I cautiously move toward the open door. I consider calling Aaron's phone, but a part of me is too curious, maybe even slightly excited. God, how sick is that?

I take a deep breath and push the door open, preparing myself for whatever is on the other side.

My jaw pops open because I wasn't expecting to find this...

Dominik is standing in the middle of my room, surrounded by papers and sticky notes. He finishes scribbling something onto a pad before he looks up at me, grinning like an idiot.

He seems completely at ease, as if he's in his own bedroom.

"What are you doing here?" I bark out.

"You're late," he states casually, which only angers me more.

"What the hell is all of this?"

I try to ignore how devastatingly beautiful he looks amidst the notes in my personal space. I'm torn between wanting to rip his throat out and to run around, reading every scattered note.

My skin burns with desire when those dual-colored eyes look at me. I hate that the most. How much I want him despite knowing it's wrong and how much I despise his existence. No matter how many times I remind myself or repeat it, my need for him remains unchanged. I'm doubting my ability to hide it at this point. My mind is consumed by the memory of his lips against mine, back when he pinned me against the wall in that dimly lit stairwell at work.

"Another gesture, I guess. This one isn't as grand though, and it's just for us, so you can't get mad at me for it." He smirks, arching a dark brow as he steps aside to reveal my bed, which is covered in purple and white sticky notes.

My legs seem to move on their own, and when I get close, I notice a beautiful hardback with delicate foil lettering and weathered design... It looks like a special edition of *The Sorrow of Young Werther* by Goethe.

Picking up the book, I grab the first note:

"*I possess so much, but my love for her absorbs it all. I possess so much, but without her I have nothing.*"

"What is all this?"

"I thought you could use a reminder," he whispers.

Suddenly, I turn around. "I don't want you here. I don't want these stupid, fake gestures."

With a delicate touch, he moves my hair to the side, revealing my neck and causing me to freeze. A shiver runs through my body, momentarily paralyzing me and making it impossible to speak or move.

"I don't believe anything you say, Zoe. Your body tells me a different story."

"Stop," I plead, but he doesn't. Instead, his fingers tighten around my hair.

"Keep reading," Dominik commands. "Please."

His voice carries a familiar desperation that tugs at me. I crouch down and collect a handful of sticky notes.

"Is this the destiny of man? Is he only happy before he has acquired his reason or after he has lost it?"

"Think of you! I do not think of you; you are always before my soul."

"Misunderstandings and neglect occasion more mischief in the world than even malice and wickedness."

"Whatever our souls are made of, his and mine are the same."

I fucking love the last quote from *Wuthering Heights*.

When I continue reading, Dominik's voice fills the air, giving life to the words as he reads them aloud.

"I cannot live without my soul."

"I have not broken your heart - you have broken it; and in breaking it, you have broken mine."

"You said I killed you—haunt me, then! The murdered do haunt their murderers."

"Be with me always—take any form—drive me mad! Only do not leave me in this abyss, where I cannot find you!"

All the things I've avoided, all the emotions I've suppressed for years, are slowly resurfacing, and it feels nauseating. I lose my grip on the book, causing the sticky notes to scatter everywhere. I shift my position to confront him, and our eyes connect in a locked stare.

"What the actual fuck is all this? What are you doing?"

"Trying to prove to you what you already know. What we both have known for so long."

I glare at him, feeling the anger surging within me. "And what's that? That you're a psychopath?"

Dominik doesn't hesitate. "That you're mine. You have always been mine and will forever be mine."

"I'm not yours. Never have been and never will be. Get it through your crazy, thick skull." My heart thumps loudly in my chest.

Dominik smiles confidently. "You already belong to me, Zoe. What will it take for you to finally see that?" His words carry a pleading tone, as if he is on the verge of breaking. "Do you want me to get on my knees and beg for your forgiveness?"

I never expected those words to come out of his mouth.

"No, I want you to get out," I grit out.

Dominik's towering presence casts a commanding aura over me as the weight of his confession overwhelms me, though I conceal it.

"I'm not beyond doing that. Begging. I may want to own

you, control and dominate you, but I am not too prideful to get on my knees and beg for your forgiveness, if that's what it will take."

"I don't want your fucking apologies, Dominik."

Frustrated by my refusal to open up, he takes a deep breath and turns away, running his hands through his hair. When he finally faces me, his eyes are glassy in the dim light. I think that shocks me more than his earlier words.

"I'm sorry I lied," he says softly. "I'm sorry for all of it: for leaving you to rot in that town with people who don't care about you, for pretending to be someone else when you were trying to explore parts of yourself that night in Boston, for impeding on your space and invading your privacy when you got to New York."

Why does his apology sound sincere? Better yet, why do I care?

"But most of all, I'm sorry for never telling Aaron how I truly felt. For not standing up for you all those years ago. I just...I'm sorry for all of it, Zoe."

Wow.

I don't know what to say.

Words, Zoe. Say words and tell him to leave.

I allow him to take my hand, feeling detached from my body as I process the weight of his confession. Dominik drops to his knees, clutching my hand against his face, and a startled cry slips from my mouth.

"I'm sorry for getting you involved in my mess. For failing you for so many years. I promise to be better, to do better by you. If you'll let me, I'll fix everything." He finally looks up at me, and I watch as a single tear crawls down his cheek.

I feel numb. Yet, his words touch my heart.

Despite my better judgment and the voice cautioning me not to, I inexplicably believe him. Deep down, I know his words hold no genuine meaning and will ultimately lead to nothing but disappointment.

But he did all this, planned all this. He has been proving for weeks that he's sorry.

No, he was just showcasing to the world his caring nature as a boyfriend. A mere facade to conceal his past actions, or maybe to win me over somehow. Eventually, history will repeat itself, and he will hurt me again. But next time, I'll be reminded of his words and what it feels like to be desired by someone I can never have.

We can never be, and we both know it.

My breath catches in my throat, overwhelmed by the weight of his vulnerability and his apology. It threatens to suffocate me as I gaze down at him. Anxious sweat coats my palms, my body instinctively tensing in response to his kneeling position before me. I desperately scan the room, seeking an escape, but all I see are more sticky notes adorned with unfamiliar quotes from books. Did he read every romance novel in existence?

I look back at him, not knowing how much time has passed, but I finally find the will to speak. My throat is drier than the Sahara desert.

"I don't want you to fix anything. Just get up."

He shakes his head. "Not until you forgive me."

I choose to confront him directly, lowering myself to a kneeling position in front of him. "There is no one here. You don't have to pretend to care."

"I'm not pretending, Zoe. It was never fake for me. It's always been you. Everything I've done is because of the way I feel for you. I'm mad about you, Zoe. Can't you see that?"

Closing my eyes, I try to force my own tears back. "Stop. Please stop talking."

"No. This is the way it's going to be from now on."

"Stop," I plead. "Why do you even care? You've never cared before."

The silence is overwhelming, prompting me to open my eyes, only to be met by the gaze of a broken man. Something cracks in my chest as a pang of sadness runs through me, filling me with a need to reach out and pull him in.

"I've always cared," he confesses, and my eyes fall to the open book lying on the floor beside me.

Picking up the copy of *Wuthering Heights*, I press it into Dom's chest. "Our story ends just like this book: in tragedy."

He takes the book and places it on the bed, then grabs another hardcover and passes it to me.

Jane Eyre.

"I read all these books in the last few weeks. Trying to find reason in what we're going through, to figure out if our story is just a repeat of one that has happened in the past, if there is meaning behind all of this. I know you don't care for this stuff, or maybe you do, and that's why you try so hard to push it away. But I care. I've always cared a little too much."

He grabs the back of my neck, pressing his forehead roughly to mine as our harsh breaths mix.

"And our story will not end in tragedy. There are only happy endings in our future, and I'll make sure of it. Just like Jane and Mr. Rochester, who eventually realize they can't escape one another. And if that's not good enough, Zoe, you'll find our story, the one I wrote for us amongst that pile on your bed."

Dominik forcefully pulls himself away from me, abruptly getting up and storming out of my room. The space between us is engulfed in a heavy silence as he pauses at my doorway, his back facing me.

"I won't give up on us, even if you have. I refuse to ever give up on you. This is not how we end because our story doesn't have an ending, little butterfly. You're stuck with me until the end of time."

And then he disappears, leaving me surrounded by sticky

notes covered in quotes from fictional novels about unforgettable love.

This is so unlike the Dominik I know. The side that cares and tries so hard to convince me of...what? Even if I felt the same, even if I wanted to try, my brother would never allow it. He would make this impossible for us. It's just not in the cards.

When I finally stand, I move the sticky notes aside to find copies of *The Great Gatsby, Romeo and Juliet, Tess of the d'Urbervilles,* and *The Hunchback of Notre Dame.* I want to roll my eyes, throw the books against the wall, and curse him. What's the point of all of this?

There is no version of reality where Dominik and I will get a happy ending. There is too much standing in our way and too much pain from the past.

I collect all the sticky notes and books, locate an empty box in my closet, and toss them inside. Out of sight, out of mind.

As long as I stick to the original plan, everything will be okay.

Just stick to the plan, Zoe.

Stick to the plan, I repeat over and over again, trying to ignore the fluttering in my chest.

"Is she coming, man? We have to get going soon." Our assistant coach is pacing, glaring at his watch every two seconds and just about ready to ream me out.

I messed up again. The pilots need to take off in less than ten minutes, and my woman isn't here yet. Knowing Zoe, she's doing this on purpose to make me sweat.

I really want to pull up the tracker app and check on her whereabouts. But after everything that went down in my closet, I made a crucial choice to rid myself of all the toxic behaviors that hurt Zoe. If I truly want to regain her trust, it's important she learns to come to me on her own terms. Even if I do refuse to leave, I need her to count on me.

I want to start fresh. Show her I'm capable of change.

As I glance down at my phone, I notice my last text to Zoe. It contains all the information about our flight for today, including the location and details. This is the first time she's joining me for an away game, and unfortunately, we have done no preparation beforehand. Now she'll be stuck in a plane with me and my team-mates for hours.

Maybe she decided to bail on me today because the last time I saw her, I laid my heart bare on her bedroom floor only for her to look at me as if I had lost my fucking mind. And maybe I have. But I needed her to understand the effect she has on me. How she consumes my thoughts incessantly, how I ache for her constantly. I know a part of her desires me. It's there, even if she has buried it somewhere deep inside. I felt it in the way she kissed me in the stairwell. It's the same desire from the masquerade ball when she didn't know me, but it's even more charged.

If I have to pursue her until she confronts her emotions, then I will go to the ends of the earth to do so. The line between us is blurry right now. I delved into many books to convince her that our love story is eternal, similar to the timeless classics found in romance novels. Regardless of how much time passes, or the obstacles in our way, we will always gravitate toward each other, forever intertwined. This bond will endure in this universe and every alternate one that exists, forever orbiting one another.

Everything is heightened for me.

The other night, I left her room as if I were on fire. Needing to get out of there before I said those dreaded three words. The words I know she doesn't want to hear, and even if I said them, she wouldn't have believed me. I don't even know if this is love. Maybe it's just a form of insanity and I've painted it the same color as love to justify my words and actions. Or maybe I've always loved Zoe.

Maybe she is the only one I have ever loved, and that scares me more than anything else.

Fuck.

After running my hand through my hair for what feels like the eightieth time, I finally turn around to face the charter flight, aware that everyone is waiting for me.

She's not coming.

Rolling my shoulders back, I sigh in defeat as I begin making my way toward the plane's staircase. They're all going to ask me why she bailed after I covered everything, and I have no idea what I'm going to tell them. I'm sick of lying. Sick of hiding from everyone.

Why isn't Zoe coming, Dom? Oh, thanks for asking, team. Because I'm a piece of shit who lied to her, used her, and doesn't deserve her forgiveness or her time.

The bitter chill of the February wind assaults me mercilessly as I make my way up the rattling, metal staircase. Just as I reach the halfway point, I hear a car screech from behind, making me almost lose my footing when I turn back.

The pure relief and joy I feel watching Zoe step out of the yellow taxi cab is indescribable. Her golden hair whips around in the wind, creating a breathtaking sight. I don't even feel the cold anymore as I take her in.

She's here. She showed up for me.

My heart lurches up into my throat as I watch her gather her things, looking all shades of flustered and so fucking cute that it sends a shot of adrenaline through my veins. Like she's a drug I just hit up for the first time. It feels as if she ignites a spark within me, spreading warmth and intensity throughout my body. No one else has ever made me feel like Zoe does just by simply existing.

I rush back down the stairs to help her with her bags, breathless when I finally reach her.

"You came."

She glances up at me, annoyed. "You told me to. It's in the contract."

I don't bother holding back my smirk. "A contract we never signed."

Zoe stops and places her hands on her hips, looking like such a brat that it makes my cock instantly hard.

"It was a verbal agreement. Do you want me to leave?"

"No way in hell I'm letting you out of my sight now." I grab her, pulling her in as my lips melt against hers. I kiss her with such hunger because I can blame this kiss on my teammates watching through the plane windows, knowing their eyes are on us right now. And because I don't know when I'll get the chance to do this again. I expect her to pull away or not open up to me, but she welcomes me almost greedily, pressing her chest against me. I can sense her heart beating rapidly, perfectly in sync with mine. Our mouths align flawlessly, and the intense heat between us intensifies, igniting a blazing fire that engulfs us both.

I don't care if we never make it to the game. There is nothing in the world that's going to pull me away from her right now.

Time seems to lose its meaning until I hear a whistle, and Zoe pulls away.

"You can do that in here, love birds. I promise we won't bite. Maybe we'll just join in."

I don't know which asshole said that, but I'm going to pummel someone's face in later for that comment. Zoe turns red before she looks at the plane and waves.

She doesn't bother looking at me or picking up her bags. She simply struts to the stairs, climbs them, and disappears inside.

God, she makes me so giddy.

I adore the way she carries herself, with that unapologetic sass that makes her truly unique. And deep down, I know that even if I rein in the rebellious part of her, that feisty side will always remain because it's an integral part of who she is, and that's exactly what draws me to her. Zoe couldn't care less about my disapproval; she lives by her own rules, and I suspect she derives pleasure from defying expectations. I'm going to personally ensure she gets off on it multiple times when I finally punish her for all this disobedience. I'm going to make her beg for it.

I'm getting hard just thinking about her tied up and in my control. Needy and exhausted from hours of edging.

Quickly adjusting myself, I bend down to retrieve her belongings and head for our late flight.

As I step inside the plane, the deafening cheers of the guys fill the air, their mocking tones aimed directly at me, branding me as Zoe's little boy toy. But I don't even care. They've been teasing me since I started all the grand gestures, and honestly, it might have bothered me by now if it were anyone else or if I were doing this for show, but all of it has been genuine. So yes, technically, I am her bitch. Her slave. Whatever else they want to call me, they can because it's all true. I belong to her as much as she belongs to me.

I am hers. I always have been and forever will be.

"Alright, that's enough." I find an empty slot in the overhead bin and shove Zoe's suitcase inside.

"What does it feel like to have Dominik-fucking-Lewis wrapped around your finger, Zoe?" Liam asks, his body turned to face her.

"I honestly never thought the day would come. I didn't think it would happen even if there were only one woman left on the planet. I always figured Dom would just buy a spaceship and go find an alien planet in search of more holes," Jameson jumps in.

I pay no attention to the others as I unbutton my suit. Slipping it off, I carefully fold it and lay it down on the vacant row in front of my seat. The plane is spacious enough that each of us has a row to ourselves, leaving the seats in the front and middle aisles mostly empty, reserved for our pressed suits.

When we're on our way to an away game, it's protocol to dress up, ensuring we're seen in our best outfit upon arrival. But during the flight, none of us want to be miserable for hours. First, it's uncomfortable. Second, it would cause our suits to become creased, resulting in a disheveled look as we travel from the bus to the stadium at the other end.

Looking around, I notice I'm the last one to get undressed. That's what I get for waiting outside like a simp for my girl.

Unbuttoning my dress shirt, I slip it off and repeat the process. Locking eyes with Zoe, I notice she's pulling down on her collar and her face is completely flushed. Either the bantering has quieted down or I don't even hear them. Instead, I'm enjoying watching Zoe get turned on by this.

She has the same look right now that she did when I undressed in front of her in my foyer a few weeks ago. I can't believe so much has happened between us in such a small amount of time. It feels like that night set off a bomb between us, and although a lot of it has to do with my bad temper, I'm kind of grateful it all happened the way it did. I don't know how much longer I would have lasted after that night.

"What are you doing?" she hisses, leaning forward.

I give a sly wink. "Like what you see, little flutter?"

"Dominik," she warns in a hushed tone.

"Look around. We all get undressed as soon as we get on our flight. We don't want to ruin our outfits."

Zoe glances around, observing the attire of the other guys. Some of them have headphones on, engrossed in their phones. Surprisingly, a few of the guys are already fast asleep, and we haven't even left yet. It seems like we're getting ready for departure though, which means I need to pick up the pace.

"Oh my God," Zoe gasps, covering her eyes.

"Nothing you haven't seen, Zoe. It's okay. We've all seen it too."

"Shut up, Noa."

"Awe come on, Cap. You know I love you." Noa laughs.

A couple of the guys start laughing too.

"Okay, I'm sorry, but I have to ask." Liam stands, leaning his arms on the headrest and looks directly at Zoe. "How do you deal?"

I'm going to kill him if he's about to ask what I think he is.

Zoe just stares at him, looking confused.

"You know..." Liam tilts his head toward me, his eyes shifting to my crotch right as I pull up my gray sweatpants.

"Oh my God," Zoe mutters, burying her face in her hands.

"Leave her alone, Liam. And if you're curious about my dick, why don't you visit Pornhub?"

"I would laugh at that joke, but your dick does belong on there, man. And that fucking bar. I was just curious." Liam's eyes turn into dinner plates, and he glances at Zoe. "Let's pretend I didn't say that, and also, I have an above average dick."

"Stop talking, Liam," Ben says without looking up from his phone.

Liam cringes and quickly turns, crouching in on himself and likely dying from embarrassment. I pull my shirt over my head and take my seat beside Zoe.

I feel her eyes on me.

"You good?" I ask, buckling my seatbelt right as the flight attendants begin going over the safety procedures.

"Yes," she says, but I can sense there is more. I finally glance down at her, and she's looking at me curiously.

"What?"

Zoe bites her lip. "What did Liam mean when he said 'and that fucking bar?'" She air quotes the last bit, and I can't help but laugh.

A sick part of me wants to reach for her hand and run it down my pants so she can feel the metal of my cock piercing. But if she does that, I'd have to make sure she becomes part of the mile high club, and I'm not sure we're there yet.

"You'll find out soon enough."

"Excuse me?"

I arch a brow at her and see her visibly swallow. "Whatever

you're thinking, it's probably right, so if you want confirmation, baby girl, you're going to have to take my pants off."

"You're sick," she says.

I lean close to her ear and feel her shudder. "Yeah, so fucking sick. And so needy for you."

She distances herself from me and retrieves her headphones from her bag. I grab them out of her hand.

"What the fuck, Dom."

I keep my eyes on the flight attendants standing near the front of the plane and keep my voice low so only Zoe can hear me. "You're here with me because we can't stand the thought of being away from one another. And because you were so excited to accompany me to a game. So you're going to behave like a good girl, show some respect, and talk to me. Everyone is watching and listening, so for the next day or so, we're both going to pretend like we're mad for one another." I steal a glance at her and notice her shocked expression. "You got it?"

She nods, and we don't talk for a while. It's not actually until after we've taken off that Zoe finally breaks the silence.

"How long is the flight to Vancouver?"

"Just over five hours," I answer.

Five hours of uninterrupted time with Zoe where she can't escape me, no matter how much she might want to.

9

ZOE

Five whole hours stuck on a plane with people I barely know. Fantastic.

Scratch that, not just people, hockey players. Famous, professional hockey players with unlimited charm and sex appeal. How am I not supposed to want to jump out of this plane?

Sitting next to Dominik right now feels suffocating for many reasons, despite it being the ultimate fantasy for most women. I steal a glance at him, finding his presence both overwhelming and magnetic. His perfectly chiseled features and intense gaze make it nearly impossible to focus on anything else. His mere existence leaves me feeling vulnerable and exposed. Dominik is determined to dismantle the carefully constructed walls I've spent years building around myself, and the power he holds over me makes me want to rage. I hate that I've lost control.

I shouldn't have come here. It wasn't part of my plan, but as I paced my room, anxiously checking the time and biting my nails, I felt compelled to go. In the end, I hastily threw some things into an overnight bag and called George, asking him to help me find a taxi. I couldn't resist the urge, even though I tried.

What is happening to me?

What happened to being mad at him?

But all those notes...his scribbles and thoughts in all those books.

He read the books.

What if he hired a professional romancer to do it? He's crazy enough for that.

But why? What do you have to offer for him to want you this much? You're a lost cause. A piece of shit. No one wants you, least of all Dominik.

Unfortunately for me, I agree with the voices in my head this time.

"Did you even crack open the books, or did you just throw everything in the garbage?"

Glancing down at my watch, I realize there is no way I'm going to dodge this uncomfortable conversation with him. We have four hours and forty-eight minutes left.

Fuck my life.

"I opened them," I say, fidgeting with my ring.

Dominik remains silent for quite some time, and as I glance up, I notice his furrowed brows and intense gaze fixed on the digital map displayed on the seat in front of us. His eyes are locked onto the minuscule plane icon, seemingly motionless, despite the fact that we still have a considerable distance left to go.

"And you didn't message me? There were no burning thoughts you wanted to talk about? Maybe even yell at me a little?" He turns, pinning me instantly with those eyes.

I wanted to talk to him about all of it. To tell him I finally caved and went through every single page in those books. I stayed up all night and read through the notes he had on *The Sorrow of Young Werther.* I couldn't believe how much I related to it.

I wanted to express to him that with every page turned and

with every word read, I felt seen. As if it was safe to hide amongst his thoughts, like I finally belonged somewhere.

But I won't be saying any of that.

"Did you pay someone to read every book and make comments?"

He shifts, turning to face me. His face looming inches away from mine. I instinctively lean back, feeling the side of the plane pressing against my back. The flight crew dimmed the cabin lights some time ago, and I quickly glance past Dominik, hoping no one notices his intimidating presence above me. To my relief, it seems everyone is either preoccupied or fast asleep. Darkness envelops us.

"Are you fucking kidding me?" he grits out.

Pressing my lips together, I shrug. "It just seemed all too deep and rehearsed. Fake, much like the way we are." I point my pointer finger back and forth between us.

He snickers. "You're unbelievable. What's it going to take?"

"I don't like meaningless grand gestures. They make me uncomfortable."

"Get used to it, because they're not meaningless. There is nothing fake about the way I feel about you. Never has been and never will be." Dominik inches closer, not backing down.

"It's all been one giant lie. From the very beginning. Even who you said you were at the ball was a lie," I say, not backing down either.

Dominik's jaw ticks. "It was still me, just masked like everyone else. And I asked if you were sure, and you said yes. I only hid my identity from you because I wanted to know what it would be like to have one night with you without all the bullshit."

"But you lied after too. To yourself, to my brother, to me."

"I did, and I'm done lying. I don't care what Aaron wants anymore. I'm going after what I want from now on. No more hiding."

I don't want to make assumptions about what he just said, so I sweep all but one comment under the rug.

"So you've told him all of this?" I cross my arms, matching his fervor head on.

Dominik looks away briefly. "Not yet, but I plan to."

"No, you won't. We made an agreement to make it seem like we're dating, and you're sticking to it. We're all sticking to the original plan."

Dominik presses his nose against mine.

He smells incredibly good, making it difficult to focus. "I don't give a shit about that anymore. Why are you fighting this so hard? Do I need to force you to see it? Is that what it's going to take?"

"You wouldn't dare," I taunt.

He arches a bow. "Is that so? Are you challenging me? Because let me make something perfectly clear: you're no match for me."

"I'm not scared of you, Dom. Not anymore. Now that I've seen who you really are."

Dominik gives me a devilish smile, making me want to bite his lip, but I shove away those thoughts and silently curse myself.

"Do you want to find out, little butterfly?" The threatening tone in his voice should shake me, make me want to retreat and shy away from the commanding force that is Dominik right now.

He's revealing a new side of himself, and logically, I should be afraid. But all I feel at this very moment is inexplicable excitement. I can't even begin to make sense of it.

I ignore his question. "You and I don't have a future. Aaron will always be our number one priority, and let's face it, you just want to get your dick wet. There are plenty of women for you to do that with. I'm sure you have been this whole time anyway," I mutter quietly.

The moment the words escape my lips, an immediate sense

of regret washes over me. I find myself averting my gaze, desperately wishing I could simply disappear into the space between the seats and beneath the floorboards. It's become clear to me that I seriously need to work on my self-control, but I can't help but place the blame on Dominik for influencing the things I say and causing me to reassess everything.

This isn't me, and no amount of apologizing should matter. No grand gesture, not even if he writes a full novel. The fact remain the same: nothing lasts forever. Not even the good moments.

Everything eventually comes to an end.

"There hasn't been anyone else for a long time. Not since you walked back into my life. And I'm choosing you now. I'll choose you over and over again. It's you, little butterfly. We should have been together all along. There is something about this," he says, caressing my cheek, and the electricity from his touch lights me up. "Something about us that makes me want to rewrite our history. I'm going to give you everything you deserve, everything you've been afraid to want in life. You can try to run, but there are some things we can't fight, and I'm done trying to fight this connection between us."

All I can do is blink because my brain isn't registering what's going on.

Closing my eyes, I try to process his words, but I can't. I've never experienced anything like this, never allowed myself to even imagine I was enough for someone to want me this way. It can't be real.

"Stop."

His hand slides to the back of my neck as an onslaught of shivers avalanches down my back. "I can't. I've never been able to. Not with you."

"You're acting crazy. Can't you see that? You rewrote the tragedy in *Wuthering Heights*!"

I intended to hurt him with my words, but they seem to have the opposite effect. "So you went through it. Did you read all of it?"

"No."

"Don't lie. It makes me want to punish you, and I can't do that here."

Oh, sweet Jesus. I pull free from his grip and turn to face the seat in front of me, crossing my legs.

Dominik leans in, his lips brushing past my ear. "Press those thighs tighter for me, baby. I know you crave to be punished. Just say the words, Zoe. I'll take you to the back of this plane and have you screaming out my name so every last person on this flight knows who you belong to."

I'm pretty certain I'm going to combust at any second.

"Dominik, please," I plead, hoping he stops tormenting me like this.

"Suit yourself," he whispers, and I close my eyes.

His fingers gently move my hair, and then his lips graze just below my ear, causing tingles to dance along my neck. I sense a slight nip on my lobe followed by a gentle suction as he exhales in perfect harmony with his movements. A surge of desire tightens and pulses inside me, eliciting a primal ache that tugs at my very core. A need that has me wanting to straddle him right here with his teammates all around us. I don't even care if they watch; I want them to watch, actually. The thought of fucking Dominik with eyes on us turns me on so much, I can barely stand to sit here.

I forcefully push myself away and stand up, quickly moving past him without caring that my breasts are practically in his face. Right now, my priority is creating some space between Dominik and myself.

Ignoring eyes on me, I almost run toward the restrooms in the back of the plane. I lock myself in the small space and splash some stale airplane water on my face.

"Get a hold of yourself. You're better than this."

But I'm not sure that I am. Not anymore. I don't even remember why I'm holding on to this anger so tightly. The longer this drags on, the worse these thoughts are going to become, and I'm not a good enough person to stop this. I don't even know if I want to anymore.

I miss the raw sexual chemistry I had with Runi in Boston. I miss being chased in the woods. I want to be punished, abused, and fucked until I can't remember my own name. Until there isn't a single thought left in my head. And knowing Runi was Dominik this entire time, it takes away the difficulty in finding that again. He's right here, and he's after me.

He's chasing *me*. He wants *me*.

He lied. He stalked you online. He pretended to be someone else. He ruined your first BDSM experience. He lied about his identity. He cares about Aaron, not you.

That is all true, except for maybe that last part, and I could look at it that way, or I could look at it from a different light. Dominik was the one who introduced me to BDSM, and he protected me from a potential predator. From the very beginning, he made me feel secure because he understood me. Perhaps he knew that revealing his true self to me would have driven me away or led me to engage with someone else who might have crossed boundaries.

Now you're making excuses for him?

Ugh. This is a disaster.

How am I going to survive the next twenty-four hours? I wish Sammy or Via were here—they'd know what to do, or she'd kidnap me. Except I'm not sure I'd even tell her about any of this.

The constant struggle between right and wrong, my desires and dislikes, is driving me to the brink of madness. I can somewhat understand the emotions Dominik must have experienced that night I entered the mansion. It's easier to pretend there was no connection between us, to start fresh rather than carry the burden of our past.

I just want to hit pause, but life doesn't work like that.

I'm going to have to figure out a way to push through this and come out relatively whole on the other side.

10
ZOE

Entering the arena from the back with the crew and team strutting in front is such a unique experience. I take pleasure watching everyone come together, each person knowing exactly what to do since they have this dance down to the second. I'm sure after all these years, this feels like second nature to the guys. But it's obvious they don't enjoy it. Walking through one by one, they tilt their public masks into place, dressed in suits that accentuate their features and athletic physique.

Dominik's getup is absolutely lethal. But what's even more entertaining—or torturous, depending on how you look at it—was witnessing him take off and put on his formal attire. I couldn't help but feel like I was missing a bag of popcorn while glaring at him on the plane. And the worst part? He fucking loved the way I couldn't seem to look away.

I drank him in like a thirsty bitch. Did I even try to stop myself? Nope.

Did I pretend like I was checking out the other guys? I intended to, but then I melted into my seat while watching Dominik.

My body desires him in a way I've never felt before. It's a type of need I've never truly experienced until now. I didn't even let myself miss Runi too much because I knew I would never see him again. It was always one night, but now, everything has changed. Having Dom so near, so deeply involved, alters things significantly.

It's just sexual attraction. It'll fade.

Maybe I can find a quick fuck just to forget about him. We're not actually together, and hey, it would be great payback for everything he's done to me. It's too bad I don't want anyone else.

Jesus Christ, I really am a lost cause.

A familiar excitement washes over me as I make my way down toward the ice, where family and friends of the team have assigned seating. The Vancouver arena is like the New York one, a bit smaller but with a similar feel. The sound of excited chatter, the smell of popcorn and hot dogs, and the sea of fans dressed in team colors create the perfect pre-game setting.

The game finally kicks off, and the arena erupts into a symphony of loud clapping and hollering. The game's rhythm syncs with the pounding of my heart. Dominik focuses intensely, and I follow his every move, jumping to my feet with every near miss and holding my breath whenever he has the puck. The infectious energy in the air is electrifying, rapidly spreading amongst the fans. I suppose that includes me now too, since I'm on the edge of my seat.

While my intention to help Dominik and uphold our agreement remains unchanged, I truly wish for his success. He's incredibly talented, and I know how hard he has worked to win the Cup this year. How much it would mean to him and all the boys to bring the Cup to New York. I can imagine every player on every team dreams of that moment. So to actually achieve it, to chase and grasp the one thing you've wanted for so long, it must feel completely surreal. Something they'll never forget. Not to mention, it'll boost their careers instantly.

Minutes turn to hours, and the score remains deadlocked. The tension is palpable as the final period begins. The crowd is frenzied, and the Vancouver fans are loud, booing us whenever the puck ends up with the Slashers.

I feel my phone vibrating in my pocket. Although I'm engrossed in the game, I could use something to distract me from Dom.

SAMMY

You look so cute, boo! And like the perfect, supportive girlfriend.

ME

What?

I alternate between watching the gray bubbles and the game.

SAMMY

You were on TV a little while ago. They were talking about Dom's performance, and the camera switched to you sitting there all pretty and cheering on your man.

ME

Yep, that's me. But you know I'm just playing the part.

I might have shared more with Sammy than I initially planned to, but it happened after I discovered Dom's hidden secrets in his closet. With no one else to confide in, I was going insane, pacing back and forth in my room. Even two workouts a day weren't enough to ease my mind, until I finally opened up to Sammy about what had happened.

SAMMY

Sure, babe. Keep telling yourself that. But I
know you, and if you want my opinion…

ME

I don't.

SAMMY

I think you're being too hard on the guy. I wish
someone wanted me enough to pull all that
shit. Besides, he's apologized in a hundred
different ways. Forgive him.

ME

Is he paying you to say all this?

SAMMY

Oh, stop. You're being dramatic.

ME

You're supposed to be my friend.

SAMMY

I am your friend and I love you. So stop being a
pain and get in there. You know you want to.
Love youuuuu

ME

I don't love you. Say things I want to hear.

SAMMY

Nope, that's not how I roll. And you love me for
it. PS: you look hot.

Rolling my eyes, I smile and tuck my phone away, glancing
up in time to see Dominik swoop in with a lighting-fast maneuver, sliding past defenders and launching the puck into the net.
The buzzer doesn't go off since we're at an away game, but the
few New York fans in the crowd cheer loudly. I leap from my
seat, my voice lost in the crowd. The scoreboard flashes,
displaying a score in favor of The Slashers.

We score two more times, with Dominik getting one assist,

and before I know it, the final buzzer sounds, marking the end of the game. The team floods out and embraces one another, fans cheering, and the air is thick with a sense of pride. It doesn't even phase me that most of the stadium has cleared out. I'm lost, watching Dominik wear a proud smile. He is soaking it in, and something about his happiness seems so genuine. So real and innocent. I love watching him like this, completely in his element.

His eyes meet mine unexpectedly, and a mischievous wink makes my cheeks blush, turning them a shade of crimson. I can't look away from him, as if our eyes are magnetically drawn to each other in this moment. Through his playful gesture, I feel a bond, a shared closeness that makes me feel.

"YOU WERE AMAZING OUT THERE," I say, following the sweat trickling down Dominik's forehead as he wipes it away, panting.

The sweat on his neck... I just want to...

Knock it off.

His smile is dazzling, and I can't help but wonder how I missed noticing such things before. Lust is a powerful feeling.

"Real or fake?" he leans in, whispering in my ear. His words force me to pause and stare up at him.

"What?"

"Your compliment. No one can hear you. Was it real or fake?" The way he's staring at me makes me feel exposed, as if he can read my thoughts without me saying a word.

"R-real," I stutter.

Dominik's eyes twinkle as he smiles brightly. "It was for you,

you know. I wanted to make this game extra memorable. Make sure you had a reason to watch and cheer loudly."

I'm at a loss for words, so I bottle up all my emotions, pushing them deep down inside. I glance around at the bustling crowd, still in high spirits from the victory. The team is gathering at the end of the dark hallway, still glowing from the win, as reporters line up to steal a moment with the hockey players.

I nod my head in the general direction. "You should go. I'm sure they want to talk to you."

"The team is going to a popular club here in downtown Vancouver after the interviews. Do you want to go?"

I shake my head. "You can go ahead. I'm going to get back to the hotel. I'm tired."

"Alright. I won't be too late." Dom sighs, keeping his eyes locked on something behind me as he leans in and places a mandatory kiss on my temple.

"Do what you like. You don't have to come back early for me. I don't care," I say.

"Keep telling yourself that." Dominik grabs my ass, pinching hard and causing me to yelp. I want to bite him so badly for doing that here, in front of so many people. The proximity is almost unbearable, the desire to touch him nearly overwhelming. Why is this happening to me now? He wrote some words on pieces of paper, and suddenly I'm losing my head over it? It doesn't matter what his intentions were or are right now, what matters is his selfishness and what he took from me.

The lies he told.

That's all I should be focusing on right now.

People don't make mistakes. They're not sorry for them. They're only sorry they got caught, and Dominik would have kept those secrets forever had I not found the black box in his closet.

"Have fun."

Behave, he mouths, smiling at me as he turns and walks toward the line of players speaking into mics and staring at giant cameras propped on shoulders. Press is always standing in the exit hallway, waiting to get a few words in.

I pull on my jacket, trying to figure out a different way to exit through the back, when I hear a reporter ask Dominik a question.

"Another killer game tonight, Lewis. Is there something inspiring your unbeatable streak lately?"

"Yeah. My girl, Zoe. She makes me want to be a better man. Play better, do better, be better. It's all for her."

He turns for a second, eyes locking on mine. It feels like a thousand words are exchanged in that one singular look. And then it's all over when Dominik turns to face the reporter again. Every fiber of my being aches to rush to him, to forgive him. Yet I restrain from going down that slippery road because I'm not sure I can stop once I start. The sound of my pounding heart fills my ears, drowning out the world around me. No matter how intense the desire, I know, deep down, it's a path destined for disaster.

It's bound to end. Period.

Well, if that's the case...why not enjoy it while it lasts?

Because it would be messy with him. Because I don't want to ruin his relationship with my brother. There is no room for me in this equation. There never was. I can't quite comprehend why he has developed this sudden infatuation, but I am confident it will fade with time. I just have to be patient and resist the surface-level temptations.

He'll get bored and move on in no time.

Turning, I make my way toward the doors that lead to the side of the arena. Ignoring the chatter around me, I resist the urge to look back, sensing his gaze fixed on my retreating back.

11

ZOE

The driver drops me off outside the team's hotel. According to Dominik, everything's arranged; I just need to approach the reception desk, give them my name, and collect the room keys.

The hotel oozes luxury from every corner—cloaked in brown marble, boasting grand pillars both indoors and out. It screams extravagance, far beyond what I could ever afford. A lengthy hallway guides me to the massive, circular reception desk at the far end. The high ceilings draw my gaze upward, showcasing intricate glass art suspended in midair. A scent of mint and eucalyptus permeates the entire space, tempting thoughts of a relaxing massage, but that's out of my financial reach. Maybe a long soak in the room's tub could be a more practical compromise. Honestly, I just need some alone time right now to forget about that plane ride and everything that's happened since. I need to drown out the incessant nagging inside my head. Suffocate this growing desire inside me.

"Hey, Zoe! Hold up," someone calls from behind me, and I turn to see Dominik's assistant coach approaching quickly.

"Hi, Coach—" I cringe, biting my lip.

"Bradley," he finishes for me, smiling and completely at ease. He seems happy after that win.

"Sorry. I'm bad with names."

"It's okay. I totally get it. There are a lot of us."

I nod, smiling. "You didn't join the guys at the club?"

He laughs, repositioning the strap of his backpack on his shoulder. "I'm way too old for that shit. I need my beauty sleep. How come you're not there?"

"It's not really my scene, and I'm exhausted. I was just going to wait for Dominik here."

There's a hint of doubt in his narrowed eyes, as if my words are not convincing enough. "Okay. Well listen, I'm glad I caught you. I upgraded you and Dom to a king-size bed because the hotel is overbooked and we had to put a few of the guys in the same room. You were both in a queen adjoining room before. I hope that's okay. I figured you two would end up in one bed anyway, and this way, you'll have more space."

Panic internally until you get inside the room, Zoe. It's all going to be okay.

"Wow. Thank you. You're sooo right. We're inseparable," I gasp out, forcing a smile and feeling my cheeks stretch super wide.

Dial it down, dumbass.

All I want to do at this very moment is to turn and bolt the other way. Panic fills my veins at the thought of spending a night alone in a room with Dominik with his teammates staying on the same floor as us.

How the fuck am I going to escape all of this now?

Coach Bradley's brows knit together, creating a ripple of wrinkles. "Are you sure you're okay?"

I nod feverishly. "Perfect. Thank you. That's really thoughtful."

"Okay, well, if you need anything, I'm in room 1720. I'm sure the guys will be back soon. Do you want me to give you the address of the club in case you change your mind and want to join them?"

"No need. Dom already gave it to me."

"He wasn't with them," Coach takes pause, inspecting me as if I'm under a microscope.

This is feeling more and more like a trap. I need to come up with something quick.

"Right. He said he was running an errand and he was going to meet up with them there. And he also told me he wouldn't be staying out too late. Just a drink to celebrate the win with the boys."

Coach Bradley sighs in relief, smiling. "Yeah, he's an excellent captain. Thanks for understanding, Zoe. I'll see you both tomorrow for breakfast."

"Good night!"

I try to suppress my smile and swiftly make my way toward the reception desk, silently urging my heart to calm down.

"Hi. I'll need the room keys for Zoe and Dominik. Dominik Lewis."

The receptionist offers me a smile, clicking her long, red nails against the keyboard. "Certainly."

I pull out my phone to text Dominik.

ME

Where are you? I just got hit with an unexpected surprise.

DOM

At an appointment. What's wrong? Do you need me to come?

What type of appointment would anyone be at after a game and at this time of night?

ME

What appointment? Why didn't you tell me? And I just spoke to Bradley. Apparently the hotel is overbooked and we got roomed together since we're such a happy couple. *vomit emoji*

DOM

Oh, okay. You didn't answer my question.

He doesn't comment on the room update.

ME

I'm fine. It was just that. You didn't answer my question about your appointment. And no comment to the room fiasco?

I watch the gray bubbles appear and disappear before another text comes through.

DOM

Where I am doesn't concern you at the moment. And the room situation is the cherry on my cake tonight. I think my luck is finally turning around. See you later, little butterfly. *wink emoji*

ME

Stop calling me that. And you won't see me later because I'll be jumping off the balcony.

DOM

You think a little dark humor is going to deter me? Don't you know I won't hesitate to jump after you and chase you through hell? Because we both know that's where we're ending up...together.

I blink at my phone, dumbfounded.

Can the guy get any cheesier? Jesus fucking Christ.

"You're all set! Do you need anything else?"

I jump in surprise, momentarily forgetting where I am before taking the cards from the receptionist.

"No, that's everything. Thanks so much," I say, pausing before I leave the desk. "Actually, when does the pool and hot tub area close?"

"It's open all night, and you'll need your access card to get in."

"Perfect. Thank you."

She smiles. "Of course."

I run for the elevators, needing to come up with a plan before Dominik shows up and ruins my sleep. This was supposed to be a weekend away with minimal stress, and now my entire body feels like it's coming alive with the anticipation of spending an entire night locked in a room with Dominik.

Unrelenting, persistent, mouthwatering Dominik.

I'm in big fucking trouble.

THE ROOM IS JUST as luxurious as the rest of the hotel. A bit dated, but well-maintained and the cleanest hotel room I've ever stepped foot inside. Pretty sure I could set up camp on the padded carpet and it would still be comfortable. There is an idea. I'll make Dominik sleep on the floor.

But then, in the middle of the room, sits a colossal wooden king-sized bed making my core tighten with an unwanted need. I lack the courage to even approach the bed. As I get closer, the floor-to-ceiling window on the twenty-first floor catches my eye. It showcases the stunning night view of downtown Vancouver, wrapped in darkness.

An image of me and Dominik, naked and pressed against the

glass, flashes through my mind and nearly has me gasping for air. I have some serious problems, and right now, the inner chaos inside me is threatening to swallow me whole.

As I pace around my room for what seems like an eternity, a realization finally hits me—I have both room keys, which means I can slip away to the pool without worrying about running into Dominik down there. And the rest of the team will be at the club for a few more hours. Hopefully, the pool will be empty. I can swim and compose myself, find some calm, and strategize on getting through this overnight trip with no regrets.

I change into my bathing suit, put on the hotel's white robe, slip on my flip-flops, and head outside.

Leaving the elevator, I don't notice anyone as I approach the full glass doors at the end of the winding, creme hallway. My room key beeps against the card reader as it flashes green. Pulling open the handle, I step inside the serene oasis of the hotel's pool and notice it's completely deserted. The blue water gently shimmers in front of me as the sound of my own footsteps slap against the tiles.

Dropping my robe on a nearby lounge chair, I slip into the heated pool and feel my body relax for the first time in hours.

This feels amazing.

The water surrounds me, its warmth embracing me like a gentle hug as I completely submerge my body. Swimming with steady strokes, my arms slice through the water as I try to release every anxious thought floating around inside my head. Hoping it all bleeds out of me right here and leaves me devoid of emotion by the time I'm done. I'm wrestling with myself. I have been for weeks.

I never actually allowed myself to feel everything that happened the day I discovered who Dominik is. That he was behind darkhorse, he was Runi in Boston. My Runi...

I didn't even allow myself to think about all the intimate

moments we shared. That it was him who saw me at my most vulnerable, leaving me raw and abused and wanting more. It was him on that couch, forcing me down until I whimpered his name, soaking his fingers.

I didn't allow myself to face the fact that, despite everything, I felt an overwhelming sense of comfort with him. With Runi. With Dominik.

And in every scenario, in every fantasy, I still want more of him. Knowing everything I know now hasn't changed that. It's made me angry, but the desire to be with him hasn't dissipated. The boundaries I vowed I'd never cross are still there, but somehow, they are fading into the background, and I think I hate that the most.

No, I hate him.

I hate his stupid hair and the way his clothes stick to his perfectly chiseled body.

I hate his stupid fucking tattoos, and how I just want to trace my fingers over them while lying on top of him.

I hate the way he looks at me and the way his eyes linger on mine, making me feel exposed to the world.

I hate the way my body reacts to him.

Fuck him and his beautiful smile, and those dual-colored eyes that stupefy me without effort. He doesn't even realize the pull he has on me. And out of all the things I hate about him, that one is at the top of the list.

It's all wrong.

The promises, our past, our present...the weight of what could be.

But the forbidden element only intensifies the fire within me. If anything, my attraction toward him has only increased. The struggle to resist is becoming more and more difficult.

And being close to him like this, sharing a room with him and getting stuck on a flight with him is only making me itch. He's a force that draws me closer despite my every attempt to resist. When our eyes meet, a spark ignites between us, sending shivers down my spine and jolting me to my core. It feels like the universe is conspiring to keep us intertwined, tormenting me with the fact that I can't have him.

It's more than just the physical appeal that engrosses me. It's the way he challenges me, the way he stimulates my mind with his sharp wit and intellect. I think that's the most surprising part about all of this, how well we seem to be matched in that way. I've never found anyone who has kept me on my toes like he has. The last time I felt anything close to this was with Runi, and how ironic to find out all these years later that it was Dominik.

It's always *been* Dominik.

Each conversation leaves me craving more, longing for the connection that I know we can't have. A line we cannot cross. We've been there once, and we can't go there again.

Aaron would never forgive me.

I need distance. I need to run, to escape this infuriating pull that threatens to destroy me. But a part of me secretly hopes for a moment of weakness, when the boundaries blur and I finally give in to him. Maybe if I give in, if I allow myself to enjoy a night with him, this desire will fade.

I could get him out of my system, could I not?

The forbidden temptation is making both of us a little crazy at the moment. My resistance only motivates him to try harder, but if I were to give in, we could both move on. It's the only thing I haven't tried. And it might be the one thing that finally sticks.

Emerging for a breath, I squeeze my eyes tightly, persistently circling the vacant pool. The rhythmic movement of swimming acts as a comforting remedy. My muscles start to ache, yet this only motivates me to exert more, stroke after stroke.

Lift, breathe, submerge.

The water drowns out my thoughts, providing me with a fleeting moment of peace.

I touch the wall, flip, and repeat the cycle until my lungs protest. But I refuse to stop because I need my emotions to cease control, stop causing me to doubt the line between right and wrong. I'm struggling with the inevitability of what I know is the truth.

Gasping for air, I surface, resting my elbows on the tile. I keep my eyes shut, waiting for the stinging sensation to fade. I finally open my eyes and startle, finding Dominik crouching just a few feet away, staring at me with a smile on his face.

"Goddamn it. How the hell did you get in here?" I wheeze.

With a smirk, he quickly reveals a hotel card before swiftly tucking it away in his pocket. Looking freshly showered, he dons a casually stylish ensemble consisting of black jeans, white sneakers, and a perfectly fitted gray sweater that accentuates his physique. His sleeves are messily rolled up, unveiling an array of tattoos that make me weak.

I'm curious about the appointment he had that made him dress up like this.

Maybe he was on a date.

Shut up. He wouldn't jeopardize everything we've done so far to take another chick out on a public date.

Maybe it wasn't public.

What do you care? I shouldn't, and I don't.

But he looks so fucking good that I need a second to compose myself. I wish the pool water were cold. Taking in a deep breath, I quickly disappear underneath, staying submerged for as long as possible.

When I come up for air, he's like a statue. Watching me curiously in the same position as before.

"Sorry if I scared you. I checked the room and saw your

clothes on the chair and a robe missing, so I figured you'd be down here," Dominik explains.

"Great work, Sherlock Holmes."

A lopsided smile tilts his lips. "Do you always have to give me a hard time?"

"Yes," I blurt out, liking the way he keeps up with me.

"I'll break you in, Zoe. Guide you into submission," he whispers, his voice a low, seductive rumble. He gracefully lowers himself before me. Tracing a finger along the curve of my neck, capturing a single droplet of water crawling over my frantic pulse. The sound of my pounding heart echoes in my ears as his touch lingers, sending shivers of anticipation through my overheated body. "Tame you exactly the way you want."

His words hang in the air, heavy with promise as our eyes remain locked. I push away, swimming to the center of the empty pool where I'm safe.

Dominik stands up, crossing his arms and flashing me a victorious smile.

My poker face is failing miserably.

"Where were you?"

"Wouldn't you like to know," he teases.

"Actually, never mind. I don't care," I express, cooling my features as I face away from him and swim toward the steps leading out of the pool. I'll go marinate in the hot tub until my body turns to jello. My plan is to exhaust myself, maybe have a drink from the hotel room bar, take a hot shower, and pass out as soon as my head hits the pillow.

I'll ignore Dominik, and in the morning, we'll head down for breakfast, pack up our shit, and leave for New York. That can't come soon enough.

My bathing suit clings to me snugly as I adjust the straps, preparing to step into the cozy, circular hot tub next to the swimming pool. While Dom's eyes roam across my body, I attempt to dismiss the electrifying sensation.

"Can I join you?" Dominik doesn't wait for my response as he starts removing his shoes.

I pretend like I'm playing with the bubbles gurgling in front of me, but from the corner of my eye, I can see him slip out of his jeans. I try not to stare down at the tight white boxers he has on and instead focus on his face and the smile he flashes me right as he grips the back of his sweater by the collar and pulls it over his head.

Sweet lord...I am going to melt right into this fucking hot tub.

He lays a towel on the ground, plops down onto it, and drapes his legs in the water while leaning back on his hands and staring at me.

I open my mouth to tell him off but notice a large, white, square bandage covering his chest, right over his heart.

"What happened?"

He nonchalantly brushes a hand over it. "A new addition."

"A tattoo? Is that where you were?"

He tips his chin down.

"Why here? Isn't your artist in New York?"

Dominik shakes his head. "I have a few favorite spots all over. One of them happens to be in Vancouver, and I've been wanting to get this particular ink for some time."

He has a multitude of tattoos, and I can't deny that I have a strong desire to trace each one and uncover the inspiration behind each piece of art. What every ink dot signifies to him, and whether some hold no meaning at all.

"What did you get?"

Dom dips his head, smiling down. "It's hard to explain, but I'm sure you'll see it once it's healed."

"Is it similar to those ones?" I say, pointing to the ink all over his left arm, shoulder, and on the side of his chest. Abstract lines, numbers, and words intertwine with each other. The different symbols, although impossible to decode, seem to be connected somehow.

"Somewhat. But this one is the main piece, right over my heart."

I glance up at Dominik to see his eyes on me, watching as I take in his tattoos.

I point to a strip of text and numbers all trickling down his forearm. "What do all these say?"

Dominik is quiet for a long time, and when he speaks, he's careful with his words. "They remind me of someone."

"Who? Your dad?"

With a smirk on his face, he casually shrugs, as if he has no intention of telling me anything. I roll my eyes, losing interest in the conversation. "You didn't have to check on me, you know. I told Coach you'd be joining the guys for a drink."

"I'm not checking on you. I want to spend time with you."

Leaning my head back, I stare up at the ceiling. "I don't want to spend time with you."

"That's not true."

"You're such a cocky bastard."

"And you're a brat."

Anticipating yet another argument, I quickly step out of the hot tub. Boiling water splashes around me, accompanied by swirling steam. Just as I put some distance between us, Dominik's hand abruptly grabs my arm, preventing me from walking away. I turn my head and look down at him, feeling an inexplicable surge of anger building up inside me.

"Don't leave. Please," he declares, his eyes heavy with exhaustion. The same type of fatigue I feel from our constant back and forth.

"Why? We're just going to fight if I stay."

"Then let's not. Can we just stop for one night? I'm tired of fighting with you. Can we just have one normal night where you pretend you don't hate me? I don't want to fight." His voice is quiet as he waves an imaginary white flag in front of my face.

Everything inside me is screaming for me to surrender the anger. Because in truth, I'm tired too. Tired of feeling angry and defeated all the time. Tired of feeling like an utter failure and that I can't do anything right. I'm tired of fighting off whatever this has become between us.

"I don't want to fight either," I confess.

A ceasefire sounds like exactly what I need right now.

"Let's call a penalty box timeout."

My chest tightens. "A what?"

"A timeout. Where we step into a box and leave all the bull-shit outside. A breather," he whispers as his hand trails down my arm and pulls me to sit down beside him, our fingers intertwined. I'm not doing anything to stop it either as I lower myself, planting my wet ass on the cold tile.

"Here," Dominik says, moving off the towel he was just sitting on to offer me the space. Even though I'm already wet and he's sitting in nothing but white, skin-tight boxers.

Don't look down.

God, just remembering how Runi suffocated me with his dick has my core tingling.

Cut it out.

I can't help it.

"It's okay. You take the towel. I'm already wet." I try to move off the towel, but he stops me.

Oh, fucking hell, why did I just say that?

He laughs, biting his lip. "Wet already, huh?"

"I'm going to cut you."

Dominik closes his eyes, groaning in pleasure. "Don't threaten me with a good time, little butterfly."

For God's sake. I'm losing this battle quickly.

Maybe I can lower my angry mask for the night and take a momentary pause. Not like I can go stay anywhere else, because then the team would think we got into a fight. It would be in my best interest to make the best out of a shitty situation that's not in my control.

Resting my hand on his thigh, he gently traces circles on my palm with his thumb. We sit in silence, our legs immersed in the warm water. I fix my gaze on the rhythmic movements of his thumb, observing its repetitive pattern.

The hot tub's gurgling suddenly stops. Despite the heavy silence, I can't bring myself to interrupt the intimate hand dance between Dominik and me. The silence feels dense, like the steam surrounding us.

"What are we doing, Dominik?"

I feel his body shift closer to mine. "We're figuring it out. One day at a time."

"There is nothing to figure out. There is no future here. I need you to let me go."

His touch disappears, and my hand remains on his thigh. I pull away and look up. He's staring at an empty cement wall by the pool. His expression seems lost, as if he's grappling with something profound. Maybe my honesty offended him.

Finally, he turns toward me. "I wish you could see inside my mind. I wish you could feel everything I've always felt for you. How hard it's been to try to forget you. If you could feel just a fraction of it, if you could see it...you wouldn't dare tell me to let go. There is no letting go, Zoe. You're my endgame."

I blink at him, unable to truly grasp his words, or maybe my brain is short-circuiting, because I don't understand.

"Stop fucking saying shit like that. Don't tell me words that mean nothing. I don't want to hear it."

Dominik tightly grips my throat, pulling me in toward his face and stealing the air from my lungs. "I don't give a shit what you want or don't want to hear. This is the truth. It's my truth, and you're going to hear it."

"I don't want you."

"Then what do you want?"

Nothing. Everything.

Something...

I want to forget who I am and step into the unknown.

I want an escape, even if it's just for a short time.

"I don't know," I stammer out, unable to keep my eyes on him as I feel my cheeks burn with that realization. Dominik senses it as he releases his grip on me, forcing me to inhale deeply.

"I think you do, and I think it scares you. I think you want this, but you don't know how to ask for it or even allow yourself to feel it. I'm fighting for you—for us—for this because it's so much bigger than you and me, Zoe. Can't you feel that?"

"No, you're wrong. I can't feel anything."

His eyes darken. "That's not true. You can feel everything, and you feel it too much. It's too heavy and too painful, so you shut yourself out. You walk away before things get too emotional or messy. Before you start to care."

I shake my head, fighting the growing knot forming in my throat. "Please stop talking." Closing my eyes, I take a deep breath before I feel his palm press into my cheek.

"It's time to put the pain down, Zoe. You don't have to carry it alone anymore. You don't need it. Let me take the burden for a little while until you realize you're so much more than the pain. Until you can finally release it and never look at it again. Put it down and let me carry it for you."

Before I even realize it, a tear rolls down my cheek, and by the time I notice, it's too late to prevent it. I can't hide or withdraw anymore because Dominik gently wipes it away with his thumb, and in that moment, I understand it's all over.

I know he's seen a glimpse into me, and I can no longer hide.

His gaze lingers on me, filled with a type of genuine need I haven't experienced before, not a trace of disgust or disdain. It's comforting to be seen like this but simultaneously terrifying. I'm struggling against this vulnerability—I hate feeling so exposed.

I don't want any part of this.

Pain is easy. It's formulaic. Sadness. Revenge. Hate. Anger. They are all simple emotions. Need. Desire. Affection. Love... Those are all hard emotions. Some are even impossible.

I need to get out of here. Fuck the pause. I can't think straight.

Rising to my feet, I don't bother looking down at Dominik as I rasp out an apology before bolting toward the exit. I hear Dominik call out my name, but I don't stop, my eyes blurring as I push past the glass doors and head for the stairwell.

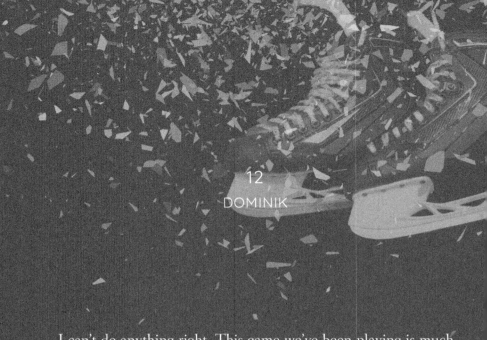

I can't do anything right. This game we've been playing is much more fragile than I realized. Zoe needs more than gestures, apologies, and time. She requires a firm foundation and proof that I won't leave. If only I could filter my words and think before speaking, I would. I hate that I'm making her uncomfortable, but I also think it's necessary in order to break through to her.

And I will fucking break through if it's the last thing I do. I'll do whatever it takes to prove to her that this is real.

That it's always been real for me.

After she left the pool area, I took the elevator up to the room, only to find it empty. It's been over ten minutes now, and I've been waiting for her to walk in. If she doesn't show up soon, I'm going to check the stairwell. I'm worried that she might be having another panic attack all alone.

I meant every word I said tonight about shouldering us through this. I'm beyond eager—I want to take her pain, lift the weight off her shoulders, and provide her with a sense of safety, a chance to trust her heart. But she won't let me. She's resisting at every step. All I've ever wanted was to make her feel alive, cherished, and loved. I'm going to give that to her. I've never shied away from a challenge, and I don't intend to start now, especially when it involves the most significant undertaking of my life.

Pacing the length of the hotel room, my gaze remains fixed on the door, straining to catch any hint of approaching footsteps in the hallway without looking outside. Time slips away as I continue my restless pacing, each step making me more impatient. Suddenly, I hear the familiar beep before the door opens.

Zoe walks in, her body still wet, and she's not wearing any shoes. As if she rushed from the pool area in a state of frenzy, worried I might chase after her. I bet a part of her would have fucking loved that. Throw her in a closet somewhere and have my way with her.

Not yet. Not like this.

Gasping for breath and with wide eyes, Zoe seems shocked to see me standing in the middle of the room.

"Are you okay?"

"Yeah, I'm fine. I just needed some air."

"Stale air from the stairwell?" I arch a brow at her.

She glares at me, unimpressed. "Yes. Away from you."

"Do you hate me that much?" I tease, but she doesn't crack a smile.

"I can't do this with you anymore. *We* can't do this," she yells, her hand waving between us. "You want me to forgive you? Fine. I forgive you. Now, please, for the love of God, leave me alone."

"That's not how this works," I whisper.

"Why? Why do you care so much? Do you want to win? You have, okay? You won. I have nothing to give you, Dominik. I'm done."

I advance toward her with deliberate steps, my heart pounding against my ribcage. On the outside, I'm forceful, but on the inside, I'm about to fall apart. The floodgates reverberate under the weight of everything I've been holding back. Emotions surge through me, crashing against my walls, threatening to overflow and devour me entirely.

"Well, I'm not done, Zoe. I made a mistake, and I will apologize for the rest of my life if you'll let me. And even if you don't, I'll still be here because I can't let go. This isn't an act, okay? I need so much more than your forgiveness. Please let me prove to you how sorry I am. Let me make it right."

"There is nothing to make right. What's done is done, and we can't go back or move forward. We're hopeless."

"We're not. Let me prove it to you, please," I beg.

"No."

"Why?" I take another step toward her, and she reacts to the small space between us.

"Because I fucking hate you," she yells out.

"Say it again, but this time, keep your eyes on me."

Zoe shakes her head, her expression filled with disappointment until it morphs into something else entirely. She doesn't look at me once before disappearing into the bathroom and locking the door.

Goddamn.

"You can stay in there all night long. We're not leaving until we settle this."

I've never felt a stronger urge to forcibly break down a bathroom door in my entire life.

The sound of running water fills the room, giving me a moment to collect my thoughts while Zoe is in the shower. I feel lost, unsure of what to do, desperately searching for a way to mend the remaining shattered pieces of us. The weight of the situation is overwhelming as I realize how close I am to losing her forever.

I can't allow that to happen. But every effort I make to fix things only seems to make the divide between us worse. I don't have the answers, but I desperately want to repair everything that's damaged between us.

Falling down on the edge of the bed, I cradle my head in my hands, going over every memory, when I hear the bathroom door open.

As I glance up, my breath catches in my throat.

As Zoe exits, the gentle bathroom light highlights her glistening, completely exposed skin. Her damp hair cascades in undulating waves, carrying the enticing scent of fresh shampoo. The sight of her perfectly peaked nipples sends a jolt of desire through me, causing me to clench my teeth and tightly grip the comforter, desperately attempting to ground myself to the bed.

"I changed my mind. I want to call a pause." Her gaze fixes on me, and her posture is completely rigid, owning the entire room as if she's in total control.

Fucking Christ, is she ever.

She could ask for the entire world right now, and I'd place it in the palm of her hand.

Zoe takes two steps toward me.

"What are you doing?" I barely get out.

"I'm done fighting. You want me, right?"

I'm about to kick myself in the teeth. "Yes, desperately. But not like this. Not after you told me you hate me."

Zoe looks down at herself, a playful smirk on her face. "That's a shame. I've been fantasizing about Runi for so long."

Jesus fucking Christ.

"You have?"

Zoe tips her chin up, biting her lip. "Mm-hmm."

Fuck doing the right thing. I have to have her or I'm going to need to be checked into an insane asylum.

"You want me to forgive you?" she says seductively.

"Yes," I choke out.

"Good. Get on your knees and crawl to me," Zoe demands.

"What?" I think I'm in shock.

"On your knees, Dominik. Show me how sorry you are."

I groan, my cock getting hard at Zoe's display of dominance. I don't know how this entire thing flipped on me, but it doesn't matter because I can't concentrate on anything else right now. All I see is her perfect body, naked and open, ready for me to take as I please. I'm dying to taste her. To lick every inch of her skin and bury myself deep inside her.

"I'm tired of fighting, and if we're forced to stay here tonight, I want to fuck. So it's now or never. Show me how sorry you are," Zoe repeats.

Without hesitation, I slide to my knees and begin crawling toward her. She's never been more beautiful. Standing tall and looking down at me—this should evoke feelings of shame or powerlessness. It should make the dominant side of me recoil, but all I feel is pride toward Zoe. I am proud of her for finally embracing this aspect of herself and being unapologetically selfish with her own needs.

I pause at her feet, staring down at her red toenails as I consider my next move.

Zoe nudges my chin up with her finger, forcing me to look up at her.

"Look into my eyes," she commands, making me fall for her a little harder. "Now apologize with your tongue in between my legs."

Fuckkk me.

She holds on to my hair to steady herself, raising her leg and placing it on my shoulder. Gripping her ass, I plant kisses up her thighs, never taking my eyes off her. It's hard to believe that after all this time, the moment I've been dreaming of is finally here. I'm so happy that I might die any second.

I trace the tip of my tongue slowly along her clit, feeling her entire body shiver. Every ounce of control is working overtime right now, forcing me to take it slow. I want to savor every moment with her, consume her with desire, satisfy her completely, and make her question why she waited so long to be with me.

My girl has come a long way though. Hard to believe in Boston, Zoe was too shy to sit on my face, now she's keeping my head locked in place in between her thighs. I fucking love it.

I lick her softly, knowing she needs so much more than what I'm giving.

I feel Zoe's body sway rhythmically against my mouth as she pushes herself closer with each movement. I want to shove her to the ground, have her ride my tongue, but I want to torture her more. So instead of giving her what she wants and fucking her with my tongue, I stand and lunge for her. Grabbing her tight against my body before throwing her on top of the bed and climbing overtop of her.

"Do you know how long I've wanted to be with you like this? You've driven me insane with need. There is no way I'm rushing this."

Zoe is breathless and flushed but staring up at me with excitement. She pulls her arm out from beneath me and runs her delicate fingers through my scalp, brushing my hair. A shiver runs down my spine as if countless tiny needles are poking my skin.

"Since that night in Boston?"

"Longer," I murmur, kissing her neck.

I'm not sure I can hold back much longer.

The sweet scent of her breath brushes against my lips. "Show me how long you've wanted me. Everything you've been thinking about doing to me since we've been apart. Show me, Dominik."

My body quivers with anticipation, but I'm holding back and can't pinpoint the exact reason. Perhaps it's because the last time I let myself give in completely, my primal came out as I finger fucked her on my couch before leaving her there. Or maybe it's because I was hoping the next time we'd be together, it would be different, filled with more than just hate and raw desire.

But this *is* different, isn't it? She wants this, craves some part of the connection we can't seem to escape. Instead of letting words and anger consume the space between us, I have the chance to give her exactly what she wants. I have the chance to shut her brain off and call a ceasefire on this endless battle between us.

"Please, Dominik," Zoe whispers, grinding her bare pussy against my crotch.

As soon as I hear her beg, I unleash. The way she says my name, it's better than anything I could have ever imagined. I've never heard her say my name like that before. In Boston, she called for Runi, but she didn't know it was me hiding behind the mask.

She sees me right now, no mask. Completely bare, and she wants this.

I grip her face and kiss her deeply, our tongues clashing against one another like angry waves. She's a vortex, consuming my thoughts as I willingly surrender to her. I can feel that she is unprepared for the overwhelming desire that is about to come over her. The taste of her is like a powerful elixir that completely consumes me. As our tongues intertwine, I find myself sinking deeper into a maze of longing, losing myself in the desperate need to have her.

I'm a depraved prisoner who's about to collect.

Zoe doesn't waste time before clawing at my shirt, and I help, only pulling away from her lips for a brief second. We're both equally hungry, growling in unison. I've been aching to feel her like this again for far too long, a relentless hunger that only Zoe could satisfy. The intensity of this moment is overwhelming, like a blazing fire igniting every inch of my body.

I latch on to her nipple, greedily sucking and biting her flesh as her whimpers fill the room.

"You need a safe word."

She shakes her head as I bite and lick up her collarbone to her neck. Zoe moans, grinding her wet pussy against my thigh. Making it impossible not to want to line up my cock and bury myself inside her. But there is no way in hell I'm rushing this— not now, not ever.

"Safe word, little butterfly. I don't plan on being gentle with you tonight."

"I don't want you to be gentle," she breathes out, shutting her eyes.

I grab her wrists and pin them above her head. "Look at me, Zoe."

She complies, her eyes, heavy-lidded and jade-colored, meet mine as I hover over her. Her gaze traces down my body, pausing on my cock as she bites her swollen lower lip, her eyes widening slightly.

"Your dick is pierced," she breathes out.

"It is. Does that scare you?"

Her eyes flick up to mine. "Considering I couldn't walk for days after last time, not really."

I chuckle, lifting my hips and kicking her legs apart with my knees. Guiding my cock down to her slit, I run it along her wet pussy and watch as her eyes roll to the back of her head.

"You'll take it and enjoy every second of me stretching you out," I say, taking in her glorious body, wide open for me like a delicate rose. Except Zoe lacks delicacy. Especially when it comes to her bold personality and her rough tastes in bed. I fucking adore that about her.

My nostrils flare and my chest heaves as I resist the urge to grind into her, to take her right here and now. It's been a while since I've had to exercise this kind of self-control. This intense desire, this connection, it's something I've only ever felt with Zoe.

"You've always belonged to me," I grit out, pressing the tip of my dick and nudging it ever so slightly inside her opening. Zoe loses her mind, whimpering and squirming beneath me.

Keeping her hands pinned, I flip her to her stomach and pull her knees up so her ass is kissing the air. She moans into the sheets as I grip the back of her hair, tilt her face up slightly, and force her to stare back at me.

"Last chance. Are you sure about this?"

Zoe whispers, her gaze pinned on mine, "Give me everything. Every last drop, Dominik. Make it hurt."

This is what getting high must feel like. The intensity of this confession surpasses that of the night at the masquerade ball because she is fully aware of my true identity this time. She craves every part of me. Unfiltered, unbridled.

I growl and forcefully push her head down, gripping her hair tightly.

I decide to test out her brat. "Hands behind your back."

She obliges immediately, and I'm a bit disappointed, my palm itching to land on her perfectly round ass. "Stay right here, in this position. Don't move an inch."

Zoe mewls, but she remains still as I take a step back to admire her. Ass propped in the air, hands behind her back, her face pressed into the white comforter.

I scan the room, searching for something suitable to bind her hands together. Spotting my bag by the door, I retrieve the tie I had worn earlier with my suit. As I make my way back to the bed, I am met with Zoe's mischievous grin.

My little impatient slut has one hand in between her legs, touching herself and moaning softly into the sheets. I climb onto the bed and instantly restrain her.

"Fuck, you're such an asshole," she says, her voice trembling as she gasps for air in between words.

"And you're a needy brat who can't take orders." Coiling the tie over until I'm satisfied with its hold, I trace my fingers along her spine, feeling the contours of her body. Moving to her chest, I gently squeeze her nipple, eliciting a sharp cry from her. Gripping her hips firmly, I pull back my hand.

Smack.

"Disobey me again and next time, I'll slap your pretty pussy," I say, leaning over and flicking her swollen clit.

"Oh my God, Dominik," she moans.

Leaning back, I grasp her ankles, pulling them apart before separating her ass cheeks and biting the round flesh just below the noticeable red mark from my hand. I lick the traces of my teeth, admiring her body before eagerly burying my face in her pussy, devouring her as my tongue laps and sucks greedily on her clit.

"Oh, fuck. Fuck. Fuck. Fuck," Zoe screams, making my cock painfully hard.

Latching on to her pussy, I suck and lick with force, using just enough teeth to drive her crazy. I get lost in the taste of her, losing track of time, space, and reality as I fucking consume her. Zoe's screams grow louder as I feel her body vibrate. She's close, but I'm nowhere near ready for her to come yet.

I move back, and she lets out a loud groan, clearly expressing her disappointment. Her legs tremble as I slide my hands down her heated skin, then bring them back up to grasp her ass gently, appreciating her flushed and sweaty condition.

"Do you like ass play?"

"No." Her answer is immediate.

"Have you ever tried it?"

She shakes her head, still trying to catch her breath.

I start playing with her asshole, gently massaging it while kissing her inner thighs.

"Fucking...Christ... Leave my hole alone." Zoe's breathless protests are not convincing.

"Better use your safe word then."

As I delicately run my tongue along her wet core, caressing the sensitive skin, Zoe's body reacts instantaneously. Her back arches, and her restrained arms instinctively rise the moment my tongue makes contact with her puckered hole.

"Dominik," she yelps.

I alternate between her clit and her asshole, loving every second of it and watching as she writhes in total euphoria. It's intoxicating, owning her body like this. I push my finger inside her ass while my mouth focuses on her pussy. The second I use my finger to massage her insides, Zoe detonates. Her orgasm is sudden and violent, overwhelming her as I continue to caress and explore her with my mouth and finger until I feel her build up again and come all over my mouth.

"Oh my god, fuck. Dominik, stop. I can't. Please. No more." Her words are muffled.

"We're just getting started, baby" I say, biting her butt cheek before leaning back to give her a minute to collect herself. Taking deliberate care to untie her wrist, I massage the sore area as Zoe collapses onto the bed, still breathless and covered in a layer of sweat.

Fisting my hard cock, I start stroking myself as Zoe remains sprawled out in front of me, still catching her breath. I shut my eyes and lean my head back, savoring the lingering taste of her on my lips. When I open my eyes, Zoe is touching herself as she watches me. If only I could get inside her head and know exactly what she's thinking right now.

"Hold on to my shoulders."

I lower myself and grasp her, gently lifting her up while

maintaining a firm grip on her hips. She wraps one arm around my neck while the other rests lower, forcing a groan out of me as she grips my cock. Guiding me to her entrance and holding her breath, like she's bracing herself for impact.

"Nice and slow?" I ask, forcing her to look at me.

She shakes her head.

"Good girl. Now ride it," I whisper against her lips. "I want to feel you come all over my cock."

She lets out a soft moan, gently rotating her hips as she supports herself, allowing only the tip of my cock to brush against her entrance.

Fucking christ she feels so good.

I firmly guide her down onto my cock, mesmerized by the look of pain and pleasure on her breathtaking face. The sensation of her nails leaving marks on my skin intensifies as the sound of our ragged breaths and passionate groans intertwine. Zoe grips the back of my head, tugging on my hair as our foreheads press together, intensifying our connection. Her screams turn into moans, harmonizing with the rhythmic movement of our bodies. She closes her eyes, taking in deep breaths as I continue thrusting, watching my cock disappear in and out of her perfect little pussy.

I can't believe this is actually happening. Maybe it's all a dream.

If that's the case, I never want to wake up.

"Fuck, you feel so good."

Zoe's grip on my hair tightens as she moves more vigorously, her eyes remaining closed.

"Look at me."

She shakes her head and leans in for a kiss, but I instinctively pull away.

"I said, eyes on me," I growl, my voice low and demanding, and she hesitantly complies.

Right now, at this moment, it's just her and me as the rest of the entire world slips away. Everything from our past fades into darkness like it doesn't exist and never happened. We are all we need. She is all I need.

With each passing second, I lose more of myself to her.

I can sense a shift in her demeanor, as if she has become distant and disconnected.

"I hate you," she finally says.

Reaching around, I wrap my fingers around her delicate throat, holding her in place as her peaked nipples rub against my bare chest. Neither one of us stops moving as my fingers tighten around her neck.

"Say it again."

"I hate you," she sighs without a moment's pause.

Her words don't have the desired impact on me. I can feel her lack of hatred through her gentle touch, lingering gaze, and the softness of her lips when we kiss. Zoe wants to hate me, but I know, deep down, she can't. It doesn't even matter because my feelings are the complete opposite. I can't stop loving her. I love her so much that it's eating me alive. Consuming my every thought and action. I cannot stop myself. Never have and never will.

I adjust my hold carefully, applying slight pressure to limit her airflow. As she moves her hips, I release my grip and then apply pressure again, fully aware of how it heightens her pleasure. Zoe's eyes roll back, her lips parting. Leaning in, I gently nibble on her lower lip, gazing down at her and savoring her sounds.

We remain that way until she's on the verge of her third orgasm. That's when I stop.

"Hate me all you want," I growl, releasing her neck just as she comes to, looking at me, confused. "Bite me. Bruise me. Burn me. Spit venom at me. Ignore me. Run from me. None of it matters just as long as you're here, touching me, kissing me, fucking me—hate me, but you'll never escape me."

Zoe's gaze is lethal as she looks into my eyes. I can feel her desire to create distance between us, but I won't let her pull away. Instead, I start to move within her, making her fists collide with my chest. Pleasure rushes up her spine, causing her to arch her hips. I lift her slightly, sensing her core tightening around me. Even with the battle raging inside her, she keeps her eyes locked on mine.

"I fucking hate you, Dominik." Her words are even more hollow than before.

"Is that why you're soaking my cock, little brat?"

"Fuck you," she whimpers, and I simply smile.

"Forever, darling. That's a promise." Zoe is tattooed on my heart, forever part of my soul, and nothing could ever change that.

Her lips collide with mine, and I hold her head, thrusting into her. Every sensation feels magnified—the taste of her breath, the scent of passion that lingers in the air, the heat radiating off our bodies. Feeling everything engulf me in the wake of our confession, the world seems to hold its breath as it wraps itself tightly around us. I wish this moment would never end. That we could remain in this secret time and space, where I finally told the woman I've always loved how I truly feel about her. How much I fucking adore her. How intensely she is ingrained in me. How distance and time never changed how I felt about her.

Everything feels just as it should as she unravels in my embrace, like all the puzzle pieces of my life have finally fallen into place.

13

ZOE

The first thing I see as I open my eyes is Dominik lying on his stomach with his face nestled against the pillow. His breathing is calm and rhythmic, reminding me of a beautiful painting.

My mind is a swirling mix of emotions, and relentless confusion gnaws at me. I'm uncertain as to why I'm still holding onto the anger, and right now, I can't even be bothered by it. That's not to say I've forgotten everything that happened, but my apathy has grown.

And that confession last night. What am I supposed to do with that?

"Hate me, but you'll never escape me."

There's a part of me that believes he's done a good deal to prove himself, while the other part feels like it will never be enough. But I'm running out of reasons to keep up this act. Last night was amazing, and I just want more of it. Can't we have just the physical? The lies can never be completely erased, no matter how many apologies are offered, grand gestures made, or efforts put forth. It's not like there is a future here, so I should just enjoy this for what it is, shouldn't I?

Why do I feel guilty?

Aaron.

Yeah, he'd never allow it.

Knowing all that didn't seem to make a difference in the way I came alive last night. I hadn't felt that way in a long time. Even after I was sore and exhausted, I needed more of him. It felt good to enjoy something other than anger, pain, and betrayal. When he'd called for a break at the hot tub, it was all I could think about. In the midst of my anger, I couldn't help but still want him. Wanting someone like that, isn't it like inhaling toxic fumes?

Gently, I rise from the bed, cautiously watching Dominik to avoid disturbing him. I need more time to figure out what I want and where to go from here. There's still a complete flight left for us to get through before we reach home. Daylight peeks through the curtains, casting a soft glow around the room. My core tightens with need as I remember every second of our time together from last night. I lost track of how many times I came, and when I couldn't climax anymore, he picked me up and carried me to the bathroom. Took his time washing my body under the hot water, running his hands carefully along every inch of my body as if he was worshiping me. Like he was trying to commit all of it to memory, worried he was dreaming or something.

We barely got any sleep, and yet here I am, wide awake and wondering what the fuck I'm doing with my life. How do I keep finding myself in impossible situations?

I slip out of bed and begin grabbing my things quietly. I need to leave this room without waking him up because when he gets up, he's going to want to talk about what last night meant, and I can't have this conversation with him right now...or ever. I'm exhausted, confused, horny, and just done with this trip.

I just want to go home.

I quickly get dressed, stuffing everything into my bag and grabbing my phone. I feel hesitant to check for any messages or missed calls. The mere thought of Aaron's disappointment and the judgment he would cast on me if he knew what happened last night leave a bitter taste in my mouth. He has always seen me as his broken, fragile sister, someone he has to protect from everything and everyone because he couldn't save me from our parents. He has never seen me as a woman with desires and faults. I can't be the reason he loses his best friend. There is no way I would do that to my brother, the only person who has ever been there for me, who has loved me.

Why is Dominik so indifferent to everything now? Aaron's feelings used to be important to him as well, but suddenly, it feels like he doesn't care about anything else except this pursuit. His only goal is to possess me and emerge victorious. And afterward, he'll just leave. Just like everything else that has left my life.

Nothing lasts forever. Absolutely nothing. And I just need to repeat that to myself before I drown in these emotions.

It'll be over before you know it, so why not have fun in the meantime?

Enjoy yourself. Enjoy him.

That's another option. I could just toss all this messy emotional baggage aside and continue to have fun. Make Dominik my dirty little secret. He has what I need physically, and we could explore things we didn't have time for at the masquerade ball. I could finally get another chase through the woods. I've been dying to experience that again.

Just the thought makes my panties wet.

I'm crazy, but so is he. As a matter of fact, he likes my brat. When am I going to find an opportunity like this again? Go back to Rabbit Hole and post online? Yeah, I don't think so.

Is it a weakness to consider doing this? Acknowledging my

surrender in desiring him? I took that step last night, and it turned out even better than I could have imagined.

It's actually quite simple and straightforward. We could come up with an arrangement, finding the perfect times when we're certain we won't be caught, or we could simply continue doing this covertly. Last night was proof that Dominik won't reject me.

The hotel door clicks shut behind me as I tiptoe down the hallway, making my way to the lobby as I try to shake off the post-sex horniness following me around like a ghost. Thankfully, both the elevator and lobby are empty of Slasher players, which means I have some time to myself before we all need to leave for our flight.

The quiet hum of the morning hotel activities seem distant, an echo of a world I'm trying to distance myself from. I wish there were someone I could confide in about all of this. Someone to tell me what I should do and if getting more involved with Dominik is a good idea. I always do this. Get myself more into trouble by being reckless and unapologetic. I did it with Greg too, muddying the waters where I worked, and look where it led me.

If I go ahead with this, I could hurt Aaron, potentially destroying his relationship with his best friend. What kind of sister would do that for their own selfish needs?

Strolling through the deserted hallways, I stumble upon a hidden nook, far from prying gazes, where I sink into a plush armchair. The usually vibrant hotel lobby is unnervingly still at this early hour, but I'm thankful for that because it's exactly what I need right now.

I long for some personal space, a chance to sort out my jumbled emotions without the interference of my brother's or Dominik's opinions. Unfortunately, time is a luxury I currently lack. So, I close my eyes, lean my head back, and draw in a deep breath, desperate to escape.

My phone buzzes in my jeans.

I exhale deeply, recognizing that I should just ignore it but fully aware that my curiosity will ultimately dominate.

> **DOM**
> What did I say about running off on me?

My heart flutters.

> **ME**
> What are you going to do about it? Come find me and spank my ass again?

Bubbles appear then disappear before his text comes through, causing me to press my thighs together.

> **DOM**
> Nah. This time, I'll tie you up and gag you... press a vibe against your clit, and see how well you take not being able to come for hours. You won't want to disobey me after that.

Jesus Christ.

Finding it increasingly difficult to convince myself that I don't desire some casual excitement with this man, I bite my lower lip. I want him to do everything he just said...

> **ME**
> Hmmm...so far, you're all talk. Try and find me, if you can.

Glancing over my shoulder, I quickly confirm I am still alone just as the message is sent. Thanks to my overly paranoid ass, I'm sure Dom will undoubtedly come after me now that I have provoked him. Without wasting a moment, I grab my things and take off, searching for a new place to hide until it's time to leave the hotel.

What have I gotten myself into, and why am I so incredibly excited by such a disastrous idea?

I SENT a text to Dominik telling him I needed to stop by the drugstore before heading to the airport. It was a lie, of course, but I thought it was a good cover in case anyone asked why we weren't arriving together. It felt satisfying when he kept calling and texting, trying to figure out where I was, but he eventually had to return to the room to get ready. Hiding in a small coat closet at the back of the hotel lobby was a brilliant idea. I had to wait for the right moment to sneak in and out, but it was worth it. I'm not sure what would have happened if he had gotten his hands on me, and a sick, twisted part of me was strangely restless to find out.

As I begin to walk up the metal stairs, I notice that the aircraft door is propped open, and Coach Bradley pokes his head out, his face filled with relief when he spots me.

"There you are! We were starting to get worried," he yells, walking down to help me with my bag.

"Sorry. I needed to make a trip to the drugstore, and my phone ended up dying."

This one is actually true. I barely had enough juice to order the Uber here.

"Dom has been pacing the plane like a madman. He's not happy with you."

My ass is going to be bruised real fucking soon.

The moment I cross the threshold, Dominik's immediately turns to face me. His relieved expression quickly turns into fury.

"What the actual fuck, Zoe! Sending me straight to voicemail?"

He's vibrating, attempting to restrain his emotions. Honestly, I'm uncertain whether it's anger or genuine concern.

"I'm sorry. My phone died. I forgot to charge it last night, thanks to you." I whisper the last part.

"Shit. I jumped to the worst conclusion." He cringes.

"I know you did."

I maneuver around him, giving a shy wave to the guys who are staring at me. There is complete silence as I head toward the same seats we had yesterday.

"We're preparing for takeoff." The announcement comes through the speakers.

Noticing that everyone has already changed out of their formal attire, I quickly glance down at the clock and realize I was only ten minutes late. Dominik is standing behind me, practically glued to my back, and I turn to face him.

"Did the flight time move up, or is my watch wrong?"

"I tried calling you. Our departure time got moved up. We've been waiting half an hour for you. I was worried sick, Zo."

Oh, crap.

"Shit. I'm really sorry. My phone died, I swear." I flash him my dead phone, and he nods.

"I believe you, but being away from home and not knowing where you went was fucking stupid." He leans down, his lips a ghost above my ear. "You ran off on me before I even woke up and never came back."

Inching back so I can look at him, I smile. "You said you were coming to find me, so I hid. Guess I won this round."

Dominik flares his nostrils and clenches his fists, keeping his eyes on the headrest in front of him. That just makes me smile wider, seeing him worked up like this. I might be enjoying it a little too much.

He doesn't say anything as we both fasten our seatbelts. The flight attendants walk by, smiling and checking everyone over before they retreat to their seats and the plane prepares for take-off.

I recline, fixating on the minuscule airplane window, and shut my eyes as we speed up, propelling into the sky.

I must have passed out because when I open my eyes next, the entire cabin is shrouded in darkness. Dominik is sitting motionless, eyes closed and hands resting in his lap. He too must be passed out. It's no wonder we're so tired since we got very little sleep last night.

I shift in my seat, trying not to rouse the sex demon inside me by thinking about last night.

"We need to talk," Dominik says, startling me with his deep, whispered voice.

"No, we don't."

This is exactly why I took off early this morning. He probably wants to dissect everything, talk about our feelings, and I just have no interest in doing that. Even though last night woke something carnal inside me, it still doesn't change the past or everything that happened after I discovered Dom's secret. Boston was one giant lie. Another thing that was never mine.

I get angry when I remember Dominik was keeping tabs on me. He was stalking me, taking photos of me without my knowledge, and monitoring me. He lied to me and hid so many secrets. Everything about us has always been a lie.

Last night was amazing, but it didn't change anything. What I loved the most was how I didn't think about anything else when I was with him. My life outside the bedroom, our expectations, my past, my family, my brother... I even forgot my own name at times. It was perfect. And it's exactly what I've been craving for so long.

I'm tired of existing inside my head. Tired of feelings, memories, worries. I crave total oblivion. I want to forget who I am, and I think Dominik can help me achieve that. Why can't he help me do that? Why can't that be enough?

What if we just stay paused?

"Stop being so fucking stubborn," Dominik grits out.

"I don't want to talk. There is nothing to talk about."

"We can't just ignore everything and go back to the way things were. That's not how it works."

I turn to face him. "No, we can't go back and forget everything you fucking did. And I don't know where we go from here, so I don't want to move, okay? I just...don't have answers."

"What does that mean?" His forehead wrinkles, and I wish I could read him the way he seems to read me, but Dominik is a closed book. Impossible to decipher.

I shake my head. "I don't know."

"Well, I can't ignore it. I can't pretend anymore. Nor do I want to."

"So, what? You're going to tell Aaron everything?" The tightness in my chest intensifies as all the things I've tried to avoid come bubbling up.

"If that's what it takes to have you," Dominik says, his expression completely serious.

What is wrong with this guy? Has he completely lost his mind?

I'm feeling trapped, as if I can't catch my breath. That's why I quickly move past him, intending to escape to the bathroom and splash some water on my face. Maybe that will make it easier for me to breathe. I cannot have a fucking panic attack on this plane with a bunch of famous athletes.

Please God, don't do this to me.

I don't look back. I don't wait for a response. I keep moving, my eyes fixed on the green restroom sign at the back of the small aircraft. It's dark inside, but I enter and close the door without locking it.

Just as I manage to take two deep breaths, the door is forcefully shoved aside, and Dominik enters the small cabin with his massive frame. I instinctively fall back and watch him lock the door.

"What the hell do you think you're doing?" I whisper-scream.

"You're not running off on me every time something gets hard. That might work with everyone else in your life, but it won't work with me. I'm not putting up with it anymore."

"You're a fucking psychopath."

Moving in close, a malicious grin appears on his face. "I'm okay with that as long as I'm your psychopath."

"You're not my anything, and I'm not yours. I don't want to talk, so get the hell out," I yell.

But Dom doesn't leave. He remains perfectly still, towering over me in the small space.

"I'm not leaving until you tell me what you want."

"I just did, but you're too stubborn to listen." I shove his chest, but he's like a rock, completely unyielding, making my attempt seem comical.

He grips my wrist, turning us as he pins my hand above my head, slamming it against the plastic mirror as my back digs into the small sink.

"Stop lying to me. Stop hiding from me. Let me in." Dominik leans his head down, dragging the tip of his tongue up my neck to my earlobe. Shivers burst from every corner of my body.

Dominik starts sucking on my neck, giving me a hickey. Marking me.

"Start talking, or I'll stamp every inch of your skin," he says right before moving to a new spot and beginning his torturous assault.

"I want to stay paused. I don't want to talk or think about anything."

The words effortlessly slip from my lips, as if they were never mine to keep. The unwavering hunger in Dominik's gaze forces me to accept there's no turning back. I finally said what he wanted to hear. Maybe I shouldn't have, but I can't help but want him. It might be pure lust mixed in with forbidden attraction or the fact that I know he can give me what I want sexually. Either way, I crave him, and I'm willing to risk it all for a taste.

14
ZOE

"Is that what you really want? To instill a temporary pause?" Dominik's hand slides beneath my sweater. The lightest touch of his fingers causes goosebumps to spread across my body. I'm breathless, dangling on the edge of a cliff.

"Yes. Make me feel nothing," I confess.

His lips play over mine. "I want to make you feel everything. I want to make you feel alive."

"Good. Then stop talking and do it."

"Your wish is my command," Dominik says, releasing my wrists and gripping my leggings. The only thing I can hear is the sound of cloth ripping as he forcefully pulls the tattered fabric off my legs. Startled by the abrupt change in course and his impressive strength, I let out a shriek.

He falls to his knees and throws one of my legs over his shoulder.

"Dominik, not here!" I whisper-yell, knowing if his tongue touches my clit, I'm not going to be able to control my noises. His entire team is sitting out there. They're definitely going to hear us and whatever is about to go down in this tiny plane bathroom.

He peppers kisses up and down my thighs, making me slick with need. I can't decide if I want to be as far away from him as possible right now or if I want to grab his head and guide his lips to where they belong. The bastard has the audacity to edge me here, out of all the places.

Pressing his palms into my ass, Dominik groans as he finally makes contact. Every last morsel of shame and guilt fades away as he feasts on me. He leaves no space untouched, lapping and devouring me as his tongue plunges inside my tight opening. I arch my back, rolling my hips as one of my hands grips his hair. I need more.

Dominik digs his nails into my flesh, sucking on my clit as a wave of pleasure rolls through me. Good fucking god, the man is so skilled with his tongue, I can feel the orgasm licking up my spine already. I try to hold back my moans and fail miserably, getting louder as I begin chasing my climax.

And just as it's about to get good, Dominik pulls away and stands.

What the actual fuck.

I'm angry, frustrated...shocked. I'm going to—

He grabs me by the neck. "Each time you defy me, your punishments will become more severe and I won't let you come. You got that?"

With eyes wide open, all I can do is nod. My body quivers with anticipation, enthralled by the commanding timbre of his voice. I resist the impulse to shift, craving his return to his kneeling position, to resume where he left off, exploring me with his dirty mouth.

"Answer me."

"Yes, sir."

"That's a good girl," Dominik coos, pulling his hand away.

He leans back, his stormy eyes unwavering as he tugs down his sweatpants and starts stroking his thick cock.

I'm fascinated, getting more turned on just watching him. Licking my lips at the sight of the pre-cum on the head of his cock. Forget him going back down. I need him inside me right this second.

"Dominik, I need you," I whisper, glancing up at him as he continues to stroke himself.

"That's too fucking bad. You're not in control."

"What?" Panting, I notice my skin breaking out in a sweat.

"On your knees," he orders.

The throbbing deep in my stomach tightens as I stand there, staring at him in confusion. His hand clutches the back of my head as he jerks me forward before forcing me down to my knees. Dominik's hand remains on his erection as he guides the head of his pierced cock to my lips. I open up for him without a fight.

I suck his dick eagerly, as if my life depends on it. His head tips back, the sound of his deep grunts carrying in the small space we're jammed in. I'm losing my mind. Each moan coming out of him drives me wild. I need relief and feel no shame when I start to grind my clit against the back of my ankle.

His grip tightens around my hair, anchoring my head in place. With deliberate thrusts, he fucks my mouth, claiming me in a savage way. The intense violation turns me on as he continues to punish me. I'm gagging and choking, trying not to suffocate while desperately thinking about how much I need to get off. I love being at his mercy like this.

"Such a needy fucking slut. Look at you, making a mess on yourself. Do you need to come, brat?"

I nod, closing my eyes as tears run down my face.

"Don't you fucking close your eyes." His voice is ragged.

I moan, and it makes him thrust faster. His movements increase as he shifts my face up, and I urge myself to relax. He's in control right now, and the more I fight it, the harder it will be on me. So I relax my jaw, letting him violate me in the best possible way as I choke, unable to see through the tears.

"You're my brat. You do as I say. Come when I tell you to come, but not until you swallow every last drop of my cum."

I hum, cupping his balls with my hand and watching as his dark eyes intensify with fresh desire. I feel his possessive words shatter the last restraint that held me back earlier today. He awakens a deep, primal part of me that I thought had disappeared years ago.

"You got it?" Dominik groans as he drags his cock out of my mouth.

"Yes, sir," I gasp.

"Good girl. Now, reach down and touch that tight fucking pussy until you come," Dominik hisses, guiding his cock toward my mouth, painting my lips with pre-cum.

Oh, thank fuck.

Running my tongue along my lips, I taste his saltiness before shoving his dick to the back of my throat. My hand trails down, settling in between my legs as I slide a finger inside. Letting out an involuntary moan, I insert a second finger, massaging my G-spot.

Dominik's gaze is fixed on me as he tilts his head to the side. His eyes scan what he can see of my body, his expression contorted with pleasure. His movements intensify as he regains control, thrusting into my mouth. Pressing my thumb against my clit, I start to feel the waves of orgasm surge through me.

There is no turning back from this. No changing my mind now, and I don't want to. I want this, want him...every single day until I've had my fill.

"Fuck, I love watching you do that," he says. "Are you ready to come?"

I hum, half nodding since he's still fisting my hair.

"You better fucking come before I spill down your pretty little throat," he commands.

And I happily oblige, my fingers plunging in and out, my choking sounds getting louder as he picks up the pace.

"Come for me. Now," he demands, and I fall apart. Whimpering and crying his name with his cock shoved to the back of my throat. Dominic groans loudly, his body coiling tight and his movements slowing as hot cum fills my mouth. I nearly choke, but I push through, swallowing every drop and trying to breathe in between.

When we're done, he helps me up, leaning my body against the small counter. Dominik takes my slick fingers and pushes them inside his mouth, sucking them clean.

"I can never get enough of that," he delights.

Dominik keeps his eyes fixed on me while he pulls up his sweatpants, straightens his shirt, and turns to exit. He doesn't bother washing his hands or saying another word. I'm left in the airplane bathroom, breathless and reeking of sex, struggling to comprehend how the hell I'm going to walk out there and face his team.

Seeing my messy appearance in the mirror, I grab my leggings and grin.

God, I am colossally *fucked*.

15

DOMINIK

I may not know the answers to everything or even the purpose of our existence in this life or the next. I don't know what's going to happen in the next hour, next week, or even a month from now. Tomorrow is not guaranteed for anyone, and almost everything is temporary. Even the good days eventually come to an end. It all inevitably transitions into something else, except for this.

Except for her.

I have always felt this way for Zoe, and now that we're on the other side, now that I've had her in this way...as Dominik Lewis... there is no going back. Nothing and no one could ever compare to this. To her. I don't care what I need to do to win her, who I have to lose...None of it matters to me. She is the one person I refuse to let go of, no matter the cost.

She might believe that all of this will eventually fade away. That she can enjoy herself and leave when she's ready, but I won't allow her to go. The past few days have made it abundantly clear to me that this is an undeniable truth.

I'm willing to go to the ends of the earth and back to make her see that. Whatever it takes. I want her to know for certain how permanent she is in my small world.

She is always on my mind. Even now, as I get showered and dressed for practice.

I can't stop thinking about her when the guys make jokes in the locker room or talk about another team's game from last night.

I can't stop thinking about the way she looked when she was down on her knees in that aircraft with my cock hitting the back of her throat as she fingered herself.

And I especially can't stop thinking about her as I skate on the ice, warming up for practice. I know I should focus because Coach will notice, but I can't be bothered.

Not today anyway.

I texted her two days ago, asking her to come to practice tonight because there's something important I need to discuss with her. But she never responded. Ever since the guys put on a big show after she walked out of the plane bathroom, she has been acting distant again. I threatened them all one by one, but Zoe was the color of the Red Sea for the rest of the flight and barely said two words.

I feel guilty for causing her an extra headache and embarrassing her, but a part of me is fucking thrilled about it. Let them hear her scream my name. I want every last person on the planet to know she's mine.

I had the intention of reaching out to Aaron to check on Zoe, but I've been actively avoiding him. I'm unsure if I can continue lying to him once we meet face to face, and I'm anxious about his reaction, so I've been attempting to stall for time. I need Zoe to be ready before I open that can of worms. Under no circumstances am I willing to take any risks that could lead to losing her again.

So instead, I borrowed George's pass and snuck into the security room of our high-rise. I've seen her coming in and out of the building, so I know she's at least okay.

She seems torn between her desires and her own expectations for herself. I'm not sure what it will take for her to accept this situation. I know she hasn't fully forgiven me, and that probably plays a part in her struggle. Maybe she feels ashamed for wanting what she craves, for giving in to those desires, and for giving in to me. Or perhaps she's trying to numb her emotions and not let herself feel anything at all.

The whistle blows, and we all skate into position.

"You okay, man?" The sound of Noa's skates cutting ice reels me back to the present and the hours of practice still left ahead of me.

"Yeah. Just tired."

Time to put your girl problems to the side and focus, Lewis.

Minutes pass, turning into hours, and I find myself consumed by the game. Hockey's familiar rush brings me the peace I've longed for. Yet my eyes continuously scan the stands, hoping to catch a glimpse of Zoe silently cheering me on. Every time I look up, disappointment floods over me as I'm met with empty benches.

She's not showing up.

When the whistle blows, Coach gathers all of us at the bench.

"Alright, boys. I know we're all tired, but you're asleep, and I need more effort. Put yourself in your opponent's shoes. They're smarter and sharper than you right now. Step it up!" Coach hollers, shooing us away.

Are we all asleep? I believe we're just fatigued, but his words feel a bit harsh as I glide back onto the ice. The bitterness of today's disappointment lingers on my tongue. I circle around while the rest of the team takes a break, attempting to distract myself from Zoe. She was supposed to be here by now.

I noticed a change between us when we were away. It felt good, maybe even primal, but it all felt right. It was as if we finally fit together like puzzle pieces. I thought we were making progress, finally moving forward, but now I'm full of fresh uncertainty and doubts.

I quickly scan the stands, desperately hoping to find her familiar face. Just when I'm about to give up on the idea of her showing up, she suddenly appears. As she walks down the stairs toward the players' bench, a smile on her face, a feeling of relief floods through me. Yet, in a split second, my excitement morphs into something entirely different as I process the scene unfolding before my eyes. Zoe nonchalantly places her coat on a seat, and that's when I notice she isn't wearing my jersey.

That's not *my* fucking name on her back.

It's Noa's.

My heart pounds in my chest, the adrenaline from practice morphing into a different kind of intensity. I'm fucking vibrating with rage. I don't understand why she would show up to my practice wearing another player's jersey. Another player on my team!

She is deliberately trying to hurt me by seeking revenge for everything. Is that it? Is she trying to even the score? Maybe her goal is to display dominance over me, to establish that she holds power in this twisted game we're playing. I'm at a loss. I don't know what to think anymore.

The whistle blows, signaling for us to assume our positions, but my concentration is destroyed.

There is no way in hell she's going to stand there for the rest of this game, wearing someone else's number on her back.

Over my dead body.

Just then, our eyes meet, and I make sure she is fully focused on me as I silently mouth a single word: *Run.*

Witnessing her smile slowly fade away, I skate over to her, undoing my helmet and listening to the sound of it hitting the ice.

There is someone calling my name from behind me, but I barely register it. My vision is consumed by red, while the sound of my pounding heart fills my ears.

Zoe turns and starts running toward the back hallway. As soon as I remove my gloves, I sprint across the remaining icy surface, determined to catch up with her. The animal inside my bones stirs as I chase her through the padded hallway, feeling my skates puncture the floor. Glancing over her shoulder, Zoe rounds the corner toward the locker room. I know exactly what I'm going to do. Spotting a nearby closet, I speed up, my fingers itching to snatch her.

She slows down, and that's when I make my move.

I grab her waist and hoist her over my shoulder. She yelps, punching my back but I ignore her. Carrying her toward the closet door, my heart races. I pull on the handle, silently praying it's unlocked. It gives way, and I stumble into the cramped darkness of the closet. I place her on the ground. We're both breathless, and she's shocked, but there's excitement in her eyes too. I can smell it on her.

The air is thick with tension as I secure the door. She's not going anywhere. Not until I'm ready to deal with her.

Through the cracks in the door, a faint light filters in, providing minimal illumination.

"What are you doing?"

I crowd her. "What am I doing? What the fuck are you doing wearing someone else's jersey?"

Zoe's eyes widen, a mixture of fear and defiance reflected on her face as she stares up at me. The fiery intensity in her eyes matches my fury.

"This is payback." That's all she says, but it's all I need to hear.

With my heart pounding in my chest, I take a step closer, fueled by the rush of adrenaline coursing through my veins.

Determined, I grab her arm and pull her up forcefully, paying no attention to her protests. I press her against the unforgiving coldness of the concrete wall, and the sound of her gasp fills the cramped space.

"This isn't payback," I growl, my voice laced with a raw power. "This is you being a brat. You've pushed me too far this time. Now you're going to face the consequences."

"Are you going to punish me?" Zoe mocks.

As I gaze into her eyes, I desperately search for even the slightest trace of remorse or regret. Yet all I find is a fierce defiance, a stubbornness that mirrors my own. Anger and frustration blend within me, causing my hold on her to tighten.

"You're going to wish that's all I was doing."

Zoe's expression flickers with a hint of curiosity. I release my grip slightly, allowing her a moment to absorb my words as I take a step back and grab the bottom of her jersey. I pull it off her body, observing her flustered expression as her gorgeous, golden curls cascade around her shoulders. She's dressed in a white t-shirt, and it doesn't seem like the temperature will rise in here anytime soon.

I grasp the neckline of Noa's jersey and pull it down toward my skate. With force, I tear through the fabric and rip the rest with my bare hands. I then grab Zoe's wrists and press them together to bind her, making sure she can't escape.

Her brows furrow, but she doesn't put up a fight. "What are you doing? You can't keep me locked up in here."

A bitter laugh escapes my lips. "I sure can. Just until I finish working and am ready to deal with you properly."

Zoe's voice fades away, her expression shifting and her previous bratty attitude deflating as she realizes what's about to happen.

I pull her toward a metal shelf and secure the jersey material around it, trapping her inside this closet.

"You're crazy," she says, fighting to get free, but I'm already done. I test the resistance, and she's not going anywhere, not in the next two hours anyway.

"You can stay here and think about the consequences of being a bad girl. Bad girls don't get rewarded. They get punished. Hard."

I kiss her feverishly, biting down on her lower lip and pulling on the flesh as I stare down at her. Gripping the stitching on Noa's number, I tear off the fabric and shove it inside her mouth, silencing her. Her shocked expression and muffled noises rush straight to my cock. Spotting some hockey tape, I decide to use it to secure the gag, ensuring she can't spit it out. I'm careful with the placement, not wanting to catch her hair or cause her extra pain later when I pull it off. Ignoring her pleas, I leave and shut the door behind me. Readjusting my erection, I make my way to the rink, hoping no one will question why my supposed girlfriend is suddenly missing.

I MAKE sure everyone is gone and the facility staff aren't around when I finally head toward the supply room. I have no idea how Zoe is doing or how pissed she's going to be with me when I walk through the door. All I know is she's going to be inside that closet, bound to that shelf, and hopefully still gagged.

I wish I had a toy with me. I would have used it to tease her for hours until she was a weeping mess, begging me to let her come. She thought she had the upper hand, showing up wearing Noa's jersey. She might think it's payback. But I see it for exactly what it is. Another test.

She's trying to get me to leave. Attempting to push me away, hoping that I will disappear just so she can validate her belief that she was right all along. She convinces herself that she doesn't deserve anyone's effort or the fight to stay. This is her way of protecting herself and preventing the possibility of falling in love or getting hurt.

But that couldn't be further than the truth. Zoe deserves far better than the unfavorable circumstances she was dealt. Her parents, who are beyond neglectful, never taught her the true meaning of unconditional love. In fact, they worsened the situation by showering their love upon Aaron, causing Zoe to witness everything she ached for, but they made her believe she didn't deserve it. What kind of heartless sociopaths would punish a child for merely existing?

She can be a brat all she likes. I meant what I said to her at the hotel: there is no escaping us.

This.

Me.

I'm not going anywhere. And if she needs time and sexual torture to get that through her head, then so be it. I've got nothing but time.

Approaching the door, I realize I'm still wearing my hockey gear. The closet seems eerily quiet, making me wonder if she managed to escape. Perhaps someone heard her cries and came to her rescue. But as soon as I open the door, there she is, leaning against the back wall. Her shoulders are slumped, and the gag is still in place. Squinting, she looks up at me, appearing fragile for a second before her fierce mask slips back into place.

I've never fucked anyone in the locker room before, but it's always been a fantasy of mine. I've wondered what Zoe would look like naked, lying on the wooden bench by the showers, her perfect body wet and glistening as I kneel between her legs. Fuck, I'm getting hard just thinking about it.

Good thing we have all night. But even if she starts behaving now, she's not getting any pleasure tonight.

I'm taming her brat. I'm going to gradually wear her down until she becomes a trembling, tearful wreck, desperately pleading for me to stop.

Zoe groans, making half-assed attempts to get herself out of the restraints, but if she hasn't been able to do it in the last couple of hours while I finished practice, what chance does she have now? I bet she's tired and sore, dying to be set free.

"Did you enjoy your alone time?"

She glares at me, muttering incomprehensible words. Her cheeks are flushed, and she breathes heavily as I approach her. Carefully, I remove the tape and take out the gag. She swallows a few times, her lips looking dry. Gripping her face, I lean down to kiss her hard. With no hesitation, she bites the corner of my lip, making me laugh.

"You're a fucking asshole."

I shrug. "But I'm the asshole who's going to untie you, so I'd be nicer if I were you. Especially after the stunt you pulled earlier."

"That didn't merit all this," she says, lifting up her knee and trying to kick me in the balls, but I block her with my thigh.

"Drop the attitude, Zoe or I'll make you beg while it drips out of you."

Maybe I should leave her tied up longer.

"Get fucked," she snarls.

Okay, now I'm getting pissed.

"It seems like you learned nothing," I growl, untying her wrists. As soon as she's free, I crouch down and hoist her over my shoulder.

She punches my back, screaming and hollering, but there is no one here but me. She can scream her heart's content. As a matter of fact, I want her to until her throat becomes raw and achy. Until she's got nothing left in her. I want to break her and slowly put her back together, one piece at a time.

"Put me down! What the hell is the matter with you?"

Without acknowledging her, I swiftly enter the locker room, ensuring that I lock the door behind me. Making a beeline for the showers, I am immediately greeted by the humid air, which is filled with the lingering scents of sweat, leather, and equipment from the post-practice showers. Apart from that, the room remains perfectly silent, as everyone else has already left.

It's just the two of us with nothing but time.

Hours upon hours of torture.

And I'm going to enjoy every second of it.

16
ZOE

"I need to come," I cry out. I'm losing my mind from the last few hours...days? I'm not sure anymore. I'm losing grip on reality at this point. I feel like I've endured weeks of torture.

I need to fucking come.

After being imprisoned for hours, Dominik effortlessly picked me up like I was as light as a blanket and brought me inside the locker room. He placed me on a bench and tore my clothes in two as the showers ran in the background, filling the air with steam.

I wanted to put up a fight, pretend I was mad at the display of control he was forcing on me, but I had showed up at the arena wearing Noa's jersey, hoping for exactly this type of reaction. I'd known Dominik wouldn't have been able to let it slide. That he would want to make me pay for disobeying him.

I would do it again.

I'm dying to come, but I'm not sorry.

No other man has ever been able to make me feel the things Dominik has with just a single touch. It's intoxicating. I would feel ashamed, maybe even guilty, but I'm over all of that. I don't think about anything else when he's touching me like this. I've been craving this type of torture for years, only dreamt about it and never thought I'd experience it again...not after that night in Boston.

Dominik has been getting off on slowly torturing me for hours now.

As soon as we stepped inside the locker room, he shoved me down on a bench, tore off my clothes, then took the blunt edge of his skate and traced the cold metal all over my body, in between my breasts and down my stomach. His breath was hot against my skin as he bent down, staring up at me as the tip of his tongue grazed my clit. I bucked hard, my body giving me away all on its own. He's made a game out of edging me and taking back his power. Not letting me come as he plays with my body like I'm a brand new toy he wants to explore.

Then, he secured my wrists together with tape, retrieved an object from the locker room to clamp my nipples, and started a prolonged edging session that has probably lasted for hours. Driving me to the edge of insanity with his fingers, tongue, and the head of his pierced cock.

This last round, I started vibrating, a hairline away from orgasm, when he stopped, towering above me as he started stroking himself until he came all over my face and chest. Watching Dominik swirl his fingers in his own cum before shoving them into my mouth might have been the hottest fucking thing I've ever witnessed.

I sucked all of it off, hoping that would be enough to earn my release. But it didn't, and now he's dragging his fingers through what's left of it, tracing down my stomach and using it to circle my overly sensitive clit.

"Please, Dominik. Please," I finally beg.

"Do you know what type of restraint it takes to stand here and not have my way with you? To not bury my cock deep inside you, where it belongs? Do you think I like this?"

He's looming over me, naked from the bottom down and in nothing but a white t-shirt.

"I think you love this," I groan, glaring down at his fingers as my mouth waters, watching his cock get hard again. He just came, and he's already recovering, ready for more.

"You're right. I do." Dominik smiles, gripping my hair and kissing me wildly. He pulls me up, his fingers digging into my thighs as he carries us toward the shower. I'm ravenous, my nails digging into my binds as I match his intensity. Hopeful it'll make him want to finally have me. I'm desperate for a new type of punishment.

I need him inside me. Need to feel him stretch me completely.

"Fuck me," I breathe against his lips.

Dominik kisses me harder, putting enough distance between us to rob me of any friction. I am running out of patience and feel completely drained. I give up. He can have this stupid win.

"Fuck me, Dominik. Please." I say the words he's been wanting to hear all along, but it doesn't matter how much I beg, he won't move. Leaving me more frustrated by the second. It's not like I can reach down and fuck myself. If I could get some relief, we wouldn't be here right now.

Dominik smiles, simply shaking his head. I can feel his cum sliding down my chest. I arch my back, trying to grind against him.

"Say it again," he sighs, pressing my back into the cold tile as I loop my bound hands around his neck.

"Please," I whisper. "Fuck me."

He grips his cock with one hand, guiding the head to my sensitive core. "You want to come?"

I nod, biting my lip as I stare down at his gloriously thick erection.

"Show me how badly you want it, little butterfly."

I don't know what he expects me to do. I'm exhausted, my wrists are bound, and he's holding me hostage against the cold shower wall.

And then it hits me.

I have something to say to Dominik that I know he's been longing to hear—complete submission. Dominik derives pleasure from control and possessiveness. It wasn't my initial plan to say the following, but considering how Dominik is a fan of lying, I don't have to feel guilty about it.

"You have me," I whisper before leaning in to kiss him. With a sudden motion, he withdraws, clutching my chin and giving me a puzzled gaze as if he misunderstood my words.

"Louder," he growls.

"I'm yours. And you're mine."

With a deep groan, he kisses me as if it's the first time he's ever kissed me. I feel the emotion behind it, but I pretend like it means nothing. I'd rather not dwell on the meaning this has for him. Dominik releases my grip from his neck and gently sets me down on the floor. It all happens so fast. My bound wrists are above my head, my breasts pressed against the tile and my ass seated on his cock, as Dominik begins slowly grinding his erection against my clit. I lose myself to the contact, feeling the orgasm lick its way up my spine as my eyes roll to the back of my head.

He pulls my hair back, staring down at me from the corner of his eyes as his fingers circle my needy pussy.

I cry, already getting so close and needing the relief more than I need my next breath. It's almost painful at this point.

"As much as I'd like to edge you for the next two days, I want to hear you beg me to stop."

A smirk plays on his face as water trickles down his forehead, making his eyes glow.

I don't think I would ask him to stop. Give me all the fucking orgas—

Before I even have a chance to finish that thought, Dominik pulls on my nipple hard, tugging the clamp off, and I detonate. The pressure on my clit and nipple has me seeing stars. My knees buckle, but he's right there, holding me in place. His fingers still pressed to my clit.

"Give me more," he murmurs, biting down on my neck and sucking on the flesh as he slides a finger inside me.

And I do. Just like that, while listening to the firm command in his voice. I come undone, not sure if my first orgasm fully stopped before this one hit me.

It's euphoric.

Addicting.

I rest my head on his shoulder, and when I open my eyes, all I see are billowing clouds of steam.

"Bad girls shouldn't get rewarded like this."

Dominik cups my pussy with one hand while his other hand explores my body. Goosebumps erupt all over my skin, even though I'm tingling with post-orgasm heat.

"I'm sorry." And I really am.

I regret wearing Noa's jersey to practice.

No. That's a lie because if I had known the punishment would be like this, I would have done it a long time ago.

He makes me want to be bad.

To push the boundaries.

He makes me want to be bratty because some deep, twisted part of me wants to see how far I can push him before he walks away. Before I become too much for him.

Dominik doesn't let up, playing with my sensitive clit and

inching me toward another orgasm, but my body is beyond sensitive now. I try to push his hand away, but instead, he inserts a finger inside me. Watching me crumble as he massages my g-spot and clit at the same time. I couldn't stop the orgasm from crashing into me even if I fucking tried. I come again, hard.

He doesn't wait for me to catch my breath.

Turning me around, he drops to his knees and lifts my leg, looking up at me with those eyes.

I'm a panting, shaking mess. "I can't."

He smirks before burying his face in my pussy. Eating me with such passion and groaning in pleasure, as if this is his favorite thing in the world.

That's one thing I love about Dominik. The way he eats pussy could win a Guinness World record. He gets off on it, and he's so skilled at it.

But my body has been through the ringer, and it's just too painful at this point.

"Again, Zoe. I want to feel you come all over my tongue."

I fist his hair, trying to push him away but end up grinding against his mouth, moaning something before I urge him to stop.

"I can't. I fucking can't."

He looks up at me, completely breathtaking and drenched in water. The sight of him in this state makes me want this night to never end, even though I feel like I'm roasting from the inside out.

He gently rubs my butthole. "You can, and you will. It wasn't a request."

He doesn't hesitate, jumping back in as his tongue swirls around my clit. Sucking and biting the flesh with just enough force to make me vibrate. As he pushes a finger inside me, my loud moaning fills the room instead of the sounds of streaming water.

Dominik curls his fingers, electrifying me from the inside while simultaneously sucking on me. Waves of both pleasure and pain collide. The sensation is almost too much to handle. The rush of another orgasm surges through me, causing my body to vibrate and my mind to go completely blank.

I'm left breathless, my body tingling with the aftershocks of my climax, when I suddenly sense Dominik rising to his feet. My eyes flutter open, and I am immediately captivated by the sight of him peeling off his drenched shirt and nonchalantly discarding it beside me. With a strong grip on my hips, he lifts me up against the smooth tiles, guiding me down onto his cock.

When he's completely seated inside me, he begins a slow thrust, his eyes cast down on my body as he slowly drinks me in.

"Oh, God." I clutch him tightly, both of us moaning in unison. I doubt I'll be able to walk properly tomorrow.

When the pain becomes overwhelming, I scream out his name, desperately tugging at the ends of his hair in a plea for him to ease up. But Dominik does the exact opposite, pushing harder and deeper inside me as he firmly pinches my nipple.

There is no way I can come again.

I'm a puddle, a jumbled mix of emotions and chaos. My legs start to give out.

"Please stop. Please."

"Not until you use your safe word," he asserts, pounding into me and eating up my cries.

The thought of using my safe word to end this right here, right now crosses my mind, but it would feel like admitting defeat. I refuse to let him win this as well.

I shake my head and his fingers dig into the back of my head, forcing me to lock eyes with him.

"Whose name will you wear on your back from now on?"

When I don't answer, Dominik tugs harder.

"Yours," I breathe out, not sure if I'm going to be conscious in the next few minutes.

"That's right. You belong to me. And if you test me again, I'll make your next punishment much longer and more severe."

He doesn't let me rest until I have another orgasm, and only then do I go limp against his body. As Dominik wraps his arms around me, I feel myself drifting away, unable to count the number of orgasms he's forced me to have. Minutes later, I feel the comforting warmth of hot water all over my body.

When I finally gather enough strength to open my eyes, I witness Dominik reaching for the shampoo before working it into my hair. He takes his time, washing the rest of my body as he brushes his fingers gently down my skin, paying extra attention to the sensitive areas he just abused.

I find it difficult to let him take care of me like this. There's something about it that feels uncomfortable, and I'm simply not used to it. I'm not sure I could ever get used to it, but right now, I don't have the energy to bring it up and start an argument, or face another punishment. So I choose to suffer through the discomfort and patiently wait for it to be over, wait until his fingers don't feel like they're branded onto me anymore.

"Why are you so stiff suddenly? Are you okay? Did I hurt you?" Soft Dominik is back with only concern in his dual eyes.

"I'm fine."

"You're not fine. What is it? Did I cross a line? You need to be able to talk about it if I did."

I glance away. "No. This was good... You didn't push me too far. It's just—"

My words fade away as my eyes fixate on the vibrant butterfly tattoo adorning his chest. There is a monarch butterfly with the name *Parvaneh* written in cursive right below it.

I lose track of what I was saying as every thought in my head slips through my grasp like sand. I'm at a loss for words. All I can do is extend my trembling hand and trace the delicate wings of the butterfly, feeling its fragile texture beneath my fingertips.

It's beautiful and incredibly detailed.

I'm almost positive that this tattoo wasn't there before. There's no way I could have forgotten a huge butterfly inked across his heart. This is the tattoo from the away game, the same one that was covered up.

Oh my god...

What the hell is this fuzzy feeling in my gut? Must be post-sex hormones.

"Do you like it?" Dominik asks, breaking through the deafening silence.

I feel my cheeks heat as I look up at him, but I still can't find the words to speak.

Instead, he talks. "That night was the point of no return for me. Seeing you in that red dress—I recognized you instantly. I should have stayed away, should have left you alone, but after we spoke, I was ready to break every promise. Determined to face and overcome every obstacle you placed in my path. I wanted to offer you all of me, from the depths of my soul to the corners of my heart, even if it meant receiving just a small piece of you in return. Whatever you wanted to give me, I would have eagerly devoured. And that night, you gave me the best gift of all —yourself."

He grasps my hand, pressing it firmly against his chest.

"You etched yourself into my mind and heart, forever leaving your mark. This ink is just a symbol of that."

My mouth opens and closes several times, but no words come out. I feel like a fish out of water. A deer in the headlights. Whatever stupid idiom there is, it's me right now. Surprised by his crazy, romantic, doofus confession. I want to get angry, to spit in his face and storm off. And I wait for the anger to find me, but it doesn't. Instead, I'm filled with warmth. A type of warmth I've never felt before.

This confession means more to me than any of the public grand gestures. It feels different, genuine, intimate, and somehow, something more than words can express. That terrifies me more than anything else because there is a glimmer of hope now breaking through the barriers I had carefully constructed.

She's avoiding me.

I don't know why I thought I broke through to her. Maybe because that's exactly what it felt like in the locker room when she spotted the butterfly on my chest. It seemed like we were moving forward. She was emotionally raw and unprotected after our session, and everything simply slipped out. I didn't even try to put a stop to it. Told her everything I've been afraid to say all this time.

I know she's fighting this, but I thought she would have allowed herself to finally see this for what it is. Or maybe I'm wrong. Maybe she doesn't feel the same way.

I thought if I could break through...force her into my darkness...then she would feel at home, but what if I've been looking at this all wrong?

When I'm with her and we're lost in one another, it's easy to forget that Zoe doesn't feel the same way about me. She doesn't crave or want me in the same way. She's never sought me out. It's always been me chasing after her, running toward her. But I guess that's a given, considering everything I put her through. I will continue to do whatever it takes, trust blindly until I win her over and she finally lets go, knowing I'll be right there to catch her.

After the locker room, something changed. Instead of lashing out or running away, she stayed around with me. It felt like a moment of hope. I could tell she felt it too. Her eyes revealed it all as she absorbed my words, staring at me as if she actually believed me.

Like she finally forgave me.

But then, when we parted, reality came crashing down, and she pulled away once more. Shutting me out in hopes of, what? Getting me to back off?

Never going to fucking happen.

I am closer to her than I have ever been, and Zoe might think she's using me for sex, but I don't even care. I'll bide my time until she comes around or I break her apart.

My phone buzzes on the kitchen island, and I nearly trip over my feet trying to get to it.

AARON

Was Zoe at the game?

My heart sinks as I realize the text is not from Zoe.

ME

No

AARON

Second game in a row?

ME

I guess, yeah.

AARON

Did you guys get into a fight?

ME

Nope.

Not the type of fight you're thinking anyway, bro. I've actually been enjoying your sister in so many positions. Funny how I
used to feel sick about crossing that line, but now, I give zero
fucks. The longer Aaron ignores our conversation about his
parents, the more resentful I'm becoming. I don't feel guilty for
being with Zoe anymore, not if he's going to avoid what's
important.

AARON

Why are you being so cold? You've both been
acting weird, but I'm not having this
conversation over text. It doesn't look good
that she's missed back-to-back games. Might
want to have a talk with your fake girlfriend.

Gritting my teeth, I take a deep breath before typing out a
reply.

ME

She doesn't have to show up to every game.
And don't worry about it. I've got your sister
handled. Let me know when you want to have
that chat.

Bubbles pop up and disappear. The one thing these siblings
have in common is their exceptional skill at avoiding tough
conversations. Before engaging in confrontational conversations,
Aaron makes sure he has all the information neatly organized in
his mental file folder. Like a skilled detective, he insists on having
the details meticulously laid out, to give him the upper hand. If I
were to make a single change about him, it would be that. Aaron's
constant need for control makes communication feel rigid and
suffocating, which is incredibly infuriating.

But Aaron is right about one thing, I do need to talk to my girlfriend. Clicking on Zoe's chat, I send a direct message.

ME

Where are you?

ZOE

Out.

HER RESPONSE IS IMMEDIATE, but the one-word answer makes me want to put my fist through a wall.

ME

I want to see you.

ZOE

I'm busy.

ME

Doing what? Where are you?

ZOE

Don't worry about it.

I notice the purple silent mode notification appearing after a second. It forces me to check her location. I promised myself I wouldn't do it, and I've kept my word (for the most part) until now. But if she thinks she can ignore me and give me vague answers about her whereabouts, then I won't respect her privacy anymore. All bets are off.

Pulling up the app, I zoom in on Zoe's location and instantly recognize the club's name. I've been there a few times. Taboo Touches is one of the more popular BDSM clubs in New York City, and they have that reputation since their vetting process is more relaxed, especially for women. Because female clients attract more men, and that's all this club cares about.

I take ten minutes to change into an all-black outfit, grab my access card, and head out the door.

You want to play games, baby girl? I'll play all day and all night long. I feel sorry for anyone that lays eyes on her tonight. They're going to wish they had stayed home and fucked their hand instead.

THE LAYOUT at Taboo Touches is similar to most kinky clubs, with the exception that the inside of this place looks super cheap. It's as if their design budget ran out midway through and no one made the argument that an investment in this would pay off in the long run. I don't think Aaron has ever stepped inside this place, because he would definitely bitch and complain about the owners.

The type of people who venture inside this establishment are often inexperienced or don't know what BDSM is actually about. Which can be dangerous for someone seriously considering the lifestyle.

Zoe's presence here indicates her lack of research. I can't believe she would show up to a place like this without me. If I even see someone looking her way, let alone touching her, I will fuck this place up along with everyone inside of it.

I flash my access card at the door and am inside the poorly lit underground club within minutes. The bass is loud, shaking the flimsy walls as I make my way toward the bar. My night is either going to go smoothly—if I find Zoe sitting at the bar—or it's going to go to shit—if I have to break into every private room of this place.

I glance across the crowded bar with a slight sense of unease until my eyes land on Zoe, who is seated at the far end of the bar, across from...Via?

She's here with her friend.

I don't know why, but this is the last thing I expected. As I gaze at Zoe sitting at the bar, I struggle to find the right words to describe her beauty at this moment. A mix of relief and lust flood me as I adjust myself to hide the bulge in my pants.

Fucking Christ, the hold this woman has on me is well beyond ridiculous.

I could give her space for the night, let her hang out with her friend...or I could go over there and teach her a lesson about giving me a one-word answer when I ask her a question.

Leaving her alone is definitely an option, but not one I'm interested in. Plus, I have nothing better to do with my time, and I love messing with my little butterfly.

Making my way over to the very back edge of the bar, my shoulder is almost touching Via's back as I lean on the counter. My hood is still up, and I linger for a second, eyes following the busy bartender before giving up entirely and glancing over my shoulder.

Zoe is smiling, her face buzzing with anticipation as she reacts to something Via is telling her. She seems different somehow, a bit more at ease.

I wonder if she's thinking of me.

Zoe's gaze meets mine, and she does a double take. I clamp down on my cheek to stifle my laughter.

"What the actual fuck!" Zoe exclaims, causing Via to turn toward me.

I reach up and wave my fingers at them, grinning.

"I want to say 'small world,' but I have a feeling you told him where we were," Via says, her eyes turning into dinner plates as she glances around. "Oh my god, this isn't what you think. I swear."

"I don't care. I don't judge."

Via arches a curious brow at me as Zoe jumps off her stool. She struts up to me, sticking her pretty finger in my face.

"Did you fucking follow me here? How?"

I look away, smirking as I casually tip my shoulders up.

"Wow. Just wow."

"Maybe don't give me one-word answers next time and make me feel crazy." I cut her a glance, and the sheer anger in her eyes makes my dick hard.

I want to throw her up against the wall, wrap my hand around her throat, and fuck her hard, claiming that tight little pussy of hers.

"News flash: you are crazy, Dominik."

"What are you doing here? If you wanted to venture into this world again, all you had to do was ask, baby girl."

"You're sick," she mutters, pretending like she's disgusted, but her body says differently. I catch a whiff of Zoe's distinct scent of vanilla and citrus as she leans in closer.

There is absolutely no chance that I'm leaving now, not before I take a piece of her.

"Hey, Via, you mind if I steal Zoe for a second?"

Via seems caught off guard for a moment, but then she shakes her head, blushing slightly. I make her nervous. Interesting.

"What? No. I'm not going anywhere with you," Zoe protests, but I grab her arm and head out of the bar area.

She struggles briefly but soon gives up. As we reach the back of the dark hallway, I release her arm. Zoe quickly charges past me, brushing her shoulder against mine as she runs into the women's bathroom.

Does she think I won't go in there after her? Clearly, she's learned nothing.

As soon as I push through the black door, Zoe turns, her expression filled with a certain type of anger. Not the one she used to wear before, but the one I've come to recognize as her brat. The same one that urges me to push her buttons and get her to submit. But it also happens to be the same anger that always has her panting and begging for more.

She remains near the back wall in the small, dark space. The bathroom is tiny with only one stall. On the opposite wall, there is a tall mirror that reaches from the floor to the ceiling next to a modern black sink. To enhance the atmosphere, there is a strip of red light that outlines the ceiling and the corners of the room.

"Get out," Zoe yells.

I turn and lock the door, unzipping my hoodie and peeling it off as I approach her.

"You don't want me to leave," I say confidently as I run my knuckles along her chest, feeling her perked up nipples poking through her tight, black dress.

Zoe's lips part as she gazes up at me, her eyes sparkling like endless green pools. Eagerly, she waits for my next action, her chest rising and falling noticeably.

"I do," she lies.

"I'm not in the mood for your games tonight, Zoe."

"I'm not playing games; I didn't want to see you."

I nod, not buying a single word coming out of her mouth. Grabbing the hem of my shirt from the back, I pull it over my head and toss the material aside. Zoe's eyes travel down my chest, lingering on the monarch butterfly tattoo.

Little does she know that most of the tattoos on my body serve as constant reminders of her or hold some special meaning related to her. Even though I couldn't have her, I needed these reminders etched on my skin to keep her close to me. She will forever be a part of my soul, and nothing can ever alter that.

"Is that so?" I say, gripping the back of her neck and yanking her against my body.

As I kiss her forcefully, Zoe immediately reacts by fisting my hair and digging her fingernails into my shoulder. We're high off one another. The attraction is magnetic. As soon as we come near each other, an undeniable force draws us in, making it impossible for either of us to resist. She tries so hard to fight it, and I love how she loses the fight every single time.

Zoe's teeth scratch my lip while the tip of her tongue traces the curve of my bottom lip. Lifting her up, I drop her onto the counter, yanking the corners of her dress down to expose her black lace bra.

She moans into my mouth as I pinch her nipple with one hand while my other hand skates up her thighs, brushing her already swollen clit over the thin material of her soaked underwear.

What a beautiful little liar.

"Seems like you didn't learn your lesson about lying."

Zoe doesn't respond, biting down on my lip while pulling the top of my hair hard.

My little brat is feeling feisty tonight—her fire matching mine perfectly.

"This has nothing to do with you, Lewis. I'm always wet and needy."

"You're wet and needy for me. You belong to me like I belong to you," I growl, pulling on her wet panties until I hear them tear. Grabbing the material, I shove it into my back pocket, knowing exactly what I want to do when the time comes.

"Do I now?" Zoe whimpers as I massage her entrance before bringing my soaked fingers up to my lips. Fuck, she tastes so good. I repeat my movements, but this time, I shove my fingers down her throat as I bite down on the skin above her collarbone.

I suck and bite hard, knowing that when I pull away, her flesh will be angry and red. The thought of visibly marking her has pre-cum leaking out of me.

I continue to mark up her neck, pushing my finger in and out of her inch by inch, hearing the noises spill from her lips as I own her body. And once I'm satisfied with the damage, I lean back and stare at the red blotches all over her chest and neck. Zoe is breathless, staring at me through lust-filled, hooded eyes.

I bend down and suck on her nipple poking through her lace bra. Watching her eyes roll to the back of her head. I can't take it anymore.

"Playtime is over, baby."

Picking her up off the counter, I whip Zoe around and shove the bottom of her dress up until the tight material is covering her midsection. She's completely exposed and staring at herself in the mirror. She remains silent as her fingers graze the angry marks I left on her. Unzipping my pants, I pull out my hard cock, stroking myself as I stare at her in the mirror.

With a tight grip on her wrists, I place her palms onto the mirror above her head "If you move an inch, I'll slap this perfect ass. You got it?"

"Yes, sir."

Kicking Zoe's legs apart, I push her chest down and spit on my fingers, spreading it over her puckered ass and slowly probing one finger inside of her. Nudging the head of my cock at her core, I line myself up and stare directly into her eyes in the mirror.

"I own this ass, this pussy," I growl, fisting her hair as I seat myself inside of her wet cunt. "This body is mine. Your mind, your heart, it's all mine, Zoe. And if I have to mark you every day for the rest of my fucking life, I will."

Zoe moans, shuddering with pleasure as I push the finger inside her ass deeper while my cock assaults her pussy. I love watching her submit to me like this, letting me take what I want from her when I want it and knowing she gets off on it.

She watches me in the mirror as I look down, stretching her with my cock and feeling her tighten around me while my finger massages her ass.

"Look how pretty you look, taking all of me," I whisper in her ear, and she whimpers, pushing back into me.

Fucking Christ.

I'm going to lose my load soon if I'm not careful.

Suddenly, the red light switches to green, and the mirror flips for a second, displaying an audience behind the glass.

Looks like we're not alone.

"They're watching us," she gasps.

Fisting Zoe's hair, I pull her up against my chest, tilting her neck, and forcing her to stare straight through the mirror. I don't stop, and I don't plan on it unless she uses her safe word.

"They are. Does that turn you on?" My breath ghosts her ear.

"Yes," she whispers, closing her eyes and leaning further into me. I can feel her growing wetter and chasing her orgasm.

"You like the idea of someone watching as I own this perfect little body?"

Biting her bottom lip, Zoe breathes deeply and nods.

"Use your words," I urge, pulling out of her and pausing for a second before thrusting back inside her.

"Yes," she moans, her hands making a fist against the mirror.

"That's a good girl." I suck on her earlobe, feeling her shudder. "Reach down and play with yourself until you come all over my cock."

Zoe wastes no time, quickly following directions. In less than a minute, she detonates, squeezing my cock so hard that I join her, spilling inside her and filling her with my cum.

Now this is what she's going to remember when she thinks about exhibitionism at a BDSM club. She's going to remember how I tracked her down and took her into a dark room, claiming her while strangers watched. She's going to get wet remembering how much she liked it. Despite our secret audience, it was all about her and me, without our masks on.

Just Dominik and Zoe.

It was always intended to be this way, and it will continue to be like this forever.

I watch Zoe struggle with her dress while I pull my pants up.

"Where are my panties?"

"You won't be getting those back," I say, watching her reaction in the mirror.

"Why?"

Leaning down, I whisper in her ear. "Because you're going to go out there and have a good time with your friend while I leak out of you all night, my cum dripping down your leg and reminding you who this pussy belongs to."

It takes everything inside me to kiss her and turn, walking out of that room without looking back.

18
ZOE

I can't stop thinking about the other night and the way Dominik felt inside me while I watched us in the two-way mirror. Something clicked after he left the BDSM club.

For the first time, I allowed myself to be in the present without dwelling on our past. I didn't think about the lies, secrets, and betrayal. I didn't even mind how he randomly showed up there, didn't even care how the hell he'd found me. My body instinctively responded to him, even before I could fully comprehend the situation. And I hate how I loved every single second of it.

Does that mean I've forgiven him? Maybe that's too extreme, but I think a part of me finally understands how he feels—the carnal desire running through him whenever we're together. Because I feel it too. I sense Dominik flowing through me, lingering long after his fingertips have left my skin.

It's all very confusing. That night felt like every other time. Perhaps my desire for the chase is fading as I realize how much better it is to be with Dominik. He makes me experience emotions I never knew were possible. I never thought my black, soulless heart could desire someone in this way.

Intimacy has never meant much to me other than sharing a moment with someone. Getting off and getting out. But it feels different with Dominik. This whole thing is developing into something greater than I imagined. I had a good grasp on it, but now I'm feeling unsure.

I long for his touch even when we're together. Thinking about missing him later. It's stupid and crazy and makes no sense. But it never feels like enough.

I thought I would get my fill by now, that I would pull away like I always do, but the opposite is happening, and that terrifies me more than anything else.

The unknown terrifies me.

This need terrifies me.

I lie in bed, staring up at the ceiling and wishing it wasn't pissing with rain outside so I could go for a run. Maybe throwing around some weights at the gym will get my mind off Dominik for a bit. My stupid vagina needs a timeout.

Or maybe a good book.

I sigh, knowing that won't work because I've been in a slump for a few weeks, and I sort of blame Dominik for that one, too.

My phone vibrates next to me. Flipping it over, my heart skips a beat when I see his name on my screen.

DOM

What are you doing?

I should leave him on read, make him sweat a little.

ME

Nothing.

DOM

Get dressed and meet me downstairs in ten minutes.

ME

Where are we going?

DOM

You'll see. Be a good girl and do as you're told, please.

An exciting shiver runs down my spine. Despite wanting to act like a brat and ignore him, I know I'll end up downstairs. I change quickly, brush my hair and teeth, freshen up my makeup, and sprint to the elevator.

As I step out of the elevator and into the lobby, Dominik is standing there, eagerly waiting for me. His eyes light up, and a smile automatically forms on my face as he approaches me.

"You came without a fight. I'm impressed, Ms. Jackson."

He looks effortlessly stunning, as usual, dressed in casual attire—black jeans, a forest-green sweater, and a stylish, black peacoat. His signature look. Dominik's hair is slightly damp, accentuating the onyx color and making his eyes glow in contrast. God, he's beautiful.

"You told me to be a good girl." I smirk, dragging out the last two words on purpose.

He arches a brow at me, and I nearly melt on the spot. "And good girls get rewarded."

Sweet Jesus.

I'd like my reward right here in this lobby, please and thank you.

Can you be any thirstier? How pathetic. Also, what kind of response was that, Zoe? "You told me to be a good girl?" Get a grip on yourself.

"Where are we going?" I'm desperate to change the subject before my heated cheeks give me away completely.

"Before I answer that, tell me if you'd rather drive or take an Uber. I wanted to walk, but given the weather out there..."

Okay, so we're going somewhere close.

"You have a car?"

Dominik gives me a puzzled look. "Yeah, I have two."

"But you never drive."

"I do, here and there. Used to more when Aaron, Tristan, and I would go to the woods for the weekend to get away from the city. Find a new adventure," Dominik says, pushing the elevator button.

"What kind of adventures?" I poke, and he gives me a sideway glance, smirking.

"A different kind." Dominik winks at me.

Shit. Do the three of them have some kinky history? I really want to hear it, but I decide to leave it for another day, maybe after Dom has had a few too many drinks.

"You miss it?"

His brows furrow. "Miss what?"

"Hanging out with the guys all the time."

Dominik thinks about my question before answering. "Yeah, I guess. But we still see each other plenty. They've just been busy with work lately."

I'm not sure if he's trying to convince himself or me, but the disappointment is clear in his voice. It sounds like he misses their old dynamic.

"Yeah, I've heard that one a lot. Money isn't the be-all and end-all."

"Try telling your brother that," he scoffs right as the elevator doors ding open and we both step inside.

"Yeah, I've been meaning to talk to him."

Dominik remains silent, and the tension becomes palpable as

we find ourselves trapped inside the mirrored box. Suddenly, all I can think about is Dominik fucking me from behind at the BDSM club the other night. As the memories rush in, a wave of goosebumps spreads across my skin. Biting my lip, I drop my gaze, desperately hoping Dominik doesn't notice the way my heart races whenever he's around.

I can't stop thinking about him, no matter how hard I try. Now, I feel shy around him. What's going on?

Dominik, previously a passing figure in my life, has now become a forceful presence in my thoughts who I can't resist. It's a nauseating sensation, a magnetic pull that seems to defy reason. I don't know how to stop it, and I'm not even sure I want to anymore.

This type of wanting feels good.

His scent is so intoxicating, I can't help but want to be close to him. Vivid images of him on his knees right here in this elevator flood my mind, instantly turning me on.

"You okay?"

I jump at the sound of his voice. "Yep!"

Dominik breathes in, his eyes fixated on my lips. He extends his hand and lightly brushes his thumb against my lip before letting go.

"Do you need me to work out your sexual frustrations? Tell me what you're thinking."

I gasp, getting flustered. "I don't know what you're talking about."

Dominik hums. "What did we say about lying?"

The elevator doors open. He doesn't move. I'm worried he might pounce on me. Even worse, I might pounce on him if we stay any longer. I quickly pull away and stumble out, desperately trying to put some distance between us.

I can hear his laughter behind me. It frustrates me how effortlessly he seems in control.

"You know how to drive, Zoe?"

What kind of question is that? "Of course."

"Great. Take these," Dominik says, forcing me to turn just in time to catch the bundle of keys flying in the air.

I just blink at him. "Seriously?"

"Yeah... You're gonna drive."

I glance down at the keychain, noticing the Audi symbol.

"You trust me enough to let me drive your car? What car—"

Before I can even finish my sentence, Dominik casually leans on a sick red-and-black Audi R8, making my jaw hit the floor.

"You've got to be shitting me," I exclaim, hopping over to the driver's side and jumping in before he changes his mind.

"Just don't kill us, okay?" He laughs.

"No promises." I beam, dropping the keys in the cup holder and turning to press the power button.

Taking a moment, I admire the interior of the vehicle, which screams luxury from top to bottom. It's making me slightly apprehensive about even sitting here, fearing I might accidentally cause some damage. The new leather smell enhances the rich vibe, along with the cleanliness of the car and the red leather seats with black stitching.

Running my hands over the cold steering wheel, I gently trace the Audi logo with my fingertips. Being reminded just how different the boys and I are. Sometimes I forget our lives aren't even on the same caliber.

"I used to have a model car just like this one. I kept it in my closet. Aaron got it for me after we went to a luxury car show in Boston. The show was only open during school hours, so we played hookie and went to look at all the fancy cars. He said he was going to collect them one day, and I believed him, even then. I wasn't really into cars until that day, especially since Aaron wanted to take me and not one of his friends."

Looking over at Dominik, I notice how intently he's listening to me, his body turned toward me. I'm not sure why I'm sharing this with him. I guess the Audi triggered those memories.

"I saw this exact model and color in the show room and instantly fell in love. Aaron bought me the toy model as we were leaving, and I kept it hidden in my closet because I didn't want my parents seeing it and taking it away. It's funny that you bought the exact same car, even down to the color."

Dominik remains silent for a while. I begin to fiddle with the controls, getting to know the car before we go.

"That's why I bought it," he whispers.

I turn to face him, not sure I heard him correctly. "What?"

"I wanted to surround myself with things that reminded me of you."

"Why?"

Dominik rests his elbow on the center console, casually grabbing a strand of my hair. He playfully twirls it around his finger before he looks up at me, jolting my breath.

"You know why, Zoe," he says softly, right before his lips melt into mine.

I am so royally fucked, it's not even funny.

"YOU WANTED me to drive to the side of Madison Square Garden that seems to be in mid-demolition?" I say as I unbuckle my seatbelt and stare at Dominik's stupid grin.

"You know, you're the most impatient woman I have ever met."

"And you're the most confusing person I have ever met. Now, out with it, Lewis. Why are we here?"

"Will you just shut up for two seconds and get out of the car?"

I cross my arms and lean back into my seat. "Nope. Not until you tell me why we're here."

Dominik narrows his eyes and swings open his door. "Fine. Suit yourself."

I watch him walk across and reach my door. I don't get a chance to protest because he quickly pulls me out of the car. Next thing I know, he's flinging me over his shoulder.

"Are you fucking insane? Put me down! You can't do this to me every time I don't listen to your demands."

"I can do whatever the fuck I want. Especially when you're being a brat." He smacks my ass hard.

I try to push away using all my strength, strike him with my arm, but it's all no use. He's way too strong. Trying to fight against his tight grip is leaving me exhausted and ruining my hair. Despite his rough treatment, I decide to playfully pinch his ass cheek, expecting him to let go, but it just makes him laugh.

"The fact you think that would work on me is just beyond cute."

"Fuck you."

"Oh, please do. You know my favorite place to be is inside that pretty cunt of yours."

"Dominik!" I screech in total shock, and it makes him burst into laughter.

He's in a great mood tonight, laughing so much in such a short amount of time. I can't remember when he last appeared so carefree and content.

It's contagious, and I hate that I love it.

By the time we make it inside, I'm dizzy and trying not to hurl from the rush of blood to my head. Dominik puts me down, holding me up while I adjust to being back on my feet.

"That was fun," he remarks, placing a kiss on the back of my head.

"Yeah, for you. What's all this?"

I take a quick look around the dark, open space. It doesn't even resemble Madison Square Garden. It's just a huge concrete box. Plastic tarps hang all around, and bundles of building supplies are randomly scattered in the middle of the floor.

Dominik takes my hand and leads me through the plastic drapes. We enter a massive, open space that seems to stretch for miles. I never realized they had this much square footage here. Maybe it has always been here but just sectioned off?

"This is an upcoming extension they're currently developing. It's meant to be a versatile space, catering to all sorts of things like concerts, sports events, and private or public gatherings. It's still in the planning stages, and they're looking for an architectural team to lead the project."

I'm standing here, and my mind is already brimming with potential ideas for a blank canvas like this. It would be so much fun to work on a project of this size.

"That's really cool. Will it affect your games or the playoffs?"

Dom shakes his head, reaching inside his coat pocket and pulling out a piece of paper.

"You asked me why we're here. I wanted you to see the place so you could get excited for the future."

I blink at him, waiting for him to say more. But instead, he just hands me the paper and waits. I unfold it, trying to make sense of what I'm looking at.

It appears to be a job application.

With my name on it...

For... Wait...

"This is filled out. With all my personal information," I whisper, quickly scanning the rest of the page.

"When I heard they were seeking external applicants, I knew

I had to get your name in front of the panel. But I also knew if I told you about it, you'd never do it yourself."

I stare up at Dominik, dumbfounded.

He continues when I don't speak. "So, I filled it out and sent it off. I just wanted to show you where you might be working soon. It's always been your dream, Zo, and I want you to be happy."

My eyes fall back down to the paper.

My name is on a job application to be part of the architectural and design team for the remodel of the extension at Madison Square Garden. Something I would have never even found out on my own, nor would I have applied because I know I won't get it.

So now, I get to wait for more disappointing news.

"You had no right." I fist the papers and shove them into his chest.

"You're pissed?"

"Of course I'm pissed. You didn't ask me if I wanted this. You didn't even tell me. Who does that?"

"Someone who knows you better than you know yourself." He takes a step toward me.

"You don't know me."

"I know every part of you. You can try to deny it, Zoe, but I don't believe you. I know *you* don't even believe you. I'm sorry you feel like I overstepped, but don't stand here and tell me I don't fucking know you. We're inevitable. Basic chemistry."

I open my mouth to respond, but my jaw snaps shut when I realize I don't know what to say.

"Do you want me to pull your name out?" he grits out angrily.

Looking at the vast, gray emptiness around us, I consider his question. How could I even contribute to a massive project like this? I don't have any experience. I studied architecture at school but never practiced in the field. I would undoubtedly fail and get fired, which would also make Dom look bad for recommending me in the first place.

"I think you should. I'm not qualified. I'm sure I wouldn't even make it through the initial round of interviews."

Dominik sighs audibly, staring up at the ceiling for a brief second before his eyes meet mine. "Is that what you want?"

"Yes," I breathe out and he doesn't say another word. Dominik extends his hand to me, and I reach for it instantly.

We walk back to the car in total silence. It may have been harsh, shutting down his nice gesture like that, but it's a waste of time. This is for the best.

I don't want to jinx it, but life has been good lately.

Better than good, actually.

My complete focus on the ice has resulted in a series of wins for us. Even Coach has noticed the change. My sleeping and eating habits have been excellent, and it all comes back to her. The way I've been feeling lately because of Zoe has brought total bliss into other parts of my life. She is stillness, the edge of light in everything I do. It's like walking into a house and instantly feeling at home.

Things have been oddly calm between her and me. It feels as though we've resolved our past issues without ever directly confronting them.

Maybe it had to do with me pretending to listen to her at MSG when she asked me to pull her name out of the application pool for her dream job.

As if I'd ever do something that stupid.

I went with it, bit my tongue and pretended like I was listening, but I wasn't. She needs an advocate to fight for her when she lacks confidence. She needs someone to support her as she discovers her true potential and heals from her parents' hurtful actions. I will always be that person for her. Even when she tries to tell me no.

Is it a little psychotic and twisted? Sure. But it's what she needs, and when she finally gets a call for the interview, she'll thank me.

Sometimes the people we love just need a little push in the right direction.

I know she'll get there on her own. I'm just here to ensure her safe arrival at her final destination during this journey. And there's nothing wrong with that.

My phone vibrates in my pocket. I smile when I see Zoe's name pop up on my screen.

ZOE

Basement parking garage. Five minutes.

Something feels off about that text. I don't even bother with a response. I'm out the door and heading downstairs in less than two minutes. It's very telling how easily she commands me. I've been trying to get her to submit, to fully claim her, but the truth is, it's me who belongs to her.

I have always been hers.

She owns me in every sense of the word. She could say jump, and I wouldn't even hesitate. I'd walk through fire for her. I would give up everything if I knew it would make her happy. If I could erase all her pain and allow her to live a normal life without the trauma and burden from her past. Sometimes, I wonder how she would have turned out if someone had loved her like she deserved from the beginning.

Zoe texted me without any context. I'm not sure why she wants me to come to the basement at night. Maybe she wants to play hide and seek? My girl always keeps me on my toes, leaving me wanting more.

That's how it's always been with us, and I wouldn't have it any other way.

ZOE IS WEARING a mask and dressed in all black. She is leaning against my R8, giving off an air of ownership over the entire building and the cars around her. Her hooded face tilts to the right and up, intoxicating me.

She's wearing the same mask I wore the night of the BDSM ball, but mine was red while hers is glowing icy blue.

The perfect contrast.

Walking down the ramp, I don't bother hiding the smirk plastered on my face.

"I like the getup. If I had known, I would have brought *my* mask," I say.

"We can share. Are you up for a game?" Zoe's voice is muffled.

"With you? Always," I say, expecting her to follow up with instructions or something more, but she just stands there.

I move closer, wishing I could see her face.

Zoe's voice breaks as she confesses, "I don't know what we're doing anymore, Dominik. I don't know what this is, and I don't know how to stop."

"Why does it need to stop?"

She shakes her head, tugging her hood even lower over her face. "It doesn't matter."

I feel her pulling away, trying to run from this. From me.

"No? We're just going to avoid talking about our feelings, per usual?" I take a careful step closer to her.

"I'm not avoiding anything. I just don't think it's working."

I know Zoe. I know that when she feels like she's losing control, she chooses to run. She wants to put space between herself and the storm inside her mind. She believes distance and time can come between us and what we have, but it won't work. Not in this lifetime or the next.

"You pull away to prevent yourself from feeling anything. You think it'll protect you from getting hurt, but it won't. You're going to feel everything anyway, no matter what you tell yourself. Besides, the next time I hurt you, it'll be intentional and because you want it." I take another step closer, but she raises her hand, motioning for me to stop.

"Hurt me *again*, you mean?" Zoe jumps in, delivering a sucker punch straight to the gut. I guess I deserve that. "I didn't call you down here for a therapy session, Dominik."

I give her a sly grin. "What did you call me down here for, then?"

"One last apology? Maybe?"

Whatever she's battling right now, it's intense. She wants to call it off, to escape, but she can't. Because even she can't deny what this is anymore.

"One last apology before what?"

Zoe crosses her ankles, folding her arms as she shrugs. "I haven't decided yet."

"Alright. You want to chase me around, little butterfly? Want me to allow you to catch me? Take over control?" My chest tightens from everything she's not saying, but I don't let on. Treating this as a game.

She shrugs, making herself smaller. It's obvious she hasn't thought this through. Maybe she wanted a bit of underground fun to get her mind off things, or maybe she wants one last fuck before she calls things off. As if I'd allow her to do that.

I threw away all the rules when I decided to go all in. I want to win her over and show her I'm here to stay. Everything has changed, and it won't go back to how it used to be.

It can't. It's not up to us anymore.

I lower myself to the floor. The sharp, cold edges of the concrete press into my kneecaps.

"What are you doing?" Zoe stills. I know how much she loves me in this position. If power is what my butterfly seeks, power is what she will have.

"Where do you want me this time? My cock inside you while you're up against my car? Or should I throw you on top of the hood, spread you open, and bury my face in that sweet pussy?"

"Get up," she orders, but I ignore her command and press my kneecaps further into the rocky ground. The floor digs into my palms as I crawl toward her, closing the short five-foot distance between us.

Zoe has consistently challenged every law for me. With her, all my principles, feelings, and preconceived notions about love have become irrelevant. My dominant side takes a backseat when it comes to her pleasure. If this is what it takes to prove to her I'm for real, then I'll do it a thousand times over.

When I get to where she's standing, her breaths are labored, and I can't tell if it's the result of shock or anger. Glaring at the neon-blue Xs on her mask, I look beyond the shield she has up and pray my next words reach her.

"I'm sorry. I'm so fucking sorry, Zoe. For all of it. For leaving you behind in Boston. For not standing up to your parents when I had the chance. For letting your brother come here without bringing you with him. I'm sorry for staying quiet and for pretending like this didn't matter. I'm sorry for not fighting for us before. I'm sorry for the secrets and the lies, but I'm not sorry for Boston. I'll never be sorry for everything we shared together that night."

"Stop. I don't want to hear it."

I ignore her, continuing. "I'm sorry for wasting so much fucking time pretending I could forget you."

"It doesn't matter."

"It matters to me." I stand, slowly lifting the mask off her face.

"Why?" The sight of her glassy, jade eyes staring up at me nearly force me back down to my knees.

"Because you're all I've ever wanted, and now that I have you, I'm not letting go. I can't let go."

Zoe looks away, clearly uncomfortable with my words. It's obvious in the way she's trying to hold herself together.

"I don't know how to do any of this. I'm scared, Dominik. I want to shut it off and feel nothing."

I cradle her face, lifting her chin up and forcing her to look into my eyes. "Let me be your nothing."

"You already are, and this isn't even real." Zoe shuts her eyes as if she's said too much. Revealed a broken part of herself she meant to keep hidden.

"This has always been real, and you know it. It's been real from the very first moment I laid eyes on you."

Zoe ignores my confession. It's the one I've been dying to say. I've wanted to say it ever since we started this ridiculous, fake dating arrangement. I want to tell her all the ways I love her, how much she means to me, but I don't think she's ready for that yet.

"It doesn't matter. You're going to get bored and leave. I'll break your heart, self-sabotage. Nothing ever lasts." Her eyes are cold and almost empty as she looks up at me. She's trying to channel her anger, using it as a shield to avoid feeling all the emotions she's been pushing away for years.

"Let me be your nothing," I whisper, repeating the words from earlier as I plead with her.

I will never give up this pursuit. Not until my last breath.

Zoe shoots me an angry glare, snatching the mask from my

hand and moving aside. But she doesn't make it far before I catch up to her and yank her back. She screams at me, but her words fall on deaf ears as I quickly unlock the Audi and forcefully shove her into the backseat.

"Let me go!"

"You don't get to walk away from me. Not anymore."

I grab hold of her sweater and pull it off her body. "You don't get to fucking ignore me and pretend like this isn't happening."

I quickly unbuckle her jeans and forcefully pull them off. She scratches at my arms, but I only see red.

"We can't do this here. Someone could see us. Aaron could see us."

Reaching behind, I undo the clasp of her bra and toss it aside. With my hand firmly on her throat, I sit her up and press her back against the middle seat. As I secure the seat belts, I carefully crisscross them over her bare upper body.

"Did you fucking hear me?" Zoe screams.

"Let them watch how I claim you. I want the whole city to hear you scream my name."

Zoe inhales deeply just as my fingers brush against her slick panties and it becomes blatantly obvious how much of a fucking brat she is. She's an excellent actress, I'll give her that. Even if she wants to fight me off, her body will always tell the truth.

I move her panties aside, both of us staring down at my fingers pressed against her opening. "You can lie all you want, baby. But your words mean nothing when your pussy cries for me like this."

Zoe gnaws on her lower lip but remains silent. I exhale, feeling the tension, and she smirks, fully aware that she has regained her hold over me. By engaging in these mind games, she knows how to provoke my wild side. And I willingly embrace it, because I am irrevocably intertwined with her wounded heart—inseparable, like a cosmic bond.

She is naked. I am fully clothed. Her back is against the leather seat, trapped by my body. I lean down to her lips, and her eyes meet mine. There is a magnetic force between us. How can I make her feel this energy? This pull that has driven me mad since the day we met.

I need to break down her walls.

No, fuck that... I'm sick of being nice. I just want to break her.

Right now, I can't concentrate on anything other than how much I want to fucking kiss her lips and touch every inch of her body. Over and over again until the sun comes up and the basement is flooded with people.

Until she's too fucking spent to fight this connection between us.

"Are you gonna leave, or fuck me?" Zoe whispers, pulling me out of my thoughts.

"I'm never going to leave. Maybe you like pretending, or maybe you're just in denial. Or maybe you like feeling helpless and out of control. But when we're together, when I touch you," I whisper against her lips, pressing my fingers slowly inside her, watching her eyes shudder closed, "everything else fades away. It's just you and me. We're all that matters. And I'm going to make sure you always remember that."

She gently places her lips against mine, and I respond by aggressively kissing her back, growling as I feel her hands trying to undo my belt. I assist her in pulling down my pants, my dick springing free as I lower myself onto my knees in front of her. Spreading her legs apart, I sensually nibble and lick along her thighs until she is trembling with desire, nearly begging me for it.

I blow on her quivering pussy before licking up her chest and neck until my lips are on hers and we're connected again. Zoe arches her back, kissing me with such desperation. I trap her lips between my teeth and bite down until she's panting for air.

"Put on the mask," I order, grabbing the purge mask lying on the car floor and handing it to her. Zoe fumbles with the strap before placing it over her face.

"Next time you try to call it quits or doubt what we are, doubt the things I feel for you, I will not be nice about it. We are an inevitable force. You belong to me, and I belong to you."

She claws at my stomach, tracing my abs with her nails as she tries to pull me down onto her. But I'm in no rush, as I need this to sink in. Grabbing her hips, I lean against the back of the front row seats and take hold of my hard cock, circling my pierced head against her cunt. Zoe moans, fisting her hair and arching her back, losing herself to the sensation of us.

"Don't move."

"Please," she whimpers.

Fuck. My lack of control is pathetic.

"Please, Dominik. I need you. I want you."

That's all it takes to push me over the edge. I lift her ass up, burying myself deep inside her. Zoe cries out, and I nearly empty myself with the way her walls grip me. I fuck her like it's the first and last time. Like I'm a starving man eating a meal for the first time.

"Dominik," she gasps, her fingernails digging into my chest as she draws blood.

"Fuck, baby," I hum into her ear. "Your pussy is gripping me so fucking tightly."

I slam into her, my eyes rolling to the back of my head as she continues to scream out my name. But I can't come just yet. I need to explore her more. I need to be inside her for longer. I need to make time stop when I'm with her.

I need all of her.

Slowing down my strides, I lean back and unbuckle the seatbelts, setting Zoe free. I turn her around so her back is facing me before I swap our positions. I barely fit in this car as it is, and my knees dig into the front seats as I reposition myself in the back. Zoe glances over her shoulder, her mask now resting on top of her head. Sweat glistens on her forehead, but she remains as stunning as ever, both of us inhaling the misty air surrounding us.

"Ride me, Zoe."

"I don't think I can."

"You can, and you will. Try, baby." I grab her hips and guide her down on my dick as she digs her nails into my thighs. The rush from the sting courses down my spine, intensifying the feeling of her even more.

I guide Zoe, biting my lip as I help her readjust until she's completely seated on me. My hand snakes up her front, pulling on her nipple as her back presses against my chest. She rides me, crying out as her movements quicken. I curl my hand into her hair, gripping tightly and shoving her head to the side so I can have access to her neck.

My other hand snakes up to her mouth. I press my fingers against her lips, and Zoe opens up for me, sucking greedily.

"This pussy was made for my cock," I whisper in her ear before biting down on her neck.

Taking my soaked fingers, I press them against her clit. Her head falls back against my shoulder, and she lets out a cry, her movements becoming uneven as she starts chasing her orgasm.

"Dominik," she moans loudly. I could muffle her, but I don't dare; I fucking love the sounds she makes.

"No more masks."

"Okay," Zoe chokes out.

"I need to feel all of you. I want you to shatter, fall apart, and know I'll pick up the pieces. Stop running from me."

"I'll always run from you," she groans right as her orgasm tears through her. Zoe screams, shouting my name as her nails dig into my arm.

I can't hold on any longer.

"Fuck, Zoe," I sigh, my eyes rolling to the back of my head as my orgasm rips through me. I grip Zoe tightly, my world shifting as I spill inside her. Her sweet pussy milks me dry, and even though it's too much, too sensitive, I can't stop thrusting inside her. Desperate for just a second more.

Hearts pounding, chests heaving, we're both incredibly still for a long time, pressed together as we share the same limited air.

I want to possess her heart and soul. To wear her scars proudly just to make her feel less alone. She's everything I've wanted and more.

I'm in love with her. I've always been in love with her.

But no matter how badly I want this...I'm not sure she could ever love me. I don't think it'll ever matter, because I'll take whatever she gives me. Even if it's scraps for the rest of my life.

"When we're together like this, nothing exists apart from you and me. When I hold you like this, all the bullshit from our past, every dark memory, every pain point vanishes...as if it was never even there. Because you are all that matters to me in this fucked up world, and I will never give up on that."

Zoe kisses my nose. The act is so gentle, it takes me by surprise.

"I believe you," she whispers, making me the happiest man with just those three words.

Finally.

Tonight is hockey night with Via and Aaron, and just the thought of them being together again makes my stomach twist into knots. It's been a while since they were face-to-face, but after meeting him at the office, Via confessed that she felt put off by him. So much so, that she almost canceled coming with me to Dom's game tonight. Even though she's been dying to go to a hockey game. I think she's secretly hoping Aaron will bail, which is honestly likely since he's never around these days.

But on the off chance he does show up, I have no idea if the two of them will behave or if they will unleash their wrath at the arena, turning it into a battlefield for all of New York City to see.

I have been anxiously thinking about how to keep the two of them happy and away from one another as much as possible. However, tonight, something else entirely has triggered my anxiety.

Dominik is consuming all my thoughts.

Isn't he always on your mind?

That's not helping.

Lately, we've been spending a lot of time together. It's been weeks since we went out in public as a couple. Even though nothing has changed outwardly, everything feels different. *He* feels different. I used to be able to convince myself that I despised him, with no attraction or connection. But I can't lie to myself anymore. What happened in the past feels inconsequential, like a faraway dream.

How did I let go of everything so quickly?

Keeping my distance isn't even an option anymore. It's not like he gives me any space. If he did, I could convince myself that he's bored and uninterested, but no. He somehow wedged himself into the back of my head and refused to leave. Was it his relentless persistence? The way he broke through my barriers? Or did I unknowingly open a door, inviting him into a space I typically reserve for no one?

These confusing feelings are giving me a headache. I can't stop thinking about his stupid face, the way he laughs, or the dimple on his right cheek when he smiles big. The way I catch him staring at me whenever I'm busy with something. This and a million other things replay in my mind all day, every day.

I hate how much I enjoy being with him.

I've tried to regain control, to push back against these thoughts, but it's been futile. And worse than that, I don't want to stay away.

It doesn't even matter because we agreed from the beginning that this would just be sex until the public breakup happens. Something temporary to help ease the tension between us. It needs to end soon, before Aaron finds out what we've been doing behind his back all this time. He trusted me to help Dom out and likely thought nothing would ever happen, considering how much his best friend has pretended to hate me. Little does he know...

Oh, god...Aaron is going to kill me.

A good sister wouldn't do this with her brother's best friend.

Whenever I'm reminded of that, it makes me want to crawl into a hole and die. But then again, when have I ever had a secret that's been mine? Mine to hold, to cherish, to enjoy. This thing between me and Dominik will not last forever, so why should I feel bad for enjoying what's left of it?

It'll be over soon. He'll leave, and we'll go on with our lives like we did before we collided.

All that matters to me right now is how he makes me feel when I'm with him.

Wanted.

Satisfied.

Protected, even.

"This place is wild! And this box, sweet Jesus. How did you get Dom to fall so hard?" Via's voice silences the thoughts in my head. I stare up at her sweet face, reminded that we're at the hockey game.

Dominik's hockey game.

Right... Enough with the intrusive thoughts and shit you have no control over.

"You're funny." I fake a smile.

"Where the hell are you right now?" Via glares at me.

"What do you mean?" Now I'm wondering if I totally blanked out.

"We're at your boyfriend's game... You know, the famous pro hockey player who got you box tickets so you could impress your colleagues and friend? That one. Who's also madly in love with you?" Via squeezes my cheek, and I smack her hand away.

"Stop it. He's just trying to make up for the rose fiasco I spent three hours cleaning up. Or have you forgotten about that already?"

Via scoffs. "Whatever. That was so sweet. Men don't do things to just be nice."

"Via," I interrupt her unenthusiastically.

"Zoe...wake up and smell the roses... Pun intended." Via shakes her head, standing up. "Want a beer?"

I try not to roll my eyes at her as she starts to walk away. "Yes, I do. And when you come back, you're only allowed to ask me technical questions about hockey."

The stadium has filled up quite a bit since we arrived, but Aaron is still nowhere to be seen. The game is about to start, and he hasn't even sent me a text to let me know he'll be late. Maybe I forgot to mention that Via would be here... Although, I'm pretty sure he remembers how excited she was at the office when Dominik invited her and our boss, Tracy.

Tracy refuses to spend time with us outside the office because she has a strict rule. However, Via has been eagerly talking about tonight nonstop for days.

Via nudges my shoulder and sits down, offering me a beer she got from the server in the kitchenette. I can't even fathom the amount of money Dominik must be spending on this box. I wonder if he gets a discount.

You were supposed to stop thinking about him.

"Does he know we're here?"

"Who?" I bob my head to the music as I watch the Zamboni finish up smoothing out the ice rink.

"Dominik. Who else?"

"Oh, I don't know. He gave you and Tracy season tickets for the box. You're welcome anytime."

"That's not what I meant." Via looks genuinely confused.

I blink at her. She blinks back. Both our brains seem to be short-circuiting. "Don't you see him every day?" she asks.

I sigh. "I thought we weren't going to talk about this. But if you must know, no, I don't see him every day."

That's a lie. I saw him earlier. It was still dark out and I was half asleep when he woke me up with his cock.

Shifting in my seat, I gulp down my beer. "We hang out all the time. We're just both busy."

Via seems disappointed. "Oh, shows you what I know. Dating is weird."

"Are you seeing anyone?"

"Pffftt, no. I'm not going near any men right now. I'm still getting over my last shitty relationship." Via stares off, her expression turning somber.

"Do you want to talk about it?"

She gives me a quick smile before shaking her head. "Not today."

"Okay."

We stay quiet for a long time, just staring at the ice and listening as the rink fills up with more hockey fans.

"I'm not anti-love or anything, you know. Quite the opposite. I can't wait for my person. I know my soulmate is out there. And I also know he's going to sweep me off my feet once he finally shows up. I just want to make sure I'm ready for him, and I'm done wasting time with assholes." Hope flickers in Via's eyes as she speaks.

I wonder what it's like to blindly believe in love like that. I admire the pure credence in Via's voice as she talks about her soulmate. I don't think I've ever believed in that. She's the opposite of me when it comes to romance. She dreams of marriage and having kids one day. I can never see myself doing either. I have too many trust issues to settle down with someone, and there is no way in hell I'd ever bring kids into this world with my childhood trauma. The idea of being with one person for life seems absurd. Marriage feels like a dumpster fire filled with nothing but disappointment. Why sign up for something that fails more than half the time? I don't get it. But that's just me.

"I know you're not, and I know you're going to find him."

Via smiles big at that. "Yeah. I wish mine would show up in the form of a sexy hockey player. Lucky bitch."

Not this again. "Will you please stop?"

"It's just so unfair. I wish I had a brother who had hot, rich friends. You didn't even have to go through the dating apps. They're the worst."

I roll my eyes at her. "Aaron has nothing to do with this. I met Dominik first."

"You did? When?" Via twists her body around to face me.

Oh, lord. I don't want to get into this with her right now.

"Speaking of brothers, mine should have been here by now." Glancing around, I pretend to look for Aaron.

"Oh, yeah? Does he even enjoy social outings with that carrot jammed so far up his ass?"

I burst out laughing because she's not wrong. I love Aaron to death, but he's been a little unbearable lately. "You can ask him yourself when he gets here."

"Ugh, no thanks. I can't stand the guy. I'm sorry. I know he's your brother and all."

"Yeah. Why is that exactly?" I lightly nudge her shoulder, hoping for a smile, but she only appears more irritated.

Via places her drink into the cup holder and lets out a labored sigh. "The guy is a douche. He was so rude and judgmental when he was at the office. Did you notice he wiped his hand after he shook mine?"

"Yeah, I remember. What happened that day anyway?"

She waves her hand, dismissing me. "It doesn't matter."

"It matters. Listen, Aaron is a control freak. Maybe he was just having a bad day. Not to say whatever he did or didn't do was okay, but *if* he shows up, just try to ignore the past. Enjoy the game. You're here with me. And if he starts being an ass, I have no problem calling him out for it."

"Yeah, but is he going to judge me for drinking beer out of a bottle or for wearing converse to a hockey game?"

"Hello, I'm doing it too. Besides, who gives a shit what he thinks?"

"Don't you?" She arches her brow.

"No, because I know Aaron has bigger problems to worry about than what I drink. Besides, he is a nice guy. Deep down. You'll warm up to him, I promise."

Via crosses her arms, scoffing and looking into the distance. "I don't want to."

"That's fine. Just don't let it affect our friendship."

Via gasps, looking completely offended. "Oh my god, Zoe...I would never. As long as you don't hate me for trash-talking him from time to time."

When I smile, it feels genuine. Not forced at all. "In one ear and out the other, promise. Vent away."

She pulls me in and kisses my temple. I wish I had the courage to tell her what our friendship means to me and how welcome she's made me feel in the short time I've been here. How happy she's made my heart. I want to tell her that I look forward to coming to work because I know she'll be there. That I enjoy all our conversations, even the emotional ones I used to avoid. Every time I'm with her, I feel like a part of me is healing.

She would love Sammy. My other work wife in Boston. They're the only people who have always made me feel like I can be completely myself. A type of friendship that would survive any distance or time.

"Okay, good. Back to the pretentious billionaire."

I bark out a laugh. "Been Googling my brother, huh?"

Via doesn't even try to deny it. "Had to fuel my hate somehow."

"Are you sure it's hate?"

"Shut up. Don't even try that shit with me."

"Why? Because you know I'm right?"

Via wrinkles her nose as if she smells something foul. "Ew. You're such an ass and so wrong, it's not even funny."

"Whatever you say," I say, winking at her.

"Started drinking without me?" Aaron's voice startles us both.

I glance behind me to see Aaron standing there in his perfectly pressed suit and peacoat.

"You're late," I murmur.

"No, I'm not. The game hasn't started," Aaron retorts, clearly on edge.

The tension between us is becoming increasingly difficult to ignore. When our parents left and I moved back into the penthouse, things became extremely awkward between us. Or maybe I'm just overthinking it since he's never there. Is it deliberate because he can't stand to be around me, or is he truly busy with work?

Ignoring the whispers in my head is difficult. I constantly worry that Aaron has had enough of me. That he might only tolerate me out of guilt is hard to ignore at times. It makes my anxiety even more vicious.

And Via is now silent, sitting beside me like a statue, which only makes things more unbearable.

I wish Tristan were here. He would know how to distract all of us and lift the mood.

"A text would have been nice," I say softly, turning back to smile at Aaron.

Can't help yourself, can you, Zoe? Just shut up and drink your beer.

"I'm sorry. I wasn't ignoring you. Just got caught up—" I don't let Aaron finish his sentence.

"With work? Yeah, figured. It's okay, you're here now. Grab a drink."

Last stab, I promise myself.

Players from the opposing team spill out onto the ice, instantly making my stomach flip. My anxiety spikes just at the thought of seeing Dominik soon.

I've done this before. A normal game. In the team's hometown. Nothing out of the ordinary. So there is no reason for me to be this nervous.

But something feels different tonight. I can't put my finger on it.

Maybe it's you.

Aaron sits down next to me a few minutes later, no drink in his hand. "You okay?"

"Yeah. Why?"

He shrugs, looking a little bored. "I don't know. You've got an attitude tonight."

I try to school my features before turning to face him. "Excuse me?"

"Back there, a second ago. When you cut me off."

I take in a deep breath. "I'm tired of the same excuses, Aaron. You've been working a lot lately. What happened to that talk we were supposed to have? Remember your text?"

Aaron pinches the bridge of his nose. "I remember, but let's discuss it later."

"Sure," I mutter under my breath.

Typical.

Aaron doesn't say anything else, but I notice him looking at Via, who's sitting on my other side. A disapproving tick appears in the corner of his lip before he corrects it.

I don't think I've ever wanted to throat punch my brother this badly before.

"Remember my coworker, Via?"

Aaron looks away. "How could I forget?"

"Be nice," I say under my breath.

When did he even have time to start hating Via this much?

Their encounter was brief, lasting only a few seconds. However, there is an intensity to his disdain that is difficult to understand. Is it because she's a little messy and free-spirited? I don't get what his problem is.

The music suddenly shifts, transitioning to an upbeat tempo, and the referees gracefully glide across the ice as the New York players burst onto the scene simultaneously. This moment right here, without a doubt, is my favorite part of any hockey game: the pregame warm-up drill. It's electrifying—watching the players pump themselves up as they skate around the ice, carefully going through their routine, getting their heads and their bodies ready for the game. And their warm-up exercises...oh, lord.

The music thumps from the speakers, mirroring the players' motions. The atmosphere becomes more exciting as the crowd claps and cheers along.

And I'm nervously watching him, waiting for his eyes to find mine.

Or don't... It's better if they don't.

"Is it just me, or is this really hot?"

It's not just you, Via. These stretches get the imagination going, even with all that gear the guys are wearing.

"It's hot," I murmur, watching Dominik skate back and forth, spraying shaved ice with the quick jerks of his feet before he drops down to stretch his legs.

"God, you're so lucky." Via melts, but her voice drifts to the background. All I can think about is the way Dominik's hands felt gripping my hair, the other around my throat as he pumped into me.

I close my eyes, trying to erase the intoxicating memories. When I open my eyes, they lock on Dominik as he skates by.

He's magnetic, and I'm completely drawn to him. My skin is buzzing, heart racing. I feel like a fucking teenager. Goddamn it.

This cannot be happening.

It's just good sex. That's all this is, and maybe it's time to cut that off too. Especially if this is how I'm reacting to him. I wanted to have a bit more fun, explore a few more kinks, but we may be out of time. It's not helpful for anyone involved if I continue to carry this intense desire. We had our fun, I got my apology, and now it's time to walk away. The longer we continue sneaking around, the greater the risk of Aaron catching us, which is the last thing I need right now.

"Do you have a problem?" Via screeches, leaning forward in her chair.

"Are you talking to me?" Aaron matches her tone.

How long have I been ogling Dominik? My head twists between the two of them as I try to figure out what the hell I missed in the last thirty seconds.

"You're unbelievable. Why don't you keep your judgmental glares and comments to yourself?"

"Woah, what's going on?" Neither one answers me. Their heated, angry eyes locked on one another.

"Maybe you should stop thinking everything is about you. You are not significant enough to hold my attention, little girl."

My jaw drops to the floor. "Aaron!"

I have never heard Aaron talk to anyone like that.

Aaron's words catch Via off guard, and she's clearly taken aback. But within seconds, she regains her composure, rounding her shoulders and tilting her chin up toward my brother like a boss.

"If you call me that one more time, or even look in my direction, I'll cut your tiny little balls off and feed them to you."

Internally, I'm screaming because no one has ever talked to my brother like this. Am I cheering on Via? A thousand percent, yes.

"What the fuck did you just say to me?" Aaron stands, towering above her.

"Do you need your ears checked too?" Via crosses her arms, leaning back in her seat.

My eyes might pop out of my face.

I should probably do something.

When Aaron takes a step toward her, I stand and block his view. He's on the verge of exploding, his face turning a vicious shade of red.

"I think you should take a walk," I say to my brother.

His gray eyes cut to mine, nostrils flaring. "Me? What the fuck did I do?"

"I don't care, but you're ending it." I give him a disapproving look and silently plead with my lips, mouthing the word *please*. He clenches his hands into tight fists, grabs his coat, and storms off without saying another word.

Something definitely happened between Via and Aaron, and I need to find out exactly what if I'm going to resolve this feud between them before it gets any worse.

21
ZOE

"Wait, where the hell are you going?"

Via gulps down the remaining beer and deliberately avoids looking at me. "I'll be right back."

"The game is about to start!"

She grabs her purse and turns to face me. "I'll be right back, I promise." This is completely unlike her. She seems panicked, looking around like she's not sure what to do with herself. "Via, are you okay? Do you want me to come with you?"

She snaps out of it, shaking her head and smiling a bit too big to convince anyone. "No. I'm fine. Thank you though."

Via runs away before I get the chance to argue with her.

The clatter of hockey sticks and the cheers of the crowd all fade into the background as I play every detail back like a detective, but I'm drawing a blank. One or both of them better talk when they get back.

Was it just my imagination, or did it seem like she was going after him?

I'll have better luck getting Via to talk than my brother. He could win awards for his tight lips, but if he hurt my friend, I'm going to raise hell.

I should go after her, right?

Just then, I turn my head, locking eyes with Dom and losing my breath. He's staring at me as if I'm the only person in this entire arena. He smiles bright, so sincere and welcoming that it releases a flurry of butterflies in my stomach. The rush of it all engulfs me, like a wave crashing over me, while a sense of uncertainty fills my lungs, pulling me underwater.

How does he do that with just one glance?

I still hate him.

I *need* to hate him.

I'm not the committed, vulnerable, attached type. And even if I were, even if he meant everything he said, it would never work out between us. Even if Aaron forgives us for initiating something physical, I will eventually destroy it.

Because I break everything.

And then Aaron will hate Dominik. They will never talk again, and it will be my fault. I can't do that to my brother for my own selfish needs. Which means I am left with two options as I sit here, trying to focus on the game as the puck is about to drop.

Walk away, stop having sex with him, and keep things somewhat professional. Turn off my emotions, swallow them whole, and pretend like they don't exist. I'm really good at that.

Focus, Zoe. Now is not the time to sort through your daddy issues.

Right now, Dominik needs to step aside so I can figure out what's going on with Via and Aaron. Looking over my shoulder, I don't spot either of them. I decide to send both of them a text right as the buzzer goes off.

And the game begins.

"IS THERE something you want to tell me, Zozo?" Aaron asks, keeping his voice low.

Via seems to have super hearing as she snickers. Aaron turns his head sharply, shooting daggers at her. I wish I could shake them both and tell them to stop.

They got back in the middle of the first period at the same time. They sat down, and neither of them said a single word for a long time. It just made me even more suspicious.

"Okay, that's it. You two need to spill right the fuck now," I demand. Looking at both of them as they stare off, pretending like they're paying attention to the game.

"There is nothing to say." Aaron pulls out his phone, and I instantly snatch it from his fingers.

I haven't had a chance to enjoy the game because I'm worried these two idiots are on the brink of a violent confrontation in front of all of New York City.

"I'm not in the mood, Zoe. Quit acting like this and give me back my phone."

"Me? What about you two? You're both being children and ruining the entire night for me. One of you needs to talk."

"We just mutually hate one another," Via exclaims and claps suddenly, hollering after number nine as if she's been following the game this entire time.

I want to smash my head against a wall.

"Aaron?" I turn toward my brother, who is avoiding eye contact.

I was wrong. It's me who's going to start a violent battle right here. Why the hell did I think tonight would be a fun outing with my new friend and my brother? Maybe if I had known they hated each other this much, I wouldn't have asked my brother to come. I know he'd rather be at work right now anyway.

Aaron finally looks at me, grabs his phone back, and tucks it away. "How is everything going with you and Dom? I haven't received an update in a long time." I'm vibrating with rage.

"I swear to Lucifer," I growl.

You can't kill him here. You won't survive in jail.

"Are you seriously going to ignore my question?"

"Yes." Aaron looks me dead in the eyes, matching my frustration, but in the most controlled way. He's a fucking lunatic.

"See, he is such an ass... You can't blame me for loathing his existence."

Aaron's jaw twitches, and he closes his eyes, taking a labored breath. "You know what? I'm going to catch the next game with you *alone*. This woman is infuriating. I can't sit here for another second."

I'm stunned. My brother is standing up again and grabbing his coat. He's actually about to leave.

"Are you serious? You're ditching me again?"

I try not to sound defeated, but I can't help it. I had hope for tonight. I wanted to smooth things out between Aaron and me. However, every interaction with him seems to make things worse.

I watch him smooth down his coat collar and glance back at the players shooting across the ice. His dusty blonde hair shines under the fluorescent lights.

"We'll talk when you get home. Call me if you need anything."

As Aaron turns, we hear shouting and then a chilling crash.

The music abruptly stops, and whistles sound all at once.

I turn my head and follow the players' eyes as they stand up from the bench. A hushed silence falls over the crowd, replacing their previous roars of excitement. My chest tightens and time seems to stand still as I watch in terror.

On the ice, a player lies motionless, encircled by a small crowd of hockey players. Coach's voice echoes, shouting and gesturing for space.

"Oh my god," Via chokes.

"Fuck."

"Who's injured? Is it Dominik?" someone shouts from behind me.

No, it can't be. He was on the bench, wasn't he?

"Dom!" That's Aaron. My brother shouts Dom's name repeatedly.

I'm on autopilot. My legs are moving on their own as I pass through the crowd. I'm running down the steps, trying to get closer to him. My only concern is to make sure Dominik is okay and it's not him on the ice.

I just need to see him. Look into his eyes. For my own sanity.

As I reach the plexiglass, I press myself against it and try to get a better look. Two men dressed in matching navy blazers suddenly emerge from the other side, carrying a red stretcher.

The other players disperse, and I finally see him.

Dominik is not okay.

He's lying on the ice with a pool of blood around his head.

The world becomes a chaotic blur. The commotion of whispers and shouts makes it impossible for me to understand what's happening. I'm paralyzed, unable to take my eyes off what's happening before me.

This can't be real.

Someone is calling my name, but I continue to push through the crowd without stopping. I'm pulled back just as I'm about to enter through the side door. I attempt to break free from the firm grip that binds me, but I can't. I scream, my voice filled with unrecognizable desperation. I just want to be with him, to reassure him that everything will be fine. Why won't they let me do that? I just want to know he's okay.

I plead, but no one listens. Agony overwhelms me, tears blurring my vision.

"Let me through! Dominik! Dominik!"

He's not moving.

His eyes are closed. Those beautiful eyes that always search for mine in the crowd, they're closed, and no matter how hard I scream his name, they don't open.

As I watch Dominik's lifeless body being gently lifted onto the stretcher, a chilling silence settles around me. The bright stadium lights cast a harsh glow on the scene, while the distant sound of the crowd's murmurs lingers in the air. Surrounded by players shielding him from the prying eyes of the crowd and the relentless cameras, I feel a part of me crack open.

"No! No! Let me go. I need to see him," I scream.

I am trapped in a nightmare where time moves both painfully slow and incredibly fast, and there is no escape.

Dominik is gone.

He's just gone.

Everyone is frozen in a state of shell shock as the arena staff blur around me. They clean up all the blood, pretending like it never happened. Like Dominik wasn't just lying there a minute ago, completely lifeless.

What if he doesn't wake up?

The music comes back on.

The air feels heavy, suffocating as I struggle to breathe. It only took seconds for the world I knew to shatter into a million sharp pieces.

22
ZOE

"This is ridiculous. Why won't they let us talk to someone?" Tristan hasn't stopped pacing the hospital waiting room since he got here around two hours ago.

I recall Aaron guiding me into the back of his car while his driver took us to the hospital where Dominik was being treated. I don't remember the details in between though. The lack of information from the nurses and the long wait for a doctor is causing my anxiety to escalate quickly.

"Walk me through it again," Tristan barks.

I take a deep breath, trying to think of the words again, but Via comes to my rescue. "We told you everything already. He got hit hard on the ice, likely a head injury, and the opponent's skate cut the back of his head when his helmet got knocked off, or so they think. That's why there was so much blood on the ice."

I close my eyes, forcing away the wave of fresh tears.

No matter how much effort I put into it, I just can't erase the image from my mind. The sight of Dominik lying there with everyone around him in a state of disbelief. It's clear that injuries of that nature are uncommon.

What if he's not going to be okay? What if he'll never play again? What if he doesn't remember...

Stop.

A hand lightly nudges my shoulder. "Hey, hey... It's going to be okay."

As I look at Via, I feel my chin quiver, noticing the concern in her expression.

Pressing the edge of my palms to my eyes, I groan. "What is wrong with me? I'm so emotional."

"Do I really need to say it?" Via whispers.

"Please don't. I just want to see him."

"I know, sweetie. You will soon. I promise."

As I blink to clear my vision, I notice Aaron and Tristan exchanging a look, instantly grasping the meaning behind their wordless communication. Aaron will eventually confront me about what happened. I know he's been anxious about Dominik, but he's also been keeping an eye on me, trying to make sense of what happened at the game.

To tell the truth, I'm completely at a loss. I blacked out and had some sort of out-of-body experience. I was reacting, but I can't even remember everything that happened. It feels like a distant dream. At that moment, I was only aware of my feelings and the strong desire to be near Dominik, despite not being allowed within five feet of him. I need to see Dominik first before I can talk about what happened, even if Aaron wants to hash it out.

Suddenly, the metal doors on the other side of the waiting room burst open, and a mob of angry hockey players pours in. I lock eyes with Noa, and the sadness on his face forces me out of my chair as I walk over to him. With a strong grip, he pulls me close, and my emotions overflow as I cry against his shoulder.

"He's okay. You're going to see him soon. I promise," he reassures me.

I pull back to look at him. "You got an update since they took him away?"

Noa nods. "Yeah, Coach has been keeping us updated. He got hit pretty hard, but he's stable. They've been doing tests since he got here, but I think they're going to allow us to see him soon. No one has come out here to talk to you guys?"

"No."

He frowns, clicking his tongue. "That's fucked up. It's been hours."

"Tell me about it." Tristan strolls over, nodding at some of the guys.

The atmosphere in this small waiting room is completely somber. As I look at the various faces, it's clear that Dominik is respected and looked after by his team. Despite his reputation as a playboy, they genuinely love him, or perhaps they would extend this support to anyone on the team, since they are like family. These guys spend countless hours together, training and working toward a shared goal. So, when one of them gets injured, it must feel as though they've all been affected.

It's a different world for them.

I often forget Dominik is a famous hockey player. I've always seen him as my brother's best friend, the guy who was always at our house, eating our food and spending weekends gaming with Aaron. He's someone Aaron could always rely on. A brother he never had.

That's how I still see him. And sometimes, it feels strange sitting amongst the crowd at the arena, looking at Dominik and remembering how far we go back. Noa walks over to the nurses' station with some of the other teammates as Tristan tugs gently on my elbow, pulling me aside.

"Are you okay?"

"I'm fine."

"You don't seem fine. You're a mess, Zoe. What happened?"

I give him a sharp look. He's dressed in a beautiful navy suit, likely coming straight from the office. "What do you mean?"

Tristan takes a deep breath. His eyes catch on something...or rather, someone behind me.

"I heard you played the worried girlfriend a little too well at the game," he says quietly.

I blink at him, not sure if I heard him correctly. "Are you kidding me? You want to have this conversation right now?"

"Listen, I don't care what you or Dominik have been up to these last few weeks. Hell, I'm fucking happy about it. It's about time. That man has been obsessed for too long. But your brother is going to have a fucking cow when he finds out, especially if it's not coming from you or Dom. I just want to make sure you've thought it through."

I fold my arms over my chest. "I don't know what you're talking about."

Tristan arches a brow, smirking down at me. "No, baby girl. You will not play that game with me. It won't work. I know *everything*."

"Meaning what? Is that supposed to scare me?" I challenge, and Tristan's smile only grows wider.

"It means"—Tristan leans down, whispering in my ear—"I know you and Dominik have been engaging in some kinky fun and that this hasn't been fake for either of you for some time."

My heart pounds fiercely, sending shivers down my spine. "I'm not doing this with you here."

"Suit yourself, but we both know your brother won't be as nice." Tristan releases my elbow, glances back, and adjusts his jacket before walking away.

I catch my brother's gaze immediately from across the room as he leans against the white hospital wall.

His stone cold eyes are fixed on me, as if he heard the entire exchange. Suddenly, I feel like the massive problem he's been ignoring. A problem he's now realizing he's been neglecting.

I hate this feeling. It makes me want to crawl out of my skin.

The discomfort quickly turns into anger. Why should my sex life be anyone else's concern? They have no right to judge or comment on my choices, as long as everything is consensual. If things go wrong, it's up to Dom and me to handle it. I promised not to interfere with Aaron and Dom's friendship, and I stand by that. I'll continue pretending and prioritizing others' needs over my own. I'm used to that. It's where I live. So I will not feel guilty for a second longer or care about what Aaron and Tristan think.

Also, the fact that his best friends think I acted strange is fucking absurd. How else is a *loving* girlfriend supposed to behave when they witness their boyfriend getting injured on ice? Anyone else would have lost their mind too.

Yeah, but your brother knows you're not that great of an actress. It was so much more than acting, and you know it too.

But it wasn't.

"Has anyone called his mom?" one of the guys asks.

Oh my god. Leslie. I can't believe I forgot about her. She was so kind to me when I was going through hell. Now, when it's my turn to show up, I fail her in the most basic way. What kind of person does that?

A new wave of tears prickles at my eyes as I reach for my phone.

"I've taken care of it already." A firm hand grips my shoulder, and I glance up to find my brother standing beside me.

"Oh, thank you. I totally blanked out."

"I know. You want to take a walk? Change of scenery might be nice for both of us."

He looks tired. He hasn't left since we arrived. Neither one of us have. I would love to leave, but I'm worried the second I do, the doctors are going to come out to give us an update.

I shake my head. "No. I want to wait."

Aaron's nostrils flare, and I know that wasn't the answer he was hoping to hear, but again, I don't give a shit right now. Since we arrived at the hospital, he has barely spoken. He seems more distant than usual, and I understand why—he's worried about his best friend. Plus whatever else he's got going on at work that seems to be eating away at him. But I'm his sister; he doesn't need to treat me like everyone else. I wish, just once, he would open up to me.

We used to be close, and now...I'm not so sure anymore.

"I need to talk to you, and we're just waiting right now."

At that moment, the metal door beside the nurses' station swings open, and two women in white coats step out. As they walk toward us, my heart sinks, knowing this is the news we've all been waiting for.

"Is there a family member here for Dominik Lewis?"

Silence.

They're all his family. Everyone in this room cares about him in some way.

"I'm listed as his emergency contact. Aaron Jackson."

The doctor nods and approaches without verifying. The room falls deathly silent, as if everyone is holding their breath.

"Mr. Lewis sustained a significant head injury, resulting in a concussion. Since he lost consciousness, we conducted a comprehensive assessment and found no signs of a brain bleed or major head trauma. However, he needs rest over the next few weeks and must be monitored closely. Does he live alone?"

"He does," Aaron replies.

"He will need to stay with someone or find outpatient care."

The words leave my mouth before I fully process them. "I'll stay with him."

"And you are?" the other doctor asks.

"I'm his girlfriend." My voice is strong, almost unrecognizable to me.

The taller brunette doctor smiles as if recalling something. "Zoe. He's been asking for you. The nurses will need to go over some things with you before Mr. Lewis is discharged."

They know my name?

He's been asking for you.

Which means...it means he's awake.

I'm so relieved, I could cry all over again, but I don't. I just nod and thank them for the news.

"When can we see him?" Tristan asks.

"He's being transferred now. A few of you can see him at a time. It's important not to overwhelm him. He's still a bit confused and might drift in and out of sleep. He needs lots of rest."

Small chatter fills the room. Aaron and Tristan ask questions. One doctor walks off while the other answers patiently. I try to listen, but after knowing he's going to be okay, I start to zone out. Going over today from the start, highlighting every detail I can remember.

Aaron saw how I reacted. The entire stadium did. And he heard that Dom was asking for me while he was in there. Out of all the people Dom knows, he asked for me.

Knowing this shouldn't make me so unbelievably happy, but it does. It feels like a high, a welcome one after hours of worrying.

That's all it is though. Relief that my brother isn't losing his best friend. Relief that Dominik will be okay in a few weeks and can get back to his games, his life...to playing hockey.

Yeah, that's what this is. Relief.

Keep telling yourself that.

AARON and I are the first to see Dominik.

Nervousness courses through my entire body as we make our way down the hallway toward his room. Rounding the corner, Aaron pauses, looking behind us before gripping my arm to stop me.

"Is there something going on between the two of you?" he demands.

I glare at him, incredulous. "Seriously? Now?"

"You need to tell me what's happening, Zoe. Are you involved with him?"

"Wow... I didn't think you'd stoop this low, Aaron. Can't you read the room? We're in a hospital because Dominik got hurt. This isn't the time."

"You didn't deny it." He seethes, his gray eyes flashing with anger. I realize this might be the first time he's been this livid with me.

I steel myself, yanking my arm away. "What's gotten into you? No, I'm not involved with Dominik. It's all an act, a performance. We have to do this for his hockey career, remember? You were part of that conversation from the beginning, so stop acting like a control freak. It's beneath you and, frankly, getting old."

Aaron doesn't respond, simply turning and striding down the hall. His shoes click sharply against the floor as I take a deep breath, following him.

Lying is easy. I can pretend that my reality doesn't exist, and in many ways, it doesn't. Aaron doesn't need to know about the ugly parts I choose to hide. Besides, I won't be the reason their friendship suffers or ruin Aaron's trust in me over something as trivial as sex. He's the only family I've got, and I would never do anything to hurt him.

Telling him the truth would do no good, especially right now. We need to focus on Dominik.

As soon as I enter the room, everything else fades into the background. My focus is solely on Dominik's large figure resting on the hospital bed. The conversation with my brother slips from my mind completely.

All the events leading up to this point seem insignificant.

Dominik looks fragile, exposed, and vulnerable with his eyes closed. He looks so out of place, and it breaks my heart.

My instincts urge me to rush to his side, to hold him tightly, but I stop myself. Walking slowly toward him, I feel a deep fracture in my chest, like a giant wall giving way.

The thought of losing him today has been haunting me. In an ideal situation, I would detach and regain control, but I can't.

I can't do it.

For the first time, some twisted part of me understands why he might have done all those things to me. Why he lied at the masquerade ball and continued to lie for years. Maybe he couldn't help himself either. Maybe sometimes, you risk it all just to feel something.

Dominik blinks, and when his eyes meet mine, they steal the breath from my lungs. It's at this very moment that I realize I can't turn back anymore.

Is this the point of no return?

He smiles, and I sigh in relief, feeling like I've taken my first real breath since the arena. Why does it feel like ages ago?

His reassuring smile comforts me, as if he's saying everything will be fine, that it's all going to be okay somehow.

"You're here," he whispers, his voice barely audible.

"Of course I'm here, you idiot," I reply, a tear escaping.

When did I start crying again?

"I'm here too. Thanks for noticing," Aaron interjects, reminding me of his presence.

"Hey, man. Miss me?" Dominik jokes.

"What the actual fuck, Dom? Forget how to play hockey out there? Or did you just decide you needed a break at the hospital?" Aaron retorts.

Dominik laughs, but it turns into a cough. He winces, and I reach out, touching his arm. Both he and Aaron look down, and I retract my hand immediately.

Get it together, Zoe.

I don't know how to act right now. Maybe I should just leave.

"I'll give you two some space."

Without looking at either of them, I bolt out of the room, sprinting down the hall. When I know I'm away from prying eyes I lean against the wall and try to catch my breath.

What's happening to me?

My phone buzzes in my pocket, and I welcome the distraction as I pull it out. It's a New York number, so I answer.

"Hello?"

"Hi, may I speak to Zoe Jackson?" I don't recognize his voice.

"This is she."

"Hi, Zoe. I'm Tyler from Adler Architectural and Design. Do you have a few minutes?"

Am I having a brain aneurysm? Why would a design firm be calling me?

"Yes, of course."

"We received your application for the new Madison Square Garden extension. Can we schedule a phone interview for next Tuesday at ten a.m.?"

What?

"S-sure," I stammer.

"Wonderful. I'll send you the details via email. Do you have any questions?"

"Yes, actually. Was my application ever pulled?"

"Uh, nope. Was it meant to be?" Tyler sounds confused, and I probably shouldn't have asked that question, but I needed to know.

"No, no. I was just curious because I was worried I had messed up somewhere. Thank you."

"Okay, great. I'll be in touch."

The line goes dead, but I continue holding the phone up to my ear, trying to make sense of the call.

Dominik never pulled my application like he promised.

Son of a bitch.

I made it to the first round of interviews.

Maybe Dominik knows me better than I thought. Maybe he's always been here for me, holding my hand and walking alongside me when the road ahead seemed impossible or scary.

Maybe he's always seen me, even when I couldn't see myself.

23
ZOE

I'm sprinting through the hospital corridors, filled with an overwhelming desire to run as far away as possible. But there is no hiding place big enough to shield me from myself and every emotion floating freely inside me. It's all too much. These last few hours have felt like an eternity, and the white walls of this place threaten to swallow me whole.

Panic rises in my throat as I recognize the same yellow wet floor sign I've passed four times already. Are there no exits in this place?

Deep breath in. Deep breath out.

Everything I've been avoiding, everything I thought I had under control is crashing down on me, and I don't know how to deal with it. I don't even know where to start cleaning up this mess.

Nothing makes sense anymore.

Glancing over my shoulder, I try to locate the exit sign when I collide with a solid chest.

"Jesus Christ." I turn and see Tristan's concerned expression as he firmly grips my shoulders.

"Zoe? Are you okay?"

I shake my head vigorously.

"What happened?"

"Noth—hing," I stammer in between breaths.

"Zoe," Tristan whispers. His dark green eyes soften as he silently pleads with me, as if trying to bring me back from the edge.

Edge of what? Confusion? I don't even know why I feel this way. It's like depression hit me on the side of the head. A giant brick wall coming at me out of nowhere, making me want to hide in a corner and cry for hours.

I never learned how to deal with stress well.

"I'm fine," I breathe, my chin quivering while I hopelessly try to stop myself from crying for the millionth time.

"You're coming with me." Tristan grips my side as he leads us through the hospital.

"I promise I'm fine." I try to push away, but he firmly presses his palm against my back, guiding us past a bustling nurses' station and down a grand staircase, which opens up to the large hospital main lobby.

"That's nice. I'm happy you're fine. Means you're in a good mood to have coffee with me," Tristan states, not bothering to look at me.

People rush from one place to another in the crowded lobby. The majority of them appear sad or worried. People often view hospitals as a gathering place for immense sadness. Few reasons for coming here bring joy, and us being here today only reinforces that belief.

Tristan's cologne smells expensive, surrounding me as we navigate through the crowd, heading toward the rear of the lobby and the hospital cafeteria. I notice that my imminent panic attack is starting to fade away. I don't think Tristan realizes how he just saved me.

"You're too in your head, Zoe."

One second we're walking, the next Tristan is pulling out a metal chair and guiding me down onto it.

"What?"

"You need to talk about this, the way you're feeling. Everything that was thrown at you. The last-minute move to your brother's house, a new city, being thrown into fake dating a hockey player. Even though it's probably the realest thing you've had in a long time." Tristan runs a hand through his auburn hair, his eyes studying me carefully for any reaction to his last statement.

"I told you before, there is nothing going on between Dom and me."

"Yeah, and I'm telling you to cut the crap. It's just me and you. And I'm not your brother, not that he would judge you for it."

I snort. "You don't know him. He would do more than judge."

Tristan raises a brow at me. "I may not know the old version of him, the one you shared a childhood with, but I know this version of him. Aaron might be a stubborn asshole half the time, but he cares deeply about you. He just doesn't want you to get hurt. He would be livid to find out you didn't trust him enough to go to him about this."

"I know he cares, but he's also controlling and has made threats before. It wouldn't do anyone any good, Tristan. Plus, I don't need his protection."

Tristan leans over, his elbows pressing into the table as he stares into my eyes. "That's all he knows, Zoe. He's been conditioned to protect you from the very beginning because the people who were meant to never did. You two need to talk."

I look down, blinking back the tears that threaten to spill, my eyes struggling to bring the scuff marks on the vinyl cafeteria flooring into focus.

"Talk to me," Tristan whispers.

I take in a deep breath. A part of me wants to open up and just spill everything I've been holding close to my chest. It's been so hard to not talk to anyone about this. There is a lot of me that I hide, and for once, I want to just set it free. To throw aside the facade and just lean into all I've been pushing away for so long. It might feel good, but it would fucking burn at first contact, and I'd rather feel nothing than feel something.

"Zoe," Tristan calls my name, pulling me from my thoughts.

Fuck it.

"I don't know what's happening. I don't know how to feel, and I'm not really sure any of this is real. I'm terrified, Tristan."

I dig my nails into the palms of my hands, feeling the invisible crack run down the center of my chest. The floodgates are about to open, and I don't think I can stop them.

My control is slipping away.

Tristan's gaze softens, and there is no pity in his eyes, just pure understanding. "What are you afraid of?"

Everything.

Nothing.

Getting used to needing him and then rotting in familiar loneliness once he leaves. Feelings I have never experienced before. They're suffocating and intoxicating at the same time. How is that not terrifying?

"Zoe," Tristan calls out when I don't respond.

"I'm afraid of feeling everything. That what I'm experiencing isn't actually real. That I'll lose him one day. Because all things eventually pass. And then I'll be left with all our stupid memories. The lingering looks, the way his fingers feel against my skin, the sound of his heartbeat, the way he makes me feel, the words he's said to me... What will I do about all of it? I don't want to feel it, Tristan. It's easier not to feel."

Tristan stares at me for a long time before his face drops and he laughs softly.

When he stops and finally looks up at me, there is no trace of humor on his beautiful face. "You don't have a choice anymore. And you're fucking blind. You've been blind this entire time. Do you think Dominik has control over the way he feels for you? That man has loved you from the very beginning. He's spent years trying to forget you, and he's failed again and again. You are and have always been the one thing he can never let go. I may not know what romantic love is, Zoe, but I know what you and Dom have goes way beyond any of that. A type of connection that's not from this world. You need to embrace it and stop pushing him away. You need to feel it all. Haven't you ever wondered what it would be like to be loved properly?"

I want to fight back. I want to tell him he's wrong, that Dominik will grow bored. That everything and everyone changes. People promise forever, but they never mean it. It's all temporary, and I don't rely on the now.

I never have.

But the words don't come.

Because the truth is, I would kill to experience it for just a moment. To give myself permission to get lost in it, embrace the depth of that type of love for only a heartbeat. To dare to believe in an irrevocable type of love. But it doesn't believe in me, it never has.

I swallow hard, trying to ignore the fury inside me. "He lied to me. He tricked me."

"But you've forgiven him for that already, so why are you hanging on to it?" Tristan says, not missing a beat.

My gaze jumps to his, and the smug expression on his face tells me everything I need to know. I didn't think Dominik would open up to anyone about what happened, but maybe the three of them are more solid than I gave them credit for. Does Aaron know too? I doubt it.

"He told you?" I arch a brow.

"He didn't have to."

Damn... Is this guy a mind reader?

Before I can stop myself, I blurt out, "Do you also hack into everyone's business?" but Tristan isn't bothered. His deep laugh fills the near-empty cafeteria, and I'm thankful for the momentary break.

"I may dabble here and there. I like to do my research on people."

Now I'm wondering what the heck he knows about me. I feel my face grow hot, thinking that he likely knows about my tastes in the bedroom. What does it matter? I'm sure Tristan is into some wild stuff himself. He doesn't strike me as Mr. Vanilla.

Oh god, now I'm thinking about Tristan and his possible rope collection.

Please stop.

I drop my face into my hands, groaning and cursing myself out in my head. But it doesn't last long before Tristan pulls my hands down, forcing me to look at him.

"I think what happened today proved a lot to you. You care so much more than you let on, Zoe. Don't run away from that. And you also need to talk to your brother. Soon."

Right now, I think I dread that the most. My head drops back into my hands, and Tristan bursts into laughter.

But somewhere inside me, I feel comforted, knowing I finally showed a piece of myself to someone and they didn't run the other way. Tristan has so many layers, and I hope one day, he'll allow me to be there for him too.

WALKING PAST THE NURSES' station, Betty, the senior nurse who has been in rotation since Dominik was admitted a few days ago, looks up from her computer and smiles at me.

"I'm happy to see you finally left."

I bite the corner of my lip. "I've taken plenty of breaks."

Betty gives me the side eye, like I'm just full of it. Honestly, she's right because this is the first time I've actually left the hospital. Dominik is supposed to be released today, and I decided to finally go home, take a shower, and grab some essentials he might need.

"Be here around 2:30, and we can go over the at-home care instructions. That is, if you're still open to looking after Dominik while he heals."

"Of course. Absolutely."

"He's lucky to have a caring girlfriend like you." She winks, making me blush.

"Oh, it's nothing."

Betty purses her lips. "It's not nothing, dear."

Shaking my head, I make my way toward Dominik's room, feeling uncertain about the recent interaction. These past few days have been a rollercoaster of emotions, but I believe I've finally figured everything out. My focus now is to take care of Dom to the best of my ability. Once he's fully recovered, we'll have a sincere conversation about ending things on a positive note. Even the thought makes my stomach twist in knots.

But it has to be that way. It's the only way.

Walking through the hallway, I find myself on autopilot. I

pass a corridor and a double set of doors that open up to a small garden. As I continue, my attention is caught by the sight of my brother standing outside, his back turned toward me. It looks like he's watching the gentle snowfall in the sky.

I didn't know he was here.

He's alone, and for once, he's not on his phone. This might be my only opportunity for a long time. Saying a little prayer, I pull the handle and step outside. Aaron's head turns to the side, but he doesn't look at me.

"Hey," I say.

"Hey yourself."

"Are you okay? Is Dominik okay?" I ask.

Aaron slowly turns to face me. "Yeah, everyone is fine."

I wrap my arms around myself as I approach him. "Why are you still here? I thought you were leaving."

"I left, but then I came back because I was hoping to run into you. I didn't feel good about the way I cornered you in the hallway the other day when we were going to see Dom."

Oh. That takes me by surprise.

"Yeah, same here. Things have felt off between us lately." I'm surprised I just admitted that to him. But maybe it's time Aaron and I hash out whatever has been bothering him, because I'm tired of this avoidance game we've both been playing.

I miss my brother.

He nods and quickly glances at his watch. It's clear he's mentally preparing for the conversation, considering every possible outcome. Aaron never enters a situation without being fully prepared. It's frustrating how he maintains such a tight grip on his emotions and communicates so precisely. Those subtle, silent cues always make me give in, causing me to talk too much and too quickly. I know he does it on purpose to control every situation, but I wish he would stop pretending with me, just once.

He's one of the only people I trust in this world, so when he holds back, it makes me feel incredibly alone.

"Listen, I know things have been weird between us since you got to New York, and I know I've been blaming work, but it's the truth. I haven't been avoiding you, but I feel like you're hiding things from me, and I don't want there to be secrets between us."

Well, that's a start, I guess.

"I'm not keeping secrets from you. It's just hard to talk when we're not even under the same roof half the time. You're never around."

Aaron cringes. "Yeah, I get that. And I hate it more than you do, trust me."

"Do you? Because you easily shoved me aside when your parents showed up out of the blue."

"Our parents," he corrects, and it makes me want to rage. That minor word change.

"They are not my parents."

Aaron senses my harsh tone and looks away, nodding. "I'm sorry."

"What's gotten into you?"

Might be too late to pull back my little rage demon.

"What's gotten into me? What about you? Jumping at the first opportunity to play nurse for Dominik." Aaron's voice reverberates, and it's not the chilly air but his voice that sends shivers down my spine.

"Why does it bother you so much?" I bellow, shoving my hands into the air. The accusation and sudden shift in conversation from our parents make me see red.

Aaron takes two steps toward me, his jaw ticking as he fights to tame his own beast. From a young age, we've shared a temper that no one else has truly understood except for us. A silent recognition that exists between us.

"Because he's going to hurt you. And when he does, I'll have to clean up the mess like I always do. I will not stand around and watch my friend hurt you. He thinks with his dick, and you deserve so much more than that."

"Will you just stop, Aaron? You don't need to protect me anymore. I'm not some broken little girl who needs shelter from the big, bad world. Those days are over, and it should have never been your responsibility in the first place."

"This has nothing to do with our childhood!"

I stare back at him, watching as his control slowly slips. I wonder how long he's been waiting to blow up at me for this. How long he's been wondering if there is something going on between me and Dom. How much of it is driven by protection versus jealousy? Maybe a bit of resentment too, because he thinks I'm taking his best friend away from him?

No, don't think that way, or you'll lose him too.

He's already gone.

"Doesn't it? Don't you hate me a little for being the discarded piece of trash you always had to deal with?"

Aaron steps forward and takes my hand in his. "No, Zoe. Never. Don't talk like that. I've always only wanted to protect you."

Up close, with him open and exposed like this, it's obvious the anger on his face is merely a mask for all the weight he's been carrying. He looks so fragile right now, reminding me of the seven-year-old boy who tried so hard to save our broken family but never could. His love was never enough because he could never fill my parents' shoes. Maybe that's why he does everything in his power to be in charge. Because he couldn't change the one thing that was supposed to come naturally. He couldn't give me unconditional love from the two people who were meant to drown me in it. No matter how badly he wanted to, he couldn't make them see, and some fucked up part of him blames himself for it. Even though he had no part to play in any of it. Even though he's the only reason I'm here today.

The weight of being my protector shouldn't have been his to carry. He was never meant to attempt to fill my mother's and father's shoes, but he tried so hard. He was always there for me, always picking up the pieces, even though he was just a child too. I should have realized it, but I was too consumed by my own darkness to see it.

"Aaron," I say, my chin quivering.

"I'm sorry I let them hurt you, Zoe. I'm sorry I forgot about you when they showed up here. I panicked, and I hate myself for it more than you can imagine, okay? I hate myself for so many things. For all the ways I didn't save you. Please let me fix it. Let me make it up to you." His voice cracks, and just hearing it causes the tears to burst free.

"Aaron," I repeat, reaching up and gripping his cheeks with both of my hands, urging him to stop for a moment and just look at me. He looks down at the ground and inhales deeply. "I don't care about them. I care about you, and I want you to know that I'm okay. Better than okay. We made it out of that house, and I'm so much stronger for it."

"You shouldn't have to be strong, Zoe."

"Hey, look at me," I press, but he refuses. So I grab his chin and force his eyes to mine. "It's in the past. And I'm learning so much about myself these days. I don't want you to worry about me anymore. I want us to go back to being friends and family. Close family, like we used to be. Can we do that?"

Aaron's expression softens. "We never stopped."

"But we did. You're never around, and we barely talk."

He closes his eyes as a pained expression washes across his face. "I know. But that's all about to change. I promise."

"Good." I smile, feeling months of heavy tension finally beginning to lift from my chest.

Aaron pauses for a long time, watching me carefully, as if he's struggling with some internal thought. "I'm going to ask you something, and I need you to tell me the truth."

I nod, holding my breath.

"Do you love him?"

"What?"

He doesn't hesitate, repeating the words. "Dominik. Do you love him?"

I don't know how to answer that. That word, the concept, it's completely unfamiliar to me. How could I possibly experience an emotion I've never felt before? How would I ever be able to identify romantic love? I wouldn't even know where to begin.

"I care about him, but there is nothing going on between us." The lie just falls right out of my mouth, and I don't even know why. I don't think Aaron would hold it against me if I came clean, but some part of me just won't allow it.

It's years of fear holding me back.

"That's not what I asked. Do you love him?"

I laugh. "I don't know what love is."

My brother's gray eyes are piercing as he stares into my soul, gently resting his hand on my shoulder as he pulls me into a hug.

We remain like that for a long time, holding onto one another before he whispers into my ear. "I think you know so much more about love than you let on, Zoe. I think you've wanted it for so long but forced it away, and for good reason. But you deserve to be happy. You deserve to feel it all, and you shouldn't have to push anything away out of fear. Because if you're worried about me, I'm not going anywhere. Nothing in this world could tear us apart."

I can't recall when exactly the tears drenched my face during Aaron's speech. It's not his words that triggered my sadness; it's the overwhelming sense of belonging. Like I finally got my brother back. Or maybe it was hearing him say he's not going anywhere. Because someone as fractured as me needs to hear those words sometimes.

Maybe this is what it means to love. To be accepted and seen for exactly who you are.

In total darkness and in blinding light.

There is nothing worse than being confined to your bed for days. I'm not used to idleness. Athletes don't do well with this limitation. It's been four days of this torment, and I'm already losing my fucking mind. When you can't sleep or quiet your mind while stuck in bed, there are few distractions available. That injury keeps replaying in my head until it becomes painful and I have to rest. Then I wake up and repeat the entire cycle. Trying to recount every detail as if that's going to change the outcome. It's anger-inducing. I have no memory of what happened. Where did that hit come from?

I was definitely focused on the game. For the most part. It's possible that my eyes kept wandering toward the stands, unable to resist the distraction that is Zoe. There are a few unclear details though. Like Aaron and Via looking pissed off to hell. And then I started to worry, thinking maybe Aaron had found out about Zoe and me. Then again at the hospital when Zoe bolted out of the room, Aaron went quiet. He seemed to be struggling with something but dismissed it as soon as I questioned him.

I don't want to cause her any more pain. I've caused enough

to last us both a lifetime. Besides, she'll never forgive me if I'm the reason something happens between her and Aaron.

I want to be the one to tell him. I want to go to him as a friend, as his sister's protector. I want to have a chance to prove my worth. Not that I need his blessing, but I want to show Zoe that we're worth fighting for.

I planned to tell Aaron about us soon. Maybe even after that game.

I don't want to hide anymore. I want to proudly flaunt her, to showcase to the world that she is mine—without a doubt, she truly belongs to me.

I want them to see me worship at her altar.

And those feelings have only grown, especially now.

Zoe has stepped up in a way I never imagined she would. Or maybe I died and went to heaven. An alternate reality where she actually wants to be around me, and not just for sex. Because she's been here every single day after work ever since I got home from the hospital. Taking over the night shift once the nurse leaves.

We haven't really talked, even though I've been itching to ask her how she's been doing since the incident. Tristan told me she'd been quite distraught, but that seems impossible because she can barely hold eye contact. And she's been avoiding any actual conversation that doesn't revolve around my health.

She's keeping her guard up.

Even though I can do things on my own now, I've been milking needing her because it makes me feel close to her. I love the attention, even if it's done out of guilt. I'll gladly accept any attention she gives me because I'm always hungry for more of her.

My phone vibrates, and I glance down, noting the front door camera alert.

She's home.

My heart beats a thousand miles a minute, as if I didn't see her earlier today or last night. She's been such a good little nurse, and I'm going to reward her for it as soon as I can.

"Dom?" Zoe calls out to me.

"Up here," I yell back, smoothing down my black comforter and fluffing up my pillow.

I've been walking around the house in the couple of hours between when the nurse leaves and Zoe shows up. I want to get stronger so I can convince Coach to move up the physical and let me back on the ice. Missing too much time is not something I can afford. We're heading for the playoffs, and I need to be prepared for that, which will prove impossible if I'm stuck in this bed.

But I also know I can't rush it. The examination will be thorough, and if I miss by one point, Coach will potentially bench me for the entire season.

Zoe pokes her head through the door, giving me a hesitant smile before walking in.

"How are you feeling?"

"Same as yesterday."

She nods, leaning against the doorway. "That's good."

When she says nothing else, I speak. "You don't have to be here, you know. I don't need help."

"I promised the hospital I'd help look after you. You have a concussion, and someone has to keep an eye on you."

"It doesn't have to be you though, since you clearly don't want to be here." I arch a brow at her, and she narrows her gaze at me.

"Do you want me to leave?"

"No. I want you to stop ignoring me. I think I preferred it when you wanted to wring my throat."

She laughs. "I still want to do that."

I can't stop the smile from creeping onto my face. "I doubt that, little butterfly."

"Don't," she warns.

"Come here."

She sighs, biting her lip and shaking her head.

Fucking hell, that lip bite.

"Do I need to come grab you?"

She rolls her eyes, and her defiance instantly makes my dick hard.

"Why didn't you revoke my application for the architectural position like you promised you would?"

I gasp. "Did you get an interview?"

"Dominik," she snaps.

"You did, didn't you?" I'm too excited to be bothered by her attitude. This news is making my heart race. I expected this moment, and I was ready to face her fury because I knew she would be picked, not because of my intervention, but because she's amazing.

"Yes. Why didn't you pull my application?" Zoe asks again, her expression harder to read than every other time she's been upset with me.

"Because you deserve the world, Zoe. And if I can be the one to help you see that, then I'll be the luckiest guy in the world, dead or alive."

Her eyes soften for just a second before she corrects them. "You're ridiculous."

I don't even bother smothering the shit-eating grin on my face. "So, did you accept the interview?"

Zoe nods, glancing away. "Thank you."

"There is no need to thank me. This is all you."

She shifts on her feet, looking out of place, but a smile blooms on the corner of her lips, and I love seeing that so fucking much. This moment is so simple, but it might be one of my favorites. I just want to soak her up.

"Do you need anything before I go shower? I need to wash the New York subway smell off my body."

It only took me sustaining a serious head injury for Zoe to finally loosen up around me.

"I do, actually," I say, ignoring the heavy pounding in my chest. I don't know why I'm so nervous.

Jesus Christ, I feel like a teenager.

"What is it?"

"I need you."

She snorts. "No sex. I'm here to keep an eye on you, not zap your energy."

I give her a sly grin as I pull out a green cardboard box the size of a shoebox from under my bed. "That's not what I'm referring to. But you know I'll always have the energy to make you come."

Zoe gapes at the box, then looks back at me in disbelief. "Where did you get that? You went through my stuff!"

"You went through mine first. Fair is fair."

She storms over, attempting to snatch the box from my hand but ends up stumbling and falling into me instead. Steadying herself by holding onto my bare shoulder, she looks at me with wide eyes. She doesn't pull away, though. The smell of vanilla and citrus fills the air around me, and I can't help but want to draw her closer and kiss her. I want to capture every part of her so there is never any doubt in her mind that this is real, that I am here to stay.

Nothing could, or will, ever separate us. Not in this lifetime, or the next. I don't care how ridiculous or cheesy that might sound, it's the truth.

"Give that back." Zoe's voice is barely audible.

I know she feels it too. She just needs to let me inside her head.

Grabbing her wrist, I bring Zoe close to my chest so that

we're sharing the same air as her vibrant green eyes lock onto mine.

"You read the ending, and you didn't change it," I accuse.

She retorts, "I didn't read your ending."

I remember that day like it was yesterday, and I know Zoe does too. I decorated her room with post-it notes from classical romance novels. Along with the novels, I left a seemingly blank notebook at the bottom. However, it wasn't really blank. I wrote our ending in it, and I'm certain she read it. Her eyes convey everything that her lips can't.

"Don't lie, you little brat. Those dried tear stains give you away."

"You don't know what you're talking about."

Despite Zoe's attempts to run, she remains trapped. I have her cornered, leaving her with no escape. I move the box out of the way and position her with her back against my chest. Taking in a deep breath, she keeps quiet while I sneak a peek at her parted lips. I make her wait for my next move, my next words, relishing in her discomfort as I notice the goosebumps appearing between her breasts.

Fuck, I could take her right here, and I know she'd like it. I know my dirty little brat wants to be filled so badly, but she won't get that. Not until she admits to me what she's known all along. Not until she willingly submits this time.

"I know everything, little butterfly. I know you care more than you let on. That you hate how much you want me and you won't let yourself feel it. I also know you felt scared that day."

Zoe's silence stretches on, making me wonder if she's deliberately shutting me out until I let her go. Her breaths grow shorter and deeper, and her body trembles against mine. It's clear she's wrestling with her thoughts, holding back the words she wants to say. I wish I could save her from herself and fill the room with words she's not ready to hear. Instead, I stay quiet, allowing her to navigate through her emotions as I hold her tightly, reminding her she's not alone.

She'll never be alone, even when she doesn't want me there. I want to walk alongside her through every storm. Until the echoes of my existence become deafening, drowning out the pain from her past.

"Seeing you on the ice that day made me lose my mind. I don't even know what happened. I had no control over it. It all hit me at once." Her voice is so quiet. For a second, it feels like I've imagined it.

I don't know what to say. Maybe I'm dead and in a place where the woman I love wants me back. That's my ideal Heaven, if it exists—being with Zoe forever.

Her eyes fixate on the wall as she tightly clenches her hands on top of her thighs.

"I would never leave you."

She shuts her eyes, pushing back the tears.

I grab her face and force her to look at me. "Zoe, open your eyes."

She winces. "No."

"Look. At. Me," I growl.

When she opens her eyes, they are glassy, as if she's struggling to hold back tears and on the verge of losing control. I wrap my hand around her neck and pull her into a passionate, deep kiss. Zoe meets my fire with fire, the kiss enveloping us like a powerful force, chaotic and starved. It rushes through me, igniting every part of my body.

I can feel all of her in this kiss, without the masks.

Biting her bottom lip, I have to force myself to pull away as I speak against her mouth, staring down at her. "There is no place on this earth, no amount of distance or time that could keep me away from you. Not even death could get in my way. I'll turn into a fucking ghost and haunt you for the rest of your life, if I have to."

"Dominik," she whispers.

"I mean it, Zoe. I will never abandon you. Never."

"Why?" She blinks up at me.

I can't believe she's really asking me that.

My thumb grazes her chin as I hold her stare.

"Because I have loved you from the very first moment you stepped inside that school office. I was obsessed. Captured. And I have loved you every single moment since. In every pocket of time, every glance, every touch, every memory, every sunset and sunrise, everything good and bad in my life—you have been there. I never stopped loving you, Zoe. No matter how hard I tried. You were and always will be in everything. You are *everything*. You are my home, do you not understand that?"

I watch as a tear slides down her cheek. "I don't know what to say."

"Don't say anything. Don't accept it. Don't believe it. I know, actually, that you probably won't. These are just words to you, but I know you feel it. When we're together, when you thought I was gone... I know you feel it, Zoe. No matter how much you tell yourself this isn't real, it won't change all the ways in which I love you. And I will never stop loving you."

She kisses me, gently resting her hand on my cheek. "Okay."

"Okay?" I repeat and she nods as more tears fall.

"Finally," I let out, right before my lips claim hers.

Startling awake, I notice the bedside lamp is still on and my book is resting against my chest.

I must have drifted off to sleep.

Before I did, Zoe was lying naked beside me, playing with my hair as I read out loud to her. We were like that for what felt like hours. Did that really happen, or was I just dreaming? Now I'm wondering if the past few days were merely a figment of my imagination. Because they've been, undoubtedly, the best fucking days of my life.

I finally got the girl.

I got the girl.

My girl.

For the past few days, Zoe and I have enjoyed our own little paradise locked up in my room. It feels like all this time, I've been walking around with half my heart missing, and now it's finally put back together. I've watched her let loose, transforming into a carefree and open version of herself. She's let go of all inhibitions, and for the first time, I feel like she's truly letting herself be. I feel lucky to witness her blooming, let alone to be the one she shares it with. Now, whenever I close my eyes, all I can hear is her laughter and see her beautiful smile. Butterflies can't see their own wings, but I've always seen hers.

I reach for my phone and realize it's only 10:30 p.m. I never fall asleep this early. The injury has messed with my routine so badly. Or maybe it's the overwhelming sense of comfort from the last few days.

You are my home, do you not understand that?

I can't believe I said all that to her and she still stayed.

This can't be real.

The sound of a dish clattering gets me out of bed. I throw on my sweatpants and make my way downstairs to the kitchen. Zoe is leaning against the island, drowning in one of my t-shirts as she raises a spoonful of ice cream to her lips.

I've never witnessed a more stunning scene in my entire existence.

Get it together, Lewis.

I refuse to conceal anything, especially from her. I said all those things, romantic things Zoe normally runs from, but she stayed. Without saying a word, she made me feel seen and accepted. Isn't that what true love is all about?

It's multifaceted, and I want every version of love with Zoe.

"Ice cream? Are you stressed?" I call out, startling her.

Zoe shakes her head, smiling as she licks the spoon clean. "Nope. Just a little late-night snack."

I reach the bottom of the staircase, approaching her as she purposely puts on a show with her tongue. "What's tonight's flavor?"

Zoe arches a brow at me. "Come have a taste."

Fucking christ.

I take her hand and lift the spoonful of ice cream into my mouth as notes of rich vanilla bean and sweet caramel burst on my tongue. Zoe watches my throat before our eyes meet, and I can sense her observing my every movement. She licks her lips slowly, driving me wild with need. I want to put her onto the counter right this second and fuck the lights out of her.

I can never get enough of her. No matter how many times I taste her, finger her, have her...it's not enough. I'm always starved for more.

Zoe drops the spoon. It clangs against the floor as she presses her body against mine. Leaning in close, she outlines my bottom lip with her tongue. I'm frozen in place, feeling her peaked nipples underneath her thin shirt as I look into her hooded eyes.

"Mmmm, you taste so good," Zoe croons, and my eyes roll to the back of my head.

Fucking christ, I need to be inside her right this second.

Grabbing the hem of her shirt, I stretch the material until the sound of it tearing fills the air. Zoe whimpers as I grip her ass, pulling her up and dropping her on top of the kitchen counter.

"Shit, that's cold," she breathes, goosebumps covering her skin.

"It's about to get colder."

My cock throbs as I slowly drag her panties down, enjoying the sight of Zoe writhing with need. Every inch of her is pure perfection. I wish there were a way to slow the clock. I want uninterrupted time with her body, her mind, her laughter, her thoughts, her trust. And if I'm lucky enough, I'll capture her heart one day.

I place myself between her legs and softly kiss her inner thighs. She gasps for air, biting her lip as she stares down at me. With a steady hand, I grab the ice cream carton, feeling the chill of its surface against my skin. Holding it above her, I slowly pour the softened ice cream onto her stomach.

I bend down and lick up a small amount from her skin, enjoying Zoe's squirming.

"Dominik," she breathes.

"Yes, baby?"

"Stop being a tease."

I pour more ice cream onto her body, watching the cream slide down her pussy and in between her ass cheeks. She yelps at the sudden temperature change, but my mouth is already on her, lapping up the melted cream as I part her cheeks.

"Oh, my god!" Zoe screams as I suck hard, moving my tongue meticulously inside and around her opening.

"Do you like your ass sucked?"

She scratches at my shoulders, trying to pull me up. "Dominik, get up here. I need you."

"You're a needy little slut. So impatient."

Wonder how long I can tie Zoe up and edge her before she gets aggressive with need. I need to find out one of these days. Book a cabin for a week and do as I please with her. Maybe I'll even plan a kidnapping.—she'd love it.

Licking up the rest of the cream, I inch my way up her body until I'm hovering above her.

She's breathless and buzzing with lust, looking like she's ready to kill me.

Firmly grasping her chin, I open her mouth, fixating on her enticing, full lips. Memories flood my mind of her head hanging off the bed last night as she eagerly let me fuck that beautiful mouth of hers.

That bratty mouth I adore so much.

Fucking hell, man.

Leaning closer, I spit the ice cream directly into her open mouth. My fingers circle her clit right as she swallows, and Zoe calls out my name, grabbing the back of my head as she pulls me into a deep kiss. We become an instant, sticky mess. The taste of her still lingers on my tongue, mixed with notes of vanilla ice cream. We are a tangled web of desire I never want to escape from.

Zoe pulls hard on my drawstring, keen to set my cock free.

"Did you like that?"

"Yes."

"Does your pussy feel empty?"

"Yes," she whimpers.

I'm on cloud fucking nine.

"Mmmm, good girl. Are you going to beg for my cock?"

Right as Zoe's hand wraps around me, there is a loud banging on the door.

"Fuck," we say in unison as I rest my forehead against hers.

"Who the hell could that be?" I groan.

"Maybe if we ignore them, they'll go away," Zoe whispers.

"Zoe? Are you in there?" Aaron's booming voice and pounding fists echo behind my door.

"Oh my god." Zoe panics, immediately jumping off the countertop.

Gritting my teeth, I pull up my pants and silently curse Aaron for interrupting my dessert. Running my hand through my hair several times, I chuckle as Zoe hops around, looking for something to wear. Of course of all the nights to rip her shirt, it had to be tonight.

"Go hide upstairs. I'll deal with your brother."

Zoe runs for the stairs, her face filled with sheer terror as she stumbles on the first step. The control that man has on her.

It needs to change.

The lock clicks open.

Something tells me Aaron has come here looking for a fight, and I've been itching for him to pull a stupid move like this for months.

He steps into my dim foyer, hair disheveled and looking utterly exhausted, as if he hasn't slept in months. Even his tie is askew, which is so unlike him.

He seems surprised to see me in my own house.

"Is everything okay?" I lean against the kitchen island, crossing my arms.

"So, you're just not answering the door anymore?"

"Well, if you gave me two minutes before barging in, I would have."

"I shouldn't have to," Aaron snaps back.

"What's crawled up your ass? Besides, you clearly have a spare key."

Aaron ignores me, his wild eyes focusing on the carton of ice cream and my torn shirt on the floor.

"Is someone here?"

"Is that any of your business?" I keep my voice calm, even though I want to snap him in half right now.

"It is when you're *pretending* to date my sister. Where is she? You don't look like you need a nurse anymore." Aaron's anger is potent.

"Why don't we talk when you've had some time to calm down? You clearly need food and two days of sleep." I bend down to pick up my shirt, and when I stand, he's right in my face.

"Is Zoe upstairs?" I can smell the liquor on his breath.

"Aaron, you need to leave."

"Out of all the women in New York City, you had to go after my sister? What the hell is wrong with you? Getting laid means more to you than our friendship? You knew she was off-limits!"

"You sure you want to do this right now? Because you have no idea what the hell you're talking about," I say, my voice rising.

"Fucking enlighten me then." Aaron's body twitches, and my blood boils at the sight of his clenched fists.

Is he serious right now?

I step closer, towering over him. He falters for a second before holding his ground.

"Why don't *you* enlighten me on why you ditched Zoe the minute your parents showed up? Just threw her at me like she was something you needed to hide. You know how much they trigger her. You, of all people, know what they did to her."

Aaron is shaking with rage. I've never seen him this angry before. He's usually so in control. Something must have broken him tonight.

"Don't get involved in affairs that don't concern you."

"Anything, or anyone, that hurts Zoe concerns me."

"Since when?"

"Always."

Aaron's brows furrow, but he doesn't step back. "Stay away from my sister."

"You don't get to call those shots. We're both adults. And if you force me to choose, I'll choose her. Every single time."

I watch the muscles flex in Aaron's jaw as he struggles with a response.

"What?" Zoe's soft voice comes from the side, distracting both of us.

"Lying straight to my face, Zo? You could have come clean at the hospital, or anytime after then."

I'm seconds away from knocking Aaron out.

"Shut the hell up for a second, Aaron." Zoe turns toward me, her voice shaking. "What did you just say?"

"You heard me," I breathe, unable to take my eyes off her.

"Say it again," she whispers.

Zoe's dressed in black leggings and an oversized hoodie, making me remember how naked she was minutes ago, sprawled out on my kitchen island.

"I'll choose you every single time."

Is this the proof she needed?

"Jesus Christ," Aaron mutters. "You two need to end this. She's been through enough, Dominik. She doesn't need your unhealed traumas added to the mix."

"That's not for you to decide."

"You've lost your mind. And you, you're entertaining this?" Aaron directs his question at Zoe, but she's not looking at him. She's staring at me as if I'm the only person here. "You don't care about hurting her, Dom? Because we both know you will eventually," Aaron continues, dead set on ruining this moment.

"I'm not going to hurt her."

Aaron jerks away. "You will because you don't understand what we've been through. You haven't lived it. You can't be what she needs."

"Aaron, stop," Zoe mutters.

I turn toward him. "No, I haven't personally lived it. But I understand more than you know. I was there, remember? You don't get to be absent this entire time and then barge into my home to play the overprotective, caring brother."

"Stop it. Both of you," Zoe yells.

Aaron flinches. "You're right. I have been absent. I've been a terrible brother, and I'm sorry for that, Zoe."

I stare at my best friend, taking in his slouched shoulders and defeated stance. He seems lost, but maybe this confrontation is exactly what he needed. Maybe it took this for him to realize how much time he's lost with his sister these past few weeks. There's no denying the change in Aaron. There used to be so much trust between us, but something has shifted. He's become more distant, colder, and it's obvious something is going on with him.

But tonight is not about him. It's about me and Zoe. Things might not be resolved by the time Aaron walks out the door, but he's going to understand how I feel about Zoe, and I need to show her I'm not afraid of him.

"Everything I was doing before, it was to replace the loss I felt without Zoe. There's no way in hell I'm going to do anything to mess this up," I promise. "I may not understand the heartbreak Zoe has gone through personally, but it's haunted me for years. I'm sorry that her first and biggest heartbreak came from people who were supposed to love her the most. People who were supposed to be there for her no matter what."

Zoe walks towards me, and I clasp her hand in mine, my eyes falling to the back of her hand as my thumb draws circles on her skin.

"Zoe, I'm sorry that you've never been truly taken care of and have only felt pain from love. I'm sorry that you believe in endings more than beginnings. I'm sorry that the idea of love terrifies you. But I'll never be sorry for this." Her eyes glisten, and she takes a deep breath. So many confessions lately. Maybe I'll switch careers and become a poet. It's like a dam burst inside me. I can't keep it bottled up anymore. "I don't regret how things happened between us. I will never apologize for that. Without all the mess and bullshit, we wouldn't be here right now. You've been a steady light in the darkest corners of my heart. And despite all of it, you chose to see the good in me. You stayed. I promise to love you in all the ways they couldn't. Until the world fades away and we're all that remains."

Zoe throws herself into my arms, catching me off guard. It takes me a moment to register what is happening when her lips collide with mine. I'm lost in the moment, oblivious to everyone and everything, including Aaron standing in the room with us.

He doesn't say anything, and eventually, I hear the front door click shut. I lift Zoe up, and she wraps her legs around me as I carry her to my room, where we get lost in each other until the sun rises the next day.

26
ZOE

The past few weeks have felt unreal. It's been like living in a fantasy or a dream. Is it possible to be this happy? I'm trying to push away negative thoughts and just enjoy the moment. But it's difficult to ignore my anxious mind sometimes.

Every morning, I wake up expecting reality to crash down on me, to be overwhelmed by the pain of my past mistakes, leaving me paralyzed from all the ways I've failed. You know, the normal voice in my head that makes me want to crawl into a hole. But that hasn't happened yet, and it's been weird, yet wonderful.

I blink and smile, taking in my surroundings. I've lost track of how many times I've woken up in Dom's bed, but it feels like it's been weeks. Even my stuff has gradually moved from Aaron's place to here. Everything unfolded rapidly, yet it feels like this is where I've always belonged.

This feeling is indescribable. I don't even know where to start.

It's all the little things I adore. Like Dominik soothing me to sleep by reading and gently tracing circles on my back. Or the way he always makes sure I'm fed before I leave for work. And the calm nights that follow each day, with the moonlight pouring in as I lie on his chest and listen to his heartbeat while tracing his butterfly tattoo. My butterfly tattoo.

I'm so into it. So into him.

Glancing over, I'm surprised to see him lying on his side, watching me.

"Uh, good morning."

"Hey." Dominik's smile brightens as he gently brushes a stray hair from my face, his fingertips lightly grazing my forehead.

"How long have you been staring at me?"

"A while." He looks so at peace.

"Creep," I mutter, smiling and biting the inside of my cheek.

"Oh, that's creepy? Me watching you sleep in the morning is where you draw the line? Chasing you through the woods is okay, but this is weird?"

A laugh bursts from my lips. "Yes, that's hot. It's primal. This is..."

The words die on my tongue, and my heart races.

This is what, Zoe?

Sweet. Romantic. Loving.

All the things I don't understand. That I've never really felt.

"This is what, Zo?" Dominik repeats my thoughts as he arches a brow, waiting for me to finish my sentence.

"It's sweet," I finally get out.

Dominik's smile is so bright that it could generate enough power to sustain a city for an entire month. I don't think I've ever seen him this happy before.

"I take it back," I blurt.

He chuckles, gripping my hips and drawing me toward him. "No take backs. I can't believe I wormed my way into your heart."

"Nah, you can't warm your way into something that doesn't exist."

Dominik looks at my neck, gently running his fingers down

to my chest. Every touch creates shivers through me. His hand finds its place above my heart, the perfect balance of strength and softness. Meeting my gaze, his expression remains inscrutable.

"Your heart is the best part of you, Zoe. It's my favorite part. And I plan on taking care of it for the rest of my life."

"Stop," I whisper.

This should freak me out. Why isn't it freaking me out?

Dominik leans in, his lips ghosting mine as he stares at me. "There is no way I'm ever letting you go."

"Dominik," I warn.

He kisses me, and a thousand bolts of electricity trickle through my body. "I'm going to marry you, Zoe. You will be my wife. That's a promise."

Oh my god.

"I don't believe in marriage." I don't budge, just staring at him dead on, waiting for his next move.

And I really do mean it. I don't believe in forevers.

"You will. In time." He smirks, as if he already knows what the future holds.

This fucking guy.

I can't...

I—I don't even have words.

All I can manage to do is pull him close and kiss him. We intertwine, his previous statement echoing in my mind as we make love under the morning sun.

"My wife," Dominik growls in my ear, thrusting deep inside me as my orgasm grips me by the throat.

It's those two words that have me detonating around him, my pussy clenching so tightly around his cock that I feel him spill inside me a second later, both of us coming at the same time.

The most insane part is how much I enjoy being with him like this. It's more than just raw and primal sex. Don't get me wrong, that is amazing. But this feels so much deeper, and that part scares me.

Because when we're not together, something feels wrong. As if I've left a part of myself behind. I can't quite make sense of it, and I'm not even sure why I'm trying to psychoanalyze it at this point.

I'm exhausted from resisting this and the way it's changing me. I'm tired of pushing away the one thing that makes me feel whole, happy. I don't want to run from everything out of fear of getting hurt. Can anyone inflict more pain on me than what I've already experienced? The rejection from my own parents is an indelible wound that can never fully heal. So do your worst, universe.

"What are you thinking about?" Dominik's voice pulls me from my thoughts.

I'm a sticky mess, lying on my stomach for the last thirty minutes, needing to start the day but refusing to move from this spot.

"Nothing."

"Tell me."

"Seriously, it's nothing." I smile, trying to reassure him, but Dominik doesn't buy it.

"Is it Aaron?"

I shake my head. "No. Not at all. He's been great. I thought maybe he'd have another outburst after everything that went down in your kitchen, but he hasn't brought it up once. It's like he's totally okay with it, which is freaking me out, to be honest."

Dominik lets out a quiet laugh. "Then what's on your mind?"

I sigh, lying. "Just work stuff."

"Are you worried about the gala?"

I hadn't even thought about that.

The work gala in a few days is one of the biggest accounts I've ever managed, and it's also the one Boston tried to take from me.

Thanks to Jenna, my client, I'm the event organizer. All eyes have been on me for weeks, and if anything goes wrong, Tracy won't hesitate to fire my ass.

"Worried doesn't even begin to describe how I'm feeling about this gala. I'm also scared Greg is going to be there, and if—"

"I'll fucking kill him," Dominik interrupts.

"No, you won't. Stop being so dramatic."

"You want to bet?" he challenges, looking completely serious.

I try not to roll my eyes. "Settle down, Mr. Testosterone With a Budding Hockey Career. We're still in the middle of damage control from your last stunt."

He shrugs, appearing unimpressed as my eyes trace the ink on his body. I don't think I'll ever get over how beautiful he truly is.

"Meh, I have other investments. I'll be fine."

"Not if you go to jail."

Dominik flashes me a devilish grin. "Tristan and Aaron wouldn't allow that to happen."

I huff, rolling onto my back. "Okay, are you all in a gang or something?"

Dominik laughs a bit too intensely for me to take seriously. I narrow my gaze at him, but he gives me a peck on the nose and hops out of bed.

"Shower?"

I watch his perfect ass walk into the bathroom, feeling my need for him build up all over again. My libido is out of control, and sleeping with Dominik has not helped matters whatsoever. If anything, it's increased since we started having sex regularly.

Which is really not a bad thing if you're having mind-blowing orgasms on the regular.

On the regular.

Should I stop myself from thinking about this? Will I always fear tomorrow, or will there be a day when I believe he's here to stay? I wish I had the answer.

"DOMINIK?" I call out into the dark, empty apartment.

He wouldn't be asleep already. He usually waits for me to get home. He specifically said he'd stay up for me tonight because he knew I had to work late reviewing the event details for tomorrow.

"Dom?"

Nothing.

Maybe he went out. I check my phone to see if I missed a text from him, but there's nothing. Something feels off as I slide out of my shoes and drop my bag onto the bench in the foyer.

I fire off a quick text to Dominik, and a second later, I hear the ding of his cell phone coming from somewhere upstairs.

I feel a jolt of excitement run up my spine, but I don't want to get my hopes up. It's been a while since we played a kinky game, and Dominik is still recovering. Shouldn't he have brought this up and asked for consent again? We discussed it before our outdoor fun, but we haven't fully delved back into the kink world since his injury. He's been making great progress though. He even returned to work, and his coach moved up his reassessment.

The possibilities for tonight keep running through my mind. Assuming this turns into a fun little game of hide and seek.

Fuck, I hope he has his mask.

Maybe I'm just tired and reading into things. For all I know, he could be passed out in bed.

But he leaves the lights on for me when he knows I'm working late.

This is going to drive me insane. I could go looking for him, but if this is what I think it is, what fun would that be?

I take off my blazer and drape it over the kitchen stool before sneaking into the vacant dining room.

It's unlikely he's downstairs; there is only stillness on the main floor. It's almost too quiet, and it's making the hair on my arm stand straight up. Which means my only options are to venture upstairs in search of him or patiently wait until he gets restless and decides to come find me.

The second option sounds so much more fun.

I'm feeling extra bratty tonight, and if Dominik wants to play, I think I'm going to make him work for it. He'll want to punish me, and I know I'll enjoy it all the same.

Now I'll be really disappointed if he's passed out in bed.

I tiptoe toward the stairs, cautiously peering up, but all I see is darkness. Out of nowhere, my phone vibrates in my back pocket, making my heart jump.

Despite mentally rehearsing different scenarios, my adrenaline continues to surge, and my heart feels like it's about to burst out of my chest. I grab my phone, and the words immediately catch my attention, sending a wave of pins and needles throughout my body.

DOM

> What are you waiting for, little butterfly? Come find me.

Who in their right mind would actually seek the hunter? It's obvious he's deliberately luring me in, fully aware of my inability to resist. How on earth does this man know what I need and when I need it? Sometimes it feels as though he knows me better than I know myself. And in many ways, that has been true. The gala is tomorrow night; I've been working non-stop and stressed beyond belief. This is exactly the type of fun I need to forget about the world and declutter my mind.

I could wait down here, maybe make myself a snack, but my excitement won't let me.

Padding my way up the oak stairs, I hold my breath, my body on high alert for any movement or sounds from the upstairs hallway.

When I get to the top, I'm breathless from nervous energy, and Dominik is nowhere to be found. Each door, however, is slightly ajar, mirroring one another so I have to search each room. As if I'm going to walk into his trap like a helpless animal.

But you like being the prey. You're secretly loving this.

I am. I can't even deny it.

Wondering how long Dominik has been planning this, I stick close to the wall and nudge each door open. Poking my head in for just a second, making sure the coast is clear before closing the door and moving down the hallway.

The final room is his bedroom.

I've been inside this room so many times, but standing out here, alone and in complete silence, brings back sour memories—the day I discovered Dominik's box of secrets.

Secrets that had to do with me.

The masks.

The lies.

His obsession.

But inside that room, I also found pieces of myself I had buried. Emotions I had denied myself the right to experience. I discovered desire, connection, lust...a different kind of need.

Existing alongside Dominik, I discovered a whole new version of myself, finding meaning in every word, spoken or unspoken.

Everything is different again.

Inhaling deeply, I push the door open with my fingertips and enter.

My heart is beating so fast, I can hear it thundering in my ears.

The room is empty.

How is he not here? Is there a secret hideout somewhere in this apartment?

I check the bathroom, nothing.

Just as I approach the closet door, a hand clasps around my neck, and a solid body pushes against me.

Dominik's scent is intoxicating, making me tingle.

Fuck me, it's embarrassing how badly I enjoy this shit. Being snuck up on like this turns me on more than any dirty talk.

"You should always check behind the door first, little brat. We're going to have to work on your hunting skills." His voice is muffled, but still gravelly. I try to turn my head to look at him, but he jams his thumb under my chin, restricting my movements.

"You snuck up on me. I wasn't done searching."

He laughs, and I can tell he's wearing a mask. "Yeah, I was getting a little too impatient thinking of all the ways I want to punish you tonight."

I feel my heart racing as a familiar thrill takes over me. "Punish me? For what?"

"Just because I'm in the mood for taking. And for all the fucking grief you gave me before."

I snicker, rolling my eyes even though I know he can't see it. "You deserved it."

His hand wraps around my throat, tightening as he twists me around, pressing my back against the wall. "And you deserve this."

My heart drops as I stare up at Ghostface—its elongated, contorted mouth twisted into a sinister grin, does something to my insides. The mask seems to come alive, mocking me in a delicious way as my dark fantasies simmer beneath my skin. Most people might find this type of thrill twisted, maybe even a little sick, but I fucking love it. This is exactly the type of distraction I need tonight. And the fact that Dominik knew what I needed without even seeing or talking to me just makes me realize how in tune we are.

He shoves me down to my knees, his hand still gripped around my throat. He's not wearing a shirt, and I drink him in as he works his belt quickly, unzipping his jeans and pulling out his hard cock. His piercing glistens in the dimly lit room, making me want to inch forward and run my tongue along his head.

"You're going to suck my dick until I'm satisfied or cum down your throat, whichever comes first. Then I'm going to tie you up to the bed and tease you until you're screaming for me to stop."

My brat is itching to come out. He knows I don't beg, and a part of me wants to find out how far I can push him.

I don't say anything as he brings his cock up to my lips. I don't open up for him when he presses it to my mouth.

"You have one second to obey," he says, pushing his thumb down on my chin. You know what? I'm willing to risk it.

My tongue darts out as I drag the tip across his glistening head. His grip tightens around my throat, making me wish I could see his face hiding behind the mask. The wrath that must be burning in his eyes at my defiance makes me so fucking wet.

Fuck, I missed this. The primal hunger is so exhilarating, the anticipation of what's to come quiets my mind in the best possible way.

He doesn't make a move, so I tilt my head and lick down his shaft. Within seconds I'm standing, breathless as Dom rips my shirt in half. The buttons scatter across the room, their clattering sound echoing as the cool air brushes against my exposed skin. He swiftly twirls me around, and the room fills with the sound of fabric tearing as he rips my pencil skirt from behind. With ease, he lifts me and charges toward his bed, throwing me onto it.

"Jesus fucking Christ, Dom!" I yelp, barely catching my breath as he grips my thigh and stomach, flipping me around until my head is dangling off the bed.

I don't even have a chance to fight before his dick is shoved down my throat. Dominik is ruthless, thrusting in and out of my mouth to try to suffocate me. I grip his thighs, digging my fingernails into his flesh as I try to hold back my gags.

Thank every star out there I was too busy to eat much today, or I'd be puking all over his bed right now.

I focus on relaxing my jaw, letting him push into my throat as tears blur my eyes. I'm barely getting enough air when he suddenly pulls out, allowing me a few seconds to catch my breath.

I hear rattling from his bedside table before he reappears above my head. His cock is rock hard and jutting up, and I'm too distracted by it to notice Dominik tilting his mask up to the top of his head. He leans over me, and I grab his dick, running my tongue up and down his length as he groans.

In a swift movement, he finishes undressing me, leaving me completely naked on his bed.

"God, I do fucking love that sweet mouth of yours," he groans, moving my head back down as he shoves his cock to the back of my throat. I choke instantly, and he lets out a soft moan.

Buzzing goes off, and I try to look for the source, but I'm also actively trying to control my gagging. As soon as the toy hits my clit, my back arches and I gasp for air—not getting much since he's still fucking my face. I moan with a stuffed mouth and feel Dominik grow harder. I don't know how that's possible, but I can't think about anything else right now. The toy is strong, and my climax rises quickly.

My hips move on their own, and just as I'm about to come,

the sensation is stolen. Before I can even react, his hot release hits the back of my throat, and I nearly choke as it gets shoved down. When he pulls out, I'm half concentrating on breathing and half trying not to vomit. Tears soak my cheeks, and I'm beyond fucking turned on from the toy he teased me with.

Dominik shoves himself into his jeans and walks out of the room.

"Are you kidding me?" He better get back here before I chase him down myself.

I look around, trying to spot the toy, but it's gone too.

Motherfucker took it with him.

When Dominik returns, he secures the mask onto his face and retrieves a set of straps.

He doesn't address me. Dominik works quickly, strapping my wrists and ankles to each corner of the bed until I'm lying out flat like a star. Completely helpless and at his disposal.

"It's going to be a long night, little butterfly. I hope you stayed hydrated today." As the buzzing starts and the vibrator touches my clit, I can hear the smile in his voice.

I know I'll be exhausted tomorrow, but it'll be worth it. This is my happy place.

"Are you nervous?" I've been watching Zoe since we got into the limo. She's been picking at her freshly manicured nails, staring anxiously out the window as if wishing she were anywhere but here.

"Yes," she mutters, not looking at me.

I stare at her hand, wanting to reach across and hold it, but I find myself pausing. I know things have been different between us lately; we feel more real than ever. Yet I still worry that one day I'm going to push her too far and she'll run off like a scared cat. I don't want to do anything to mess this up, but Zoe knows by now that there is nothing she can do or say that would make me leave.

I'll chase after her through fire and rain.

So fuck it. Hold her hand.

Reaching across, I take her hand in mine, holding my breath for a second. To my surprise, Zoe intertwines our fingers.

"Do you want to talk about it? Before we pull up?"

She shakes her head, then turns to face me with a smile.

"Thank you, though. I wish we could have just stayed in or fast-forward to tomorrow."

"It's going to be great. You've worked for months on this project," I say reassuringly.

"But what if Tracy hates it? And I know people from Boston will be there too since Jenna is from there. I got sent here just to steal their biggest project. I'm sure Greg is still pissed," Zoe says, biting her lip nervously.

I slide Zoe across the leather seat until she's pressed up next to me. She smiles, momentarily forgetting her anxiety, and that alone makes my night.

"Fuck Boston. Fuck New York. Fuck anyone who doesn't give you praise tonight. Actually, I'll fuck them up for you. How's that?"

"Stop," she teases.

"I won't. Your wins are my wins, and your losses are my losses. I've got your back, but tonight is all about you, Zoe. Don't let anyone take that away from you. No matter what, you've earned it, and it's going to be amazing. Jenna knows it. I know it. You know it too." I brush a curl away from her face, staring at her perfectly painted red lips and stopping myself from kissing her so hard that it smears her lipstick.

Zoe pauses for a long moment, just staring at me. I'm about to ask her what she's thinking when she finally breaks the silence.

"Thank you for coming tonight. For helping me forget the past few weeks and for just being here. It means a lot to me."

Wow, what a declaration.

"Who are you, and what have you done with my Zoe?" I taunt, and she shoves my chest, laughing.

"And just like that, you managed to spoil a perfectly good moment."

Placing a gentle peck on her cheek, I shrug. "Got you to forget for a second."

Zoe sighs. "You did."

The limo slows to a stop, and she takes a shuddering breath, staring outside at the bustling crowd.

"I'm right behind you."

Zoe turns and kisses me firmly on the lips. For a brief second, I'm tempted to tell the driver to turn around and head back to my apartment.

She pulls away, reaching for the door handle, but I stop her.

"Not tonight, baby girl," I say, grabbing her hips and pulling her onto my lap. Planting a kiss on her forehead, I smile at her confused expression. Gently pushing her to the other side, I slide across the seat. Opening the limo door, I step out, surveying the crowd on the street.

It's a typical bustling night in New York City with the booming bass from the new store echoing behind me. I reach my hand out to Zoe, crouching down to meet her gaze, captivated by her stunning jade eyes. As her fingers intertwine with mine, the chaotic world around us fades into silence. I wish I could freeze this perfect moment, holding her close and never letting go.

THE VENUE ITSELF IS ELEGANT, with its soaring ceilings covered in shimmering chandeliers and ornate architectural details. Every aspect screams money, and I'm sure it was done on purpose to draw in a certain clientele.

The space is buzzing as high-end individuals gather, expensive perfumes permeate the air, blending with the sound of champagne glasses clinking.

From what I understand, tonight's gala has been in the works for over a year. Jenna and Zoe started working together in Boston, and now Jenna has expanded her business to New York City, opening this gallery along with a few other smaller ones scattered around the city. I don't really know how much money is in this line of work, but I imagine this type of event in the middle of the Upper East Side must have cost a fortune.

I linger next to the fully stocked bar, sipping my drink and watching Zoe put on her professional mask as she walks around the room, checking in with guests and going over details with her colleagues. She's in total control, comfortable and in charge. If you didn't know her as well as I do, you'd think she was completely at peace, but I can see the anxiety in the way she's holding herself. She's nervous but hiding it so well. She's mastered the art of burying her feelings and acting unfazed by them. Despite her ability to deceive most people, including Aaron, I can easily see through her insecurities.

Those parts of her are the ones I love the most.

My favorite days with Zoe are the lazy Sundays when we don't get out of bed until noon. Or the slow strolls through the park when she doesn't fight to remove her hand from mine. Watching Zoe strut around my kitchen wearing my shirt and singing into a spatula as she makes us food. Spending time on a Friday night with Aaron and Tristan, watching a movie and laughing like we're all seventeen. Those nights are rare, but I cherish them so much.

I love our wild nights too. The need to chase is a part of who I am—who we are—and that will never stop. There is so much for us to explore, so many new kinks to experience together, and I can't wait for all of it.

Suddenly, Zoe's gaze meets mine, and her smile lights up her face from across the room. I can't believe how effortlessly she moves me. With just one look, she sets free a thousand butterflies in the pit of my stomach.

Every minute, every lingering stare, every touch makes me

fall in love with her all over again, each time deeper and more intensely than the day before. It's almost unimaginable, considering I've been obsessed with her since the moment I first saw her.

I wink at Zoe, and her head falls, her cheeks turning red.

Fuck, I adore that.

I adore her. More than she'll ever know.

"You like that?"

I turn toward the voice and immediately recognize the piece of shit talking to me. Of course, it's the jackass that got my girl moved to New York. I don't like to be surprised—most hunters don't. I can't make up my mind whether to thank him for bringing her to me or to confront him for hurting her. Maybe I'll do both.

"Excuse me?" I reply, taking a good look at Greg.

I wasn't sure he'd show up tonight, but clearly the man has a death wish. Wait until Aaron gets here. I *almost* feel bad for the guy.

"I was just asking if you're into that. Because I can give you a few pointers or maybe tell you to stay away," Greg says, nodding to where Zoe is standing.

Downing the last of my whiskey, I leave the glass on the counter and approach him slowly.

"You mean the woman who is way out of your league on every level?"

"Woah. Didn't mean to offend. You know her or something?" He raises his hands.

"Or something," I mutter.

It's funny how quickly the smug expression on his face disappears.

"Shit, man... I'm really sorry. But, if I may—"

"You may not," I snap.

I don't even bother casting him a glance, my eyes following Zoe as I try to calm down and not rearrange this asshole's face right here at the bar. I can wait until the guys get here and we can quietly take him outside.

When I look back, Greg looks up from his phone, then down again, appearing more confused than a rodent about to run across a busy intersection.

"Shit. You're Dominik Lewis. You play for the Slashers! That's so cool. Wait, are you dating Zoe Jackson? There is an article here. No fucking way."

I'm sure Zoe would understand if I spilled a little blood. Wouldn't she be happy I took care of her Greg problem forever? It would be a beautiful display of affection.

Goddamn intrusive thoughts.

"Am I missing something here?" I grit my teeth, knowing I should probably leave before things get ugly, but I rarely do what I'm supposed to.

What fun would that be?

Greg laughs, and the sound irritates me more than his face.

"Sorry, I've had a few shots and my filter is gone. This event was supposed to be mine, but your 'girl'"—he puts the word in air quotes with his small fingers—"stole it from me. Her client fired me even though this was my account in Boston. So I'm a little bitter. I'm sure you can understand why I reacted like that."

Leaning in close to Greg, I smirk, making sure he can hear my next words clearly.

"The only thing I understand is that you're a small-minded man-child who can't even locate the clitoris. I'm going to leave you be right now because I know how hard Zoe worked to make sure tonight goes smoothly, and I won't have you ruin it for her. But if I were you, I'd start looking for another job. And maybe get the fuck out of here before I mess you up."

He reeks of vodka and yesterday's mistakes.

Greg looks a little stunned. "Are you threatening me?"

I remain silent as he begins to walk away, but suddenly, I grab hold of his small arm. "Oh, and one more thing. You're going to apologize right this second for what you did to her, or I'm going to make sure you'll never get off again. And after, if you so much as look in Zoe's general direction or speak her name, I'll pluck out your eyeballs and feed them to you."

His eyes widen, and he quickly pulls his arm back right as I push him away. "What the fuck is wrong with you, dude?"

I give him an expectant look and gesture toward Zoe, encouraging him to keep going. I wonder if he's going to make a run for it, but he turns and heads to where Zoe is standing with Via.

I watch the entire interaction, taking in Via's spitfire expression and immediately liking her more for protecting my girl. I note the way Zoe shrinks but doesn't show any signs of weakness on that beautiful face. Greg's back is facing me, so I have no idea what he's saying, but Zoe barely looks at him before she walks away. He turns to me and flips his middle finger. I nonchalantly wave and smile, relishing the thought of thoroughly dismantling his miserable life.

"Could you be any more whipped?" Tristan slides up next to me, already holding a drink in his hand.

"Jealousy doesn't look good on you, Tris."

He snickers into his glass. "Please. Love is for the weak."

"Whatever helps you sleep at night, big boy. You see that asshole walking off on the left?" Tristan follows my gaze.

"Yeah. Is that Greg?"

"Yes. Don't let him leave," I say, and within seconds Tristan has his phone out, texting someone.

I love that about Tris—he acts without hesitation. He may ask questions later, but not when we need him most. He trusts our decisions when we take action, especially when it comes to stuff like this. If I ever need to bury a body, Tristan will be the first person I call.

"I've been wanting to take my anger out on someone for a bit.

I'm glad Greg showed up." Tristan's laugh reverberates low in his throat.

"Yeah. I'm just sad Aaron missed that interaction. It would have been fun watching him trying to hold back. Speaking of, where is he?"

Tristan sighs. "In the building, dealing with a problem."

As I face Tristan, my brows furrow, and his expression is anything but positive.

"His parents are here. Apparently, they want to buy some art pieces and were invited by a family friend."

I wasn't expecting that to come out of his mouth. "Fuck."

"Yeah, but we're dealing with it. I had a feeling something like this would happen, and we wanted to be prepared," Tristan says.

"We? As in you and Aaron?"

Noting the change in my voice, he narrows his eyes at me. "Generally, that's what 'we' means. Feeling a little left out?"

"A little. There seems to be a lot of that happening lately."

Tristan shrugs, looking bored. "You've had a lot going on. Work problems, girl problems, and then an accident that put you in the hospital."

"Yeah, and I've handled all of it. I can handle this too. You know that," I state.

"I do, but your friends are here to ensure you don't *have* to handle shit."

Just as I'm about to respond, Tristan interrupts me by placing a hand on my shoulder.

"Listen, put all of that out of your mind for now. Because we have to deal with their parents before it ruins Zoe's big night. I have a plan, but you might need a drink first."

Tristan only demands alcohol before delivering difficult or complex news. I make eye contact with the bartender and ask for two whiskeys.

28
ZOE

"You know, if you ask anyone in the office, they'll tell you I don't hand out praise often. Which is true, except for when it's well deserved. Then I don't shut up about it." Tracy grabs me by the shoulders, smiling cheek to cheek. "This is beyond fantastic, Zoe. Jenna is so thrilled that she wants to become a permanent client of ours."

Tracy does another sweep of the grand hall, nursing her nearly empty champagne glass.

Saying I'm over the moon would be an understatement.

This night has gone better than expected. I've done four rounds and checked the list twice, so I should be able to relax now, maybe even pat myself on the back for not screwing anything up. But I can't seem to unwind. Something inside me is unsettled, like I'm waiting for the other shoe to drop.

Maybe the shoe was Greg's half-assed apology. I still can't believe he ran over and said all that shit, even though the whole time, I felt like he was being held at gunpoint.

At least the boys seem to be having a good time. Tristan and Dom managed to get Aaron to loosen up enough to start spending money on some artwork. I have no idea where he plans on displaying the pieces since his house is already filled with enough art, but I'm not about to question his spending habits right now. Not when he's making Jenna so happy.

Everything goes black as I feel clammy fingers cover my eyes. The familiar scent of Chanel perfume gives her away instantly. Whipping around, I pull Sammy in for a hug, almost breaking down in tears.

"Oh my god, you bitch! Why didn't you tell me you were coming?" I exclaim into her hair, which is a different color again. A beautiful, rich green this time.

Whenever Sammy gets bored or is having a hard time with life, she changes her hair. She's the type of person who can pull off any look, and I secretly hate her for it.

"You know how much I love surprising you. Besides, I wasn't about to miss your big break. You're definitely getting promoted. This is fucking amazing, Zoe." Sammy grabs my cheek, inspecting me like she hasn't seen me in years, but in reality, it's only been a couple of months. "Also, you look hotter than last time, which is so unfair."

"Stop," I say, rolling my eyes.

"I'm serious, bitch. It's probably all that sex with a hockey player that's giving you the glow up. I want to see his massive, pierced cock," Sammy nearly screams, and I almost lunge at her.

"Are you insane?"

"Oh, come on. Like anyone can hear me over the music and their own gossip. Did you run into Fuck Face? I have to remind myself that jail is not suitable for people like me whenever I'm tempted to throw him in front of a bus.

"Yeah, he already came by and gave me a pathetic apology." I brush it off, but Sammy's jaw nearly hits the floor.

"Shut the hell up. No, he didn't. He's been so bitter, I was sure he was going to make some sort of scene."

Interesting.

"No. But he seemed nervous when he came over. I don't even know. I walked off before he finished his speech."

"Maybe your boyfriend scared him off!" She's way too excited for her own good. I'm just realizing how much I missed Sammy's theatrics.

"Sammy." I shake my head, smiling.

She looks back at me. "You know that's hot. All possessive and shit."

"I'm just so happy you're here."

Sammy's smile vanishes as her mouth pops open in surprise. "Sweet Jesus, I know I'm into chicks, but he's even hotter in person."

I turn to see Dominik and Tristan walking toward us.

She's right. He is hotter in person. There's an aura about Dominik the camera can't capture. He's like walking sex on a stick, and with Tristan next to him, they're lethal—enough to even make a lesbian take notice.

I love that Dominik's eyes are only on me.

Wherever we go, countless people stare at him, yet he remains oblivious. He is constantly watching me, noticing how I react to him and to the things happening around us. He has been observing me from a distance tonight. I can't tell if he's been keeping tabs on me or if he's enjoying seeing me at work, being passionate about something. Maybe it's a mix of both.

The moment I walk into a room, his eyes are immediately drawn to me. They're always on me.

He belongs to me just as I belong to him.

Tristan says hi to Sammy, but before I can even introduce them, Dominik pulls me into a frenzied, breathless kiss. And after a long second, he peels himself away and leans close to my ear, sending shivers down my spine.

"This is more than they deserve, baby. I'm so proud of you."

Hearing those words does something to me.

I've only ever heard Aaron say that to me a couple of times, and I've never dreamed of hearing it from my parents. But this is different. For some reason, hearing those words come from Dominik overwhelms me. The intensity of it reverberates through me as I stare into his eyes, feeling the weight of those three words so deeply that I want to tell him.

I could just say it because I've felt it for a while now.

But I don't.

Instead, I thank him quietly and smile.

"So the famous Sammy. Zoe has told us a lot about you. It's nice to finally meet you." Tristan extends a hand out to Sammy.

"Good. I don't want to be forgotten." Sammy laughs, cutting me a sharp look.

"As if that would ever happen. Did she already ask you if you have a sister?" I ask Tristan, and he laughs, nodding before I even finish my question.

"Fuck me. Am I that predictable?"

"More like desperate," I whisper, and she shoves my shoulder.

"Hi, Dominik," Sammy says, blushing. I don't think I've ever seen her this shy before. This must be the effect Dom has on everyone.

"Sorry, I meant to introduce you two, but I got distracted." I bite my lip.

"We've already met." Dominik winks at Sammy, and her face turns a deeper shade of red.

Oh, sweet Jesus.

"When?" I blurt out.

"Just earlier," Sammy mumbles. Why is she struggling to speak?

"It's Dom. Are you surprised at this point?" Tristan jokes

right before he gently grabs my arm and pulls me aside. "Can we see you for a second?"

"What's wrong?" I quickly get out, scanning the room and looking for some sort of emergency.

"Nothing. I just need to talk to you." Tristan remains utterly calm, in stark contrast to Dominik who is watching me with furrowed brows, as if he expects me to erupt. Sammy continues to talk to him, completely unaware that he's disengaged.

"Okay."

Tristan doesn't hesitate, turning around to face Sammy with the biggest smile. "We're going to borrow Zoe for a second if that's okay. It was so wonderful to meet you, and we'll be back to catch up. We can grab a drink, and I'll tell you all about my older sister."

Sammy beams, looking at the boys before her eyes land on me. "Sounds good. Let me know if you need help with anything, Zo."

"I'll be right back. Don't go anywhere." I squeeze her hand before turning to walk out of the main gallery room with Dominik and Tristan.

I wait for someone to break the silence, but we just keep walking until I can't take it anymore.

"Is one of you going to tell me what's going on?"

"Your parents are here," Tristan casually says, but I might have misheard him. I disconnect immediately, feeling numb while concentrating on the echo of our footsteps in the quiet hallway.

"Zo?" Dom takes my hand, and I blankly look up at him.

"Hm?"

"Are you okay?"

"Yeah, I'm fine." I shrug it off.

Tristan stops by a gray door, as he pulls the handle and waits for Dominik and me to enter an empty utility room.

Tristan locks eyes with me as soon as the door shuts.

"I assume you heard what I said back there, so I won't repeat it. But I need you to follow Aaron's lead. Can you do that for me? I know you don't like to see your parents, but I promise you, this will be the last time."

"What do you mean it'll 'be the last time?' Is that where Aaron is? He's with them?"

I'm not sure why it still surprises me. I would have assumed that with each sting, the blow would become so dull that eventually it wouldn't feel like this. But it's still there—a guttural ache right in the pit of my stomach. It would be nice if there were no expectations or if there was a way to turn this off entirely, but hope is a tricky thing that never seems to disappear.

"Yes, but it's not what you think." This time, it's Dominik who speaks.

He doesn't wear the same calm and collected demeanor that Tristan does so comfortably. Dom never has. Aaron and Tristan are entrepreneurs to their core, but Dominik is all emotion, passion, and drive. That's why he's such an amazing athlete.

I just stare at them, not quite sure what's going on or why they've brought me into this room to tell me my parents are here. Who the hell cares? They always seem to show up on important days. Every single time without fail. This was the other shoe, and I'm the stupid one who didn't expect it. I should have prepared myself.

I look between Dom and Tristan, letting out a deep sigh. "Let me guess... You brought me here to hide? So they don't have to see me, and Aaron won't have to do damage control?"

"Fuck that," Dominik snarls.

"Absolutely not," Tristan says simultaneously.

That takes me by surprise.

Dominik grabs my hand, bringing it to his lips while he pins me with those dual-colored eyes I love. "It's time for your comeback, little butterfly. Right now, it's best if you have less information, so just follow Tristan and Aaron's lead. I'll be right here if you need anything. I will forever be here, standing right behind you."

It's time for my comeback? I don't understand.

"Can you please speak English?" I watch them, yet neither speaks. Tristan's phone buzzes, and he glances at Dominik before heading deeper into the lengthy utility room.

"Come on, baby. Let's go break some hearts." Dom grabs my hand, and we follow Tristan.

"Dominik, can you please tell me what's going on?" I whisper so Tristan doesn't hear me.

Dom gradually reduces his speed, creating a slight gap between Tristan and us. He eyes Tristan, and when it becomes apparent that Tristan doesn't notice, Dom pulls me closer and leans down.

"I've always daydreamed about taking revenge on your parents. What that day would look like, how I would go about doing it. If I would take my time, make them pay for every heartbreak, every tear, ever rotten word they threw at you. I imagined slowly killing them and watching the blood flowing out of their bodies. I want to make them pay. I know it won't fix what happened to you, but it would make me feel better knowing I finally did something about it."

I've thought about revenge too.

Countless nights spent lying awake as my tears scalded my cheeks. So many times, amid chaos, I wished I could disappear into another life. I want to erase the memories of those who caused me immense pain and left lasting wounds on my soul. Wounds that will never heal. I'll always have their ugly scars to remind me. No matter what I do, who I become, those memories will always follow me like a dark shadow. It's part of who I am now, and I have to accept that. I have to live with the fact that the people who were meant to love me the most, ended up leaving the deepest cuts.

Hearing Dominik's admission makes me weak at the knees. I never realized he had noticed everything that went on inside that house. For the longest time, I believed only I had seen it, experienced it. If it was all in my head, perhaps it wasn't real at all. Maybe it wasn't my reality.

But it was.

Every single day, it was my reality, and though it will always be part of my story, it doesn't have to define me. It doesn't have to determine my future; instead, it can remain in my dark, horrible past.

"I've thought about it too," I admit.

Dominik smiles, squeezing my hand. "Good. Let's go get that revenge then."

"Just like that?"

"Just like that." He winks.

Fear and excitement flood my lungs in equal measure as a thrilling sensation courses through me. Allowing myself to be swept away by the unrestrained forces of revenge brings me a profound sense of freedom.

29

ZOE

I'm gripping Dominik's hand so tightly that I'm afraid I might accidentally crush his fingers. Every part of me wants to run away, but we steadily make our way toward a pair of double doors that are slightly ajar.

Tristan's arm extends, prompting the three of us to stop. A heated argument is unfolding behind the closed door.

"Why are you behaving this way, Aaron? Sweetie, this is so unlike you." It's my mother, Elaine.

Just hearing her voice makes me want to cry. Emotional trauma responses are fucking dumb. I wish there were a way to stop them.

I really wish I could have prepared for this.

"Get used to it. This is the real me. Without guilt weighing me down. I should have approached this topic a long time ago, but I was too afraid. That's no longer a concern." Aaron's intense anger is palpable, even from the other side of the door.

"I don't fucking understand. You're being ridiculous." That's my father's voice, Bob. "She's not even a Jackson."

Who's not a Jackson?

"What the fuck did you just say?" Aaron sounds shell-shocked.

"Bob! Stop!" Elaine shouts.

"He deserves to know the truth. Maybe he'll stop this nonsense. You've been wanting to tell him for a long time, so tell him, Elaine. Tell your son what you did."

"Please, stop." Elaine's voice comes out broken.

"Someone better tell me what the hell is going on."

"Tell him about the time when you were a whore."

Wow.

"What the fuck, Dad!"

I need to go in there and comfort my brother before he does something he'll regret.

Tristan takes a step forward, trying to peek through the door, but Dominik grabs his arm and stops him.

Every inch of my skin feels pricked, and I can barely hear anything over my thundering heart.

"Bob, don't."

"Zoe is not your full sister."

Pitch-black silence.

"What?" Aaron shouts.

Silence.

My heart feels like it's going to jump out of my throat at any second.

Elaine is crying.

"She is your half-sister. Your father has never let me forget the one mistake I made, and it's okay, because I deserve it. I deserve to be reminded of what I did."

Bob is not my father?

What?

"What the actual fuck, Mom."

"She slept with some guy, and he got her pregnant. That's why that spawn looks nothing like me. She's not mine, and she will never be mine. Every day I had to look at her face and be reminded of what your mother did. How she tried to ruin our family," Bob spews. I guess he's not my father.

Never has been.

"You better watch your mouth, or I'm going to punch your teeth in." Aaron seethes, his temper growing.

"I'm your father! You do not get to talk to me that way."

"You are no father of mine when you talk about my mother and my sister that way," Aaron barks, sounding powerful and unbeatable. He might be feeling utterly confused, but he doesn't sound like it at all.

Like statues, Dominik, Tristan, and I remain silent, eager to hear more until I'm suddenly gasping for air. It all makes perfect sense now. All these years, the way they treated me, the intense hatred in my father's eyes whenever they fell upon me. My entire life falls into place like small puzzle pieces.

Despite having no role in her affair or their marriage, I was punished for simply coming into existence. Bob hated me before I was even born.

But now, I finally understand the reason behind it all. At least now, there is some clarity. And most importantly, it wasn't something I did.

It was never my fault.

"Is this true, Mom?" Aaron finally speaks.

"Yes." Her voice is barely a whisper. "I'm so sorry. I never meant for any of this to happen. There are things you will never understand, and I'm not justifying it, but I made a mistake, and I've been paying for it ever since. Your father was kind enough to forgive me."

"Forgive you?! He called you a whore, Mom. With the way he's behaving, I'm sure you had a good reason to fuck some other guy."

She cries some more, and some deep, twisted part of me

wants to walk over and hug her. Even though she never showed me the same kindness. What the hell is wrong with me? I should hate her. She gave birth to me and has been regretting it ever since. Her husband meant more to her than her own child. Instead of protecting me, she joined him.

"Stop crying, Elaine. No one wants to see your ugly tears."

"I'm going to fucking kill him," Dominik snarls under his breath.

"You're a fucking asshole," Aaron fumes. "And you, I can't believe you would allow this to happen. All these years, and for what? For him to treat you like this while you discarded your own flesh and blood? She was just a kid!"

He must be addressing both of them now.

I'm not sure if I can do this. Maybe I'm not ready after all.

My entire body shakes, and Dominik turns me around, gripping my face. "Stay with me, okay?"

"I can't."

"It's almost over, and I've got you. I won't let them hurt you." He kisses my cheek, and I steal a second of comfort from his proximity.

I can only nod and focus on my breaths. I can't walk into the room and face my demons while having a panic attack.

"Let's get in there before this gets any uglier," Tristan whispers, and Dominik tightens his grip on me, holding me close. His warmth calms me instantly. I don't think he knows how much he affects me or how safe he makes me feel.

I never imagined that we could rebuild after all that happened between us. But the transformation was almost instantaneous when I finally gave this a chance and allowed him into my life. He had always been there, waiting for me behind that door. Giving me time until I could find my way to him.

"Wait," Dom whispers, looking down at me. "Are you ready?"

"Yes," I exhale.

"Are you sure? Because you say the word, and I'll take you away from here."

"Dominik!" Tristan warns from behind him, but Dominik doesn't even flinch. He's completely focused on me.

Touching his cheek, I push the nerves aside and smile. "I'm okay. I've got you guys with me."

When I look behind Dom, Tristan smiles and winks at me, and I know that, whatever happens in that room, I'm going to be okay because these men have my back no matter what. I've never felt that type of security before. Never known with certainty until now, and that, alone, feels like a win.

As I cautiously position myself between Dominik and Tristan, tension crackles in the air like a live wire as we push through the doors and walk into the room. Aaron is rigid, his arms folded tightly across his chest as he stands locked in a fiery standoff with Bob, whose face is flushed red with anger. Elaine sits in a nearby lounge chair, her breaths shallow and ragged as she clutches her head. The room feels like a powder keg on the brink of explosion, just like my insides at the sight of seeing my parents for the first time in a long time.

I've avoided being in a room with them since they locked me up and barely fed me for a week straight. Elaine was out of town, and Bob snapped at something I had done. I can't even remember what it was; it was that insignificant. I think I had broken curfew or something. He left me a bucket and locked my door from the outside. I had nightmares about that for months.

Just the memories make me want to crawl out of my skin.

They both look at us, completely blindsided. Aaron smiles, like he knew we were coming. He must have been the one Tristan was texting, waiting for the signal to join.

Has my brother been planning this all along?

Don't get ahead of yourself. Aaron has never done that before. Why now?

No expectations. No disappointment.

I'm just going to follow their lead.

Bob turns to Aaron. "Are you kidding me with this? What's gotten into you? I can't believe you're acting this way. Why would you bring her here? You know what it does to your mother."

Aaron's tone turns venomous. "Mom or you? Now that I think of it, she was never the one to badmouth Zoe, and even if she did, I feel like she only did it to please you. What kind of monster are you?"

Aaron's face is flushed, his eyes narrowed into fiery slits, and his fists are clenched so tightly that his knuckles are white. Veins pulse visibly on his forehead, and his breathing is heavy and labored. I have never witnessed Aaron this angry before.

Right as Bob is about to open his mouth, Aaron steps in. "You know what? It doesn't matter. I'm not remotely interested in hearing your explanation. All I want to hear out of your mouth right now is an apology for everything you've put Zoe through. Both of you."

Bob's howling laughter startles Elaine so much that she lets out a loud hiccup. She looks so weak right now and it's embarrassing.

If he's not my biological father, then who is? Could there be someone out there who loved my mother enough to love me too? Maybe not, because he gave us up. But maybe he never knew about me in the first place. My mom could have disappeared.

But what if...

I can't think about that right now. Hope is the root of heartbreak, and it has no place in my thoughts.

"Over my dead body. I'm not sorry, and I never will be. Actually, scratch that." Bob throws his hands in the air like a fucking child about to have a tantrum. "I am sorry about one thing. For not forcing your mother to abort her. I should have put my foot down that day, but she was so upset, I dropped it. Didn't want to make a scene at the clinic."

Dominik moves so quickly I don't even know what's happening until Bob is on the ground, nearly unconscious. Tristan and Aaron yank Dominik off him, barely able to restrain him while Bob just lies there, groaning and holding his bloody face.

"Oh my god, Bob! Aaron, call the police."

Tristan laughs. "Yeah, that's not going to happen."

"Then I will!" Elaine sneers, acting like we're at fault here.

"You touch your phone, and I'll make sure everyone you know and love, excluding Aaron, suffers in ways you can't begin to imagine," Tristan says calmly as he turns toward my mother. She stares at him, stunned with her hand hovering over her phone.

"Are you good?" Aaron asks Dom right before he's nudged off.

"Yeah, I'm good. I just... I couldn't take that anymore."

I keep my eyes on Dominik as I speak. "It's okay. But I don't need his apology. I don't want anything from them."

"I do. I want his head," Dom sneers.

"Alright. Calm down, Henry the VIII." Tristan removes his jacket, casually placing it on a chair by the door. As he turns around, something about his demeanor shifts, and suddenly, he effortlessly commands the entire room. Even Elaine, who is seated next to Bob on the floor, watches Tristan. "Now that we've all had some time to talk about our feelings and Zoe doesn't want an apology, I'm going to get to it because I'd like to enjoy some of this night and let Zoe get back to being a wonderful event host." Tristan winks at me, making me blush. "Since we don't expect Zoe to protest, Aaron and I decided to take care of the situation ourselves.

"What is he talking about, Aaron?" Bob says, struggling to sit up.

Elaine looks so pathetic as she helps him, especially after everything he just said about her. She's still at his beck and call, like a slave. If I were her, I would have spat in his face.

Aaron seems completely composed. Meanwhile, I'm trying not to shit myself and have a panic attack at the same time.

Tristan takes his sweet-ass time speaking, purposely stalling and looking at his nail beds. "Your retirement fund, the one you've been building since your early thirties, has been moved to an account under Zoe's name. Everything you've worked hard to save now belongs to your daughter. Isn't that so thoughtful?"

I'm experiencing a brain malfunction, causing me to blink and swallow repeatedly.

What did he say?

"No," Elaine murmurs.

"What?!" Bob shouts.

"Don't get too worked up now, Billy. You don't want to have a heart attack," Tristan smirks.

I wish I were as lethal as Tristan.

"So now you'll have to work until you drop dead, or sell your house and admit to your friends you're poor. At least we left your house alone." Dominik speaks this time.

He was in on this too? For how long?

I have so many questions.

Am I hallucinating?

"We considered it briefly, but Aaron didn't want to deal with the hassle of finding you an old folks' home," Tristan turns to Dom.

"Yeah, that's a problem for another day." My brother is still seething, but he seems to have calmed down .

"How much?" I finally say, causing all eyes to fall on me.

"How rich are you?" Tristan taps his chin, staring at the

ceiling before looking at me. "Somewhere north of twenty million."

Sorry, what?

I can't help but burst into laughter. It's not just a tiny, delicate chuckle. It's a type of cackling I can't seem to rein in or control. And it doesn't seem to end.

"Think I broke her." I hear Tristan speaking to Dominik and Aaron.

As Dominik approaches me and embraces me, something strange happens. Laughter fades away, replaced by tears. It feels as though my world is crumbling yet, somehow also coming together. As though the very essence of my being is shattering, yet there is a sense of renewal, as if everything is falling into place at last.

Right now, being surrounded by these three men who have chosen to stand by my side feels beyond overwhelming. My brother's unwavering defiance of our parents' wishes leaves me speechless. The depth of his love and this unexpected gesture are hard to grasp.

Gratitude overwhelms me, like a cleansing tide, washing away all other emotions. It fills me, pushing out the fear and uncertainty that have troubled me for so long. These men, with their act of solidarity, have given me a lifeline, a small flicker of hope in the middle of darkness. And for that, I am incredibly grateful.

Smiling through my tears, I look up at Dominik and turn to my brother. "Thank you for choosing me. And for all of this. For helping me find my way back to myself," I say, glancing at Dominik and Tristan as well. "But I can't accept this money. I want to donate it. I've tried to never rely on anyone else, and I don't plan on starting now. The only part of them I will keep is you, Aaron."

My brother's face lights up with a brilliant smile as he approaches me, wrapping me in a warm, tight hug.

"I'm so proud of you, Zo," he whispers, bringing fresh tears to my eyes.

"I love you," I say into his chest.

"I love you more." He pulls away, wiping a tear from my cheek. "Do you want to leave?"

I nod, and Aaron silently signals for Dominik to take over. He's beside me in a heartbeat.

"Son, if you walk out of that door, you're dead to me." Bob is leaning against Elaine, and she's barely holding it together. Not sure if she's crying because all her money is gone or because she's about to lose her precious firstborn.

"Good. The feeling is mutual," Aaron says over his shoulder.

And then the four of us turn to walk out.

"Everyone good?" Tristan asks us, but Dominik pauses, releasing my hand and slowly approaching my parents, focusing on Bob.

"You come near Zoe again or show up to an event she's at or even walk down the same street she's on, I won't hesitate to sever your head and toss it in the river. You got it?"

Bob looks like he might lunge at Dominik. But before he can even take a step, Dominik bucks, causing Bob to stumble backwards and bump into Elaine as they both topple over.

"I'll take that as a yes," Dominik laughs, turning around as the guys snicker.

We huddle together, leaving the room as a united front, and I look up at Dominik. His smile is so light, calming the emotions raging inside me. My heart flutters with sensations I never thought I'd feel—joy, relief, gratitude, all mixed with a newfound sense of belonging.

I start crying again. Why am I so emotional right now? Maybe it's because I finally understand the true meaning of home. It's not a place with four walls and a roof, but a place of acceptance. In being seen for exactly who we are.

And when I look into Dominik's eyes, I realize he embodies everything that home should be—comfort, security, peace, excitement, and a quiet type of love. With him, I am whole, anchored to a different type of belonging, finally realizing that this is a forever type of connection that goes way beyond the physical.

He is my constant, and with him, I know that no matter where I go or how lost I get, I will always find my way back.

Back to him.

Back to *home*.

Several weeks later

I'M LASER-FOCUSED, not thinking about the countdown or what these next few minutes mean, not just for my career but for the entire team.

The final cup game.

Nope, not going to think about it.

I'm one with the ice right now, blazing to the other end of the rink. As my skates cut into the ice and I gain speed, the crowd's deafening roar increases. A drop of sweat slides between my eyebrows, threatening to distract me right as Axel pulls up on the other side, making eye contact with me.

I'm ready.

As Axel unleashes the puck with a forceful flick of his stick, time seems to slow. I snatch the puck from the air, my movements fluid and instinctual as I pivot toward the opponent's net. But I am not alone; they close in on me like a pack of wolves, taking away our window of opportunity.

Time is running out, Dominik.

Focus.

In a split-second, I trust my instincts and pass the puck back to Axel, then dart around the net, weaving through the opposing players with practiced finesse. I spot my opening.

"Axel!" I shout, my voice cutting through the din of the crowd.

He responds by taking a blind shot at me. The puck flies through the air with impressive accuracy. I react quickly, intercepting it with lightning reflexes. With a swift strike of my stick, I send the puck soaring toward the net, completely fixated on the target.

The next second, the buzzer blares, and the arena erupts into a cacophony of sound and color. Confetti rains down, blocking my vision.

Did the puck go in?

What the actual fuck.

Before I can catch my bearings, I'm flooded by a sea of teammates, their shouts mingling with the cheer of the crowd.

"Dominator! Dominator! Slashers! Slashers!" the crowd chants, and I know we won.

We won the cup.

"We won?" I shout.

"WE WON! You got us the cup, you mother effing king." I think it's Liam shouting back, but I can't be sure. There is too much going on. I think I might be going deaf.

I finally make my way out, throwing my helmet onto the ground and skating to the players' bench. My girl is already standing beside Coach; her beautiful, smiling face is everything I need to see. I embrace her, pulling her out of the box and onto the ice with me.

Zoe looks more breathtaking than ever as she begins running her hand through my sweaty hair.

"You did it, baby. Like I always knew you would."

I arch my brow. "Did you now?"

"Yes. Congratulations. I'm so proud to be yours." She nods, biting her lip.

Those words coming from her lips feel like something from out of this world.

"And I'm proud to be yours."

Zoe nervously glances around, smiling when she sees the cup being brought out. "I should go. This is your moment."

"No, it's our moment. You're not going anywhere."

"But, Dominik—"

I pull her in for a kiss. "I don't want to hear it. I wouldn't be here without you."

"That's not true."

"It is true. It's all for you," I groan against her mouth, and she bites my lip, causing a shiver to run down my spine.

Zoe gently pulls back, her gaze locking with mine as the entire stadium vanishes. All around us, everything and everyone dissipates, leaving only her and me standing on the ice.

"I love you," she whispers, turning my world completely upside down once more. As those three words escape her lips, their beauty surpasses any I have ever heard. The weight of Zoe's declaration hangs in the air, like an unbreakable promise. I am undeniably and unquestionably hers.

"I love you so incredibly much."

She throws herself at me, pulling me in for a fierce kiss, and I no longer care about anything but this moment stamped in time with her.

How did I get so lucky to get everything I've ever wanted? It's almost surreal, as if I'm in a dream. I don't deserve her, nor any of this, but I'm grateful to have it. Feeling like the luckiest man to ever walk this Earth. And I know, with Zoe by my side, I always will be.

She peels herself away, leaving me feeling sad as she retreats. She winks at me. A moment later, my team surrounds me, revealing the cup. It's larger than I remember and incredibly shiny. I can tell they put effort into polishing it just for today. My fingers itch with the need to hold it.

I can practically feel the weight of history resting on its sturdy frame, each scuff and scratch bearing witness to the countless games lost and won.

While I search for someone to take hold of it, the team waits for me.

"No." I shake my head.

"Yes. You're our captain."

With bated breath, I reach out, my fingertips tingling with anticipation as I prepare to grab the trophy and haul it over my head. Excitement and euphoria fill me, adrenaline rushing through my veins.

As I wrap my hands around the cup's cool metal, I turn to find Zoe's green eyes behind me, glistening as she witnesses this moment, sharing it with me. Every emotion I've felt since childhood washes over me. I remember everything I sacrificed to get here, to stand right here and share this with everyone in my life.

With the woman I love.

With my team.

I raise the cup triumphantly over my head, and the stadium erupts, imprinting the significance of this moment in my mind forever. We commemorate this victory as a united team. My heart is beyond full as we skate around the rink, bathed in our collective victory.

When it's time for me to hand the cup off to Axel, our assistant captain, I'm just itching to get to Zoe. I hoist her up into the air, and her laughter covers me like a warm blanket.

"You did it, Dominik. You all did it," Zoe declares.

"*We* did it, baby."

Zoe shakes her head, leaning down to rub her nose against mine. "I didn't do anything."

"You're right. You didn't do anything. You *are everything*," I say, taking her hand and pressing it against my heart. "Here and here." I keep my eyes pinned to hers as I point at my head.

"Dominik," she sighs, and I catch the slight tremble in her chin.

Taking a deep breath, I look around and cringe. "Hold on to this feeling, because you're about to hate me in two seconds."

Her brows furrow. "Why?"

I gently set Zoe onto the ice, kissing her nose before letting out a loud whistle, my eyes fixed on my marker in the stands. He immediately turns and blasts a horn. I watch Zoe as the entire stadium rises to their feet. Each person in the crowd is clutching a tiny white box. Suddenly, another whistle pierces the air, and in unison, all the boxes spring open. Purple paper butterflies, in a mesmerizing flurry, engulf the entire venue, soaring through the air.

"Oh my fucking god!" she yelps, her mouth open in complete shock.

"I know how much you love grand gestures."

She turns to me, smiling cheek to cheek. "You're in so much trouble."

I scoop her up in my arms, kissing all over her face.

Zoe looks so happy, her arms raised in the air as she catches butterflies in her hands. Happier than I've ever seen her before.

Her radiant smile lights up the ice, and seeing her happiness fills me with unparalleled joy. Holding her gently in my arms, hearing her laughter, and breathing in the sweet scent of her hair, she becomes the entirety of my world. Her happiness is the greatest achievement I could have ever hoped for.

She is, and will forever be, my greatest achievement.

EPILOGUE
DOMINIK

A year later

LIFE IS GOOD.

So fucking good that sometimes I have to pinch myself and make sure I'm not dreaming. Every day with Zoe has felt like a dream, and when it's this good, something is bound to go wrong, isn't it?

Too bad I don't believe that shit. Now that I have everything, most importantly the girl of my dreams, there is no way I'm letting it go.

I will always work hard for the things that matter and the things I want in life.

I come back to the moment, focusing on Zoe as she straddles me, riding me in the back of the car. Her perky tits bouncing up and down as a light sheen of sweat covers her flawless skin. Fuck, she's so beautiful.

The moon, grand and radiant tonight, casts a luminous glow,

enveloping the cabin in a perfect light as I etch this moment into my memory.

She looks like a true goddess in the moonlight.

My goddess.

I don't think I've ever loved anything so much, and I know I never will.

I trace her damp skin as her curls fan all around her bare shoulders. She stares down at me, eyelids heavy with desire as she rides my cock.

"Is this what you wanted?" I groan, gripping her hips and deepening our movements.

Zoe moans, biting her lip. "Yes," she breathes, closing her eyes.

"Eyes on me, baby. I couldn't hear you."

"Yes," she screams, opening her eyes as I thrust deeper, curling my hips to hit her G-spot.

She looks just as perfect as the first day I met her. She's always been perfect, just as she is. In darkness and in light. I have loved every version of her, and I will love every version that comes. I can't wait to spend forever with her.

"Good. I want you to finish because I have a surprise for you." I reach down to rub her clit, feeling her legs begin to vibrate. After a year of this, I know the exact spot to touch her, the exact rhythm of my cock to get her to come within seconds.

"No. Not yet," she moans, but a second later, she explodes, coming all over my cock as she continues to bounce.

"Come with me, Dominik. Fill me up."

Oh, fuck.

That's all I need to hear. "Keep riding me, little butterfly. Don't stop."

Zoe leans her forehead against mine, gripping my shoulders as she rides my cock hard and fast. We move in unison, perfectly in sync as our bodies sway, causing the car windows to become misty while the air fills with an intense heat.

Her moans grow louder, and I angle myself to rub against her clit.

Her eyes flutter shut, and she tips her head back. "I'm close. Fill me up, Dominik."

"Fuck," I groan. My movements become jerky as I grip the back of her head, fisting her soft hair as I empty myself inside her. Zoe shudders at the same time, screaming out my name as she comes for the second time.

That's still the best goddamn sound in the entire world. I can never get enough of this, enough of her or the way she makes me feel.

Zoe falls forward on me, both of us a beautiful, sticky mess.

"I love you," she murmurs.

"I love you more. So fucking much, baby," I say into her hair, kissing her temple.

How did I get so lucky?

I don't deserve her. I never did, but she chose me anyway. Despite everything that happened between us, despite all the lies and hurt, she chose me. And I never stopped chasing after her. I never will.

She's flourished so much in just a year. Zoe had so many offers after working on the extension at Madison Square Garden, and she landed a permanent position at a top architectural firm. I am so lucky to be able to watch her follow her dreams. Every day, she becomes more confident, happier to be doing something she's always dreamed of doing. I couldn't be more proud.

All the garbage from before is behind her, and she's moved forward, becoming stronger and better. And she did it all on her own. I just stood beside her, proud and supportive as I held her hand.

Zoe peppers kisses on my shoulder and neck before climbing

off me. I watch as my cum slips out and down her thigh. Taking my finger, I scoop up the liquid and grab her chin.

"Open up."

Zoe keeps her eager eyes on mine as she grabs my finger and takes it all the way to the back of her throat, sucking it clean. I just came, but the sight has my dick hardening already.

I want her all the time. Even right after I've fucking had her.

She has no idea the power she has over me and how she holds all of my heart in the palm of her small hand. This goes so much further than love. It's never-ending. All-consuming. Suffocating in the best possible way.

She's mine, and I am hers.

Forever.

I watch her closely while we dress, meticulously noticing every little detail as if it's my first time witnessing them. The way she effortlessly pulls up her jeans and secures the button. The delicate knot on her lace bra strap. The graceful arch of her back as she slips her shirt on.

Zoe looks over at me and smiles. "What?"

I shake my head, grinning like a lovesick puppy. "Nothing."

"Why are you looking at me like that?"

"Just admiring you."

"I'm all gross and sweaty," she scoffs.

"You're always beautiful, and hopefully somewhat satisfied?" I say, pulling her in for a kiss.

"Definitely satisfied, but I can always go for seconds," she hums against my mouth.

I need to get out of this car before I fuck her again.

Swinging open the door, a gust of spring wind rushes inside, pushing around the steam and the incredible smell of sex.

"What are you doing?" Zoe turns, looking at me with a puzzled expression.

"We're going on a little walk."

"Here? In the middle of nowhere? At night? Why?"

Arching a brow, I smile at her. "Is my little butterfly scared?"

"No, just confused and cold." She wraps her arms around herself, and I reach into the backseat, grabbing my hoodie and handing it to her before I get out of the car.

It's well after dark, and we're on the outskirts of New York City. After an amazing dinner, we went stargazing, and Zoe thought I parked here randomly because we just couldn't wait to make it back home. Which is only partially true.

Little does she know, the forest she's standing next to belongs to her.

Zoe looks around, hesitant, as she realizes there isn't a single soul in sight. We're more likely to encounter animals than other people.

I walk into the wooded area, looking over my shoulder at Zoe and waiting for her to catch up.

"Where are you going?"

"Just come."

I can hear the smile in her voice. "Wait, is this an impromptu chase?"

God, I love this woman.

I laugh, shaking my head. "So eager."

Zoe rushes toward me, her arms embracing me tightly as I lift her up. "With you, always."

"Good. I always want you hungry for more, but I didn't bring a mask."

She pouts, making the most adorable face. "Boo. You came to the woods and didn't bring masks? Are you getting too old, Lewis?"

"Watch it. If you act like a brat, I'll treat you like one and rub your face in the dirt with your ass in the air."

"Don't threaten me with a good time," Zoe coos.

I bite her chin and place her onto the ground, taking her hand

and walking deeper into the forest. Not much longer now. The cabin isn't too far from the road. I did that intentionally, wanting a perfect retreat for her but with enough open forest behind the property for us to get lost whenever we feel like it.

Turning around, I face her. "You know what? I changed my mind."

She arches her brow.

"Run, little butterfly. But remember, when I catch you—and I will catch you—I'll take what I want from you until you can't remember your own name."

Zoe crosses her arms, her brat coming out to play. "Are you kidding me?"

"Are you giving me attitude right before I destroy that beautiful pussy for a second time tonight?" Fisting my hoodie, I pull her in and plant a deep kiss on her plump lips before drawing the flesh through my teeth.

As she moves away, Zoe shudders, and a smile forms on her lips before she takes off running.

I decide to wait until she hits the clearing and sees the cabin. Everything inside me is pulling me closer to her, to this memory we're about to create together. One I have been fantasizing about for days, months, even years. I just hope she's thought about it too.

With Zoe, this could go either way.

As I run through the forest, my fingers brush against the branches and leaves, and a smile forms on my face. I gaze up at the moon, feeling grateful to the universe for granting me another night like this one, and every other night before that I got to spend with her. I'm thankful for all of it. Feeling so lucky to share my life with Zoe.

I'm always thankful, but tonight, the emotions are extra strong because, tonight, she promises to be mine forever.

I fucking hope she does.

The cabin door is wide open, and Zoe is nowhere to be found.

Even though the place is brand new, its rustic facade blends seamlessly with the natural surroundings. I had this wooden cabin built in her name, meticulously designed to match the ones she had often described to me. The type of place she always wished she could escape to when life gets a little too much. Zoe needs the quiet and tranquility of nature, and I hope this place gives her all of that and more. The interior is dark and moody, with a cozy kitchen in the corner, adorned with deep forest-green cabinets—her favorite color. All the rooms are nature themed, but the best part about the cabin is the small library, providing endless moments for my girl to escape into.

I know she's the designer, but I wanted to give her a place with a part of me in it. A tribute to her beauty and the depth she carries within her. Because my Zoe deserves the world, and I will spend the rest of my life making her happy.

Stepping inside, I trudge to the back of the cabin and find her standing in front of the bookshelves. Rows of books line the shelves, some new and some old, their spines ready to be worn from countless hours of exploration. Here, she can lose herself in worlds that make sense to her, finding solace within endless words.

The masks are sitting side by side on one shelf, a velvet box propped open in front. Zoe is frozen in place, her eyes fixed on the ring, our game forgotten. I would kill to know what she's thinking right this second.

I reach over her shoulder, take the ring out of the box, and hold her left hand.

"You already belong to me, little butterfly. You always have and always will. Remember my promise? This is just so the rest of the world knows it too." I look down at her, waiting for her refusal, but she just stares up at me as I slide the ring on her finger.

"Dominik," she breathes.

"Say it. Promise me forever."

"Yes."

"Yes, what?"

"Yes to forever with you."

The way she says those words brings tears to my eyes. Her promising me forever, her acceptance and approval, means so much to me. Zoe choosing me. I will never take that for granted.

Forever with Zoe.

"Fuck, I love you so much." I smile, scooping her up and slamming her into the bookshelves, making sure my knuckles take the impact.

"I love you, Dominik. Now make me scream your name over and over again."

"With pleasure, little butterfly." I bite her neck, ripping open her jeans.

Zoe giggles, and from the corner of my eye, I see her holding up her hand and smiling.

Her happiness is my sanctuary.

My home.

My life.

Forever my *everything*.

THE FUN ISN'T OVER...

In the middle of a snowy winter, best friends Dominik and Aaron enter what they think is an abandoned hotel, lured by the promise of a lucrative business venture. Dominik is there to support Aaron, who has decided to risk everything to meet with a mysterious partner for a chance at a successful future. But the hotel isn't what it seems—it's the famous Untamed, a secretive place where hidden desires come to life.

As the night unfolds, innocent dares turn into dangerous games, mixing reality with fantasy. The friends get caught in a web of secrets where every choice can have serious consequences. They don't realize it yet, but this night will change their lives forever. And who knows if they'll even survive. After all, no one fully escapes from the seductive and sinister twists of Untamed.

ALSO BY TINA SPENCER

Shattered Obsession

Untamed

Wonderlight

ACKNOWLEDGMENTS

For anyone that has loved, supported and shared Shattered Obsession (or any of my books). I cannot thank you enough. There are truly not enough words to say how grateful I am for you and what this means to me. You have changed my life.

I hope you enjoyed how Zoe and Dominik's story concluded. It was a difficult process, but this decision felt right in the end. They felt right. I felt a lot of pressure to give them a fitting ending, and I hope I did right by them.

Before we get into all the amazing people I want to thank (and there are so many), I have to thank the person who forced me into becoming a romance author. Because if it weren't for you, I wouldn't be here. If you had given me the love I deserved, craved, needed...I may not have written romance. I would not have been publishing my third novel in a year. I would not have met such amazing people. Friends that have become family now. This journey was my light, and you were my darkness.

This book, like every book, was only possible because of some amazing people. These people were there for me during the hardest season of my life. You guys are my pillars and I'll always be grateful. No words can express my gratitude enough. Thank you for handling my broken pieces with grace and gentleness. I love you (you know who you are).

To my children: everything I have ever done is for you. Everything. I love you so much. Forever and always.

Mom and dad: thank you for always being there for me and for being my biggest fans. I love you both. I hope you don't read these books but I just want you to know how grateful I am for having such a solid and supportive family.

Heidi: Thank you for being there for me during one of the hardest seasons of my life. I likely wouldn't have finished this book if it weren't for your encouragement and support. Thank you for saving me when I needed it the most.

To my amazing street and beta team: you ladies are the best and I'm so fucking thankful for every one of you. Thank you for believing in me, for hyping me up and loving my books. Our group chat gives me so much joy and I'm so glad books were the reason we all got to connect. I hope we meet face-to-face some day soon. Jasmine: you helped me work through the fog and get to the ending of this book, for that I will forever be grateful. Thank you for jumping in when I needed it, and for all the late night chats.

Rachel: thank you for your patience and for saving my ass with this book. I will forever be in your debt. Seriously, you're amazing. And thank you for bringing Heather into the mix as well. I really appreciate you both immensely. Rachel, your attention to detail is chefs kiss. Thank you for being such a wonderful editor and friend.

To the book community, my ARC team and the Hopeless Romantics reader group: THANK YOU. You bunch make all of this so enjoyable. If it weren't for your love and support, none of us authors would be here, pulling all nighters and losing sleep to share our stories with you. I wouldn't be here. Thank you for your continuous support. Please keep dropping into my DMs, I love hearing from you.

I want to conclude this with a final note, as I experienced one of the most challenging seasons of my life while writing this book. If you are currently facing difficulties, just remember that you are not alone. You are never alone. I hope that my words have made you feel understood. Seen. Wanted. Strong. Made you feel like you are capable of doing hard things, because I promise that you are. This too shall pass, as it always does.

ABOUT THE AUTHOR

Tina Spencer has held a lifelong passion for spinning tales since early childhood. When Tina's not spending her free time writing and agonizing over her fictional characters, she's working through her endless TBR, spending time with her family, traveling, and attempting to get *some* sleep. She enjoys writing about flawed characters and their meaningful journeys through life and love. If you're looking for emotional and inspirational books with spice, then you've come to the right place.

For more, visit www.tinaspencerbooks.com

facebook.com/authortinaspencer

instagram.com/tinaspencerauthor

goodreads.com/authortinaspencer

Made in the USA
Middletown, DE
17 April 2025

74465697R00186